The University of Wisconsin Press
1930 Monroe Street, 3rd Floor
Madison, Wisconsin 53711-2059
uwpress.wisc.edu

3 Henrietta Street, Covent Garden
London WCE 8LU, United Kingdom
eurospanbookstore.com

Printed in the United States of America

This book may be available in a digital edition.

Library of Congress Cataloging-in-Publication Data

Names: Zacharias, Lee, author.
Title: Across the great lake / Lee Zacharias.
Description: Madison, Wisconsin: The University of Wisconsin Press, [2018]
Identifiers: LCCN 2018011386 | ISBN 9780299320904 (cloth: alk. paper)
Subjects: LCSH: Michigan, Lake—Fiction. | LCGFT: Novels. | Fiction.
Classification: LCC PS3576.A18 A64 2018 | DDC 813/.54—dc23
LC record available at https://lccn.loc.gov/2018011386

Across the Great Lake

Also by Lee Zacharias

Short Stories

Helping Muriel Make It Through the Night

Novels

Lessons
At Random

Essays

The Only Sounds We Make

Across the Great Lake

Lee Zacharias

Lee Zacharias

The University of Wisconsin Press

For

Michael

and for our sons,

Max and Al

In memory of my father,

Joseph Ryan Ives

who served as a merchant marine from 1937 to 1945 but never spoke of his time on the oceans or the Great Lakes to me

For in their interflowing aggregate, those grand fresh-water seas of ours,—Erie, and Ontario, and Huron, and Superior, and Michigan,—possess an ocean-like expansiveness . . . They contain round archipelagoes of romantic isles . . . they have heard the fleet thunderings of naval victories . . . they are swept by Borean and dismasting blasts as direful as any that lash the salted wave; they know what shipwrecks are, for out of sight of land, however inland, they have drowned full many a midnight ship with all its shrieking crew.

Herman Melville, *Moby Dick*

To Lake Michigan—the only one of the Great Lakes without an international boundary—sailing masters pay the utmost respect, not only because of this Lake's long history of sudden disaster, but because of the prevailing winds that can sweep its length to roll up backbreaking seas, the scarcity of natural harbors or even man-made places of refuge, and the crowning fact that it is the trickiest of the Lakes to keep a course on, due to currents caused by a flow around the Straits of Mackinac when the wind shifts.

William Ratigan, *Great Lakes Shipwrecks and Survivals*

Across the Great Lake

1

We went to the ice. That was the year my mother died, but I do not remember her. What I remember is the ice, everywhere I looked, a world made of ice, and then the fire. But first there were the voices.

"Get up," he said.

"I can't," she said.

"You mean you won't."

"I can't."

Was I listening outside the closed door? Surely my mother taught me better, had told me that eavesdropping was not something a polite little girl would do. Such a strange word, *eavesdropping*. Did I know it then? Was I already a bad girl? Perhaps she despaired of me, I don't know. We got stuck in the ice, there was a storm, and while we were gone my mother died. My father was not a man of words, and now that so many years have passed, there is no one left to ask whether I was ever a good girl, a girl who might have deserved love, or not.

"There's other women lost a child."

"You don't know."

"I know enough."

A clot of silence seemed to thicken, though perhaps they only lowered their voices, perhaps I simply couldn't hear them.

"For the last time, get up," he said. "You've another child needs tending."

Did she answer? My father was a captain. When he spoke people listened. They did what he said. Perhaps she repeated "I can't," the only memory I really have of her, those two words in her voice. Or perhaps, when my father offered me as a reason for her to get back up and live, she said nothing at all. I had just turned five years old. In the hallway there was a yellow light in a sconce. It was a grand house, set against the hill on Leelanau Avenue, but the light had scorched a spot on the wallpaper, and there was a water stain near a seam, a small, brownish lake in the green-and-gray print. I used to spend hours perusing those blotches, as if imperfection was what my eyes sought from the start, though I don't remember whether I noticed them that night.

"All right then," my father said. "I'm taking the girl."

Surely neighbor women would have cared for me, as they did later, after my mother died. I suppose it's possible he never meant to take me, only to frighten her back into life. A railroad car ferry, those women would tell me later, their voices hushed because he was a captain and in our town a captain was beyond reproach, is no place for a girl, and in the dead of winter too. But my mother must have sunk back into her pillow and said nothing, because I went to my room, and not long after, he came in and dressed me in heavy woolens, pulled a cap down over my ears, and wrapped a scratchy scarf around my face. It was dark when we left the big house on our side of the harbor, the pretty side. He had an automobile, and we drove the snow-crusted road through the welcome gate with its model ferry on the crossbar around to the other side, where the boats docked and the men who worked on them lived behind their sagging porches in shabby little houses sided with tarpaper brick.

I had never seen the loading before. There was a great clanking as the railcars, those big freight cars, loomed up out of the darkness and rolled onto the vast lower deck of the ship, the flagship of the Annies, as the townspeople called the Ann Arbor Railroad ferries, though my father always called his ship a boat, as if it were no bigger than a dory. Later, in

4

the summertime, I would sometimes sit on the Elberta bluff with my stepmother, watching his ship pass between the stub piers into the big basin enclosed by the breakwaters and beyond, because a captain is never home and for the people who belonged to the captains and crews, such rituals are what passed for family life. Even from that distance anyone could see that it was not a boat such as you might take out to fish, but a huge and powerful ship with a tall, handsome pilothouse and big smoking stacks, no place for a girl, though I loved it, I cannot tell you how much I loved it. I came to know it inside out. I knew more than my father knew. Because it was not his job to watch me. He had a ship to command. No one on such a ship was in the habit of minding little girls, and no one on a ship in trouble could have spared the time. Today you would say I slipped below the radar, but there was no radar then, only a magnetic compass, lead and log lines. They forgot me, all of them except Alv, and I loved being a forgotten girl, a secret girl, a girl whose life began to speak to me down on the car deck and below, in the bowel of the ship where I was not supposed to be, a girl who believed her real life was beginning.

As the cars loaded I listened to the buzz of the men's voices and burrs of their laughter, barely audible beneath the loud wheels, metal on metal, the boom of the sidejacks and stanchions and ringing of the chains, then the groaning of the ropes and hiss of steam as the big seagate came down and closed over the stern. When the whistle shrilled, I was taken to my father's cabin and set on the bunk above its built-in wooden drawers, across from the desk with his instruments, his charts, and his log, where even before the ship heaved away from the dock I drew a house with a stick mother and father and child beneath a spoked sun, which was another thing a good girl ought not have done. It was the captain's log, a book for grown-ups, not children's doodles, but it must have looked so dull, all those words on the page with no pictures. So I made that little gift for my father. Then the horn sounded, the engines sent a shudder up through the floor into my feet, and we went to the ice.

2

$\mathcal{M}$y father's ship, which came to be known as the Bull of the Woods, was named the *Manitou*, for the two islands in the fishing grounds to the north, where captains often sought shelter from high seas. It was a lake, but they called the waves seas, for it was a lake as big as a sea and in a gale or a storm such a lake is more treacherous than the ocean, its waves just as steep but sharper and closer together. And of all the Great Lakes, my father's, the one the Ojibwe named Michigami, great water, is the trickiest to navigate. If you could walk its deep floor, you would have to skirt a litter of beams, timbers, and bones from all the ships it has claimed. Every child in Frankfort knew about the seventeen men who perished when the *Westmoreland* failed to outrun a blizzard in a northwest gale and sank in Platte Bay. We knew about the nine hundred lives lost on the *Eastland* at the far south end of the lake and the fifty-two sailors who perished on the *Milwaukee*. Our heads were full of proper nouns. The *Alpena, Andaste, Lady Elgin, Mahor, Rising Sun, Rosabelle,* and *Rouse Simmons*. That was the Christmas tree ship that was never found though its cargo of balsam and spruce came up in the fishermen's nets the next spring. We knew how Captain Peter Kilty went down on the *Pere Marquette 18*, knee-deep in water on the flying bridge as he waved good-bye, taking twenty-seven of his crew with him, knew all the wrecks and close calls, the hotels in town that had burned, the Royal Frontenac, the Yeazel, their names seared into our memory even before we were born. The chief engineer who had survived when the crippled *Ann Arbor 4* sank beside the south pier was our neighbor. He liked to show us the pocket watch that had hung frozen in ice on the engine room bulkhead until the ship could be raised the next spring, liked to put it to our ears so we could hear how it still kept perfect time.

Even the islands that gave my father's ship its name drew their own from disaster. It was our bedtime story, the Ojibwe legend about the mother bear and two cubs who swam all the way across Lake Michigan in order to escape a forest fire raging in Wisconsin. When they arrived, the mother climbed the steep bluff that became Sleeping Bear Dune, but the cubs were too tired, and when they drowned they became the North and South Manitou Islands, the very islands our fathers sought in storms as safe harbor. Every night we mourned those cubs as we rode the sheltering arms of our parents up to our rooms. Why would their mother have left them to die? Why didn't she turn around, why didn't she save them? Those baby bears spoke to us in a way all the other tragedies the lake held did not, even those of us whose fathers were captains and mates and chief engineers, our fathers who might perish on the most routine journey, more than fifty ships lost in the Manitou Passage alone. For our sake our mothers muted their worry. I think people were more stoic then than they are now, but what they kept from us we knew because we passed news of disasters the same way children pass the truth about Santa Claus and still later their first inklings and misinformation about sex.

It was 1936. We were children of the Depression, though I can't say any of us knew what that meant. The ferries ran as it seemed they always had, always would. I lived in a tall house on Leelanau Avenue with my mother and father, and there was work to go around, even for the shanty boys who lived in Elberta. It is true: the ferries saved us, up there in our remote little corner of Michigan, just as the new cement breakwaters that angled two thousand feet out into the lake protected our harbor. And if the railroad had once been more prosperous, how was a child to know? Santa Claus didn't do as much for children as he seems to these days. We didn't love him, we didn't love those sunken ships or the men who died, but we did love those two little cubs.

And we knew ice. There in Michigan's north woods we grew up like the Eskimo boys and girls who learn a hundred words for snow. If we didn't know that salt makes sea ice porous, we did know that lake ice is dense. The harbor, where we skated each winter, often froze all the way to the bottom; some winters the whole lake froze shore to shore, an ice field more than one hundred miles across. My father's ship came to be known as the Bull of the Woods not because it was the newest or fastest in the fleet, but because it proved to be the best icebreaker and was often called to help other ships, even when it got stuck itself, as many as three of them trapped together behind a range of tall windrows. Even when he was home my father might be called away any minute. Fully loaded, the *Manitou* had a draft of eighteen feet, but a few feet above the waterline there was a sharp slant to the aft, the Annies' trademark cutaway prow, which allowed it to ride up on the ice in order to crush it with the ship's weight, though the path it broke was so narrow sailors called it a horse's tail.

But the ice we went to was not the ice I had known, not the slick on the sidewalks and steep front steps to my house, where I fell and broke my arm the year before, or the glaze on the road that sometimes kept my father from coming home even when the *Manitou* was docked across the harbor in Elberta. It was not the hard-packed hill where we rode our sleds, the ragged escarpments that rose along the breakwaters, or even the spray that froze midair around the lights at the ends, those giant white sculptures that took the faces of fairytale monsters and goblins. What I knew was the scrim of frost on our windowpanes, the ice in my father's eyebrows, the crystals that were my breath caught in the pores of the scarf stiffening around my face, and the enormous fangs that hung from our eaves and the ships' bridges, icicles so long you could see them all the way across the harbor, along with the heavy crust like salt all over the sides that made the ships look like giant deer licks, for in the winter deer often walked out on the ice, and sometimes, when it was not so thick, they fell into the cracks between the floes and drowned, though no one thought to name an island after them.

Crossing the lake that February of 1936, I would learn more of winter's names: sheet ice, which is a field when it is attached to something and a floe when it is not, and blue ice, which is a kind of sheet ice that is nearly transparent but very hard even for the Bull of the Woods to break up. White ice is older, more forgiving because it holds more air. White ice can be rammed, but to ram the anchor ice that builds around slips would damage the docks, and the pack ice that piles against the piers goes even deeper. In spring I liked to stomp and splatter the slush of melting snow in the gutters with my rubber galoshes, but all winter long in the basin between the breakwaters slush ice piled atop the sheet ice, sticking to the sides of the ships and creating more drag than the shallow harbor could handle. Ships rode up on it and stuck as if they had fetched up on a sandbar. That February it was ten degrees below zero as we crossed a continent of icy plains and windrows, those mountains that the wind heaves up when it shoves ice sheets together, forcing chunks up and down through the cracks into thick walls ten and fifteen feet high and as deep as twenty-five, so many miles long that later, in school, when we learned about the Great Wall of China it was those endless white mountains on the lake that I pictured.

3

There was a ghost on my father's ship, but I can't tell that story yet. Because ghosts take their time. They keep their secrets. A ghost never comes at you straightaway.

4

*M*anitou, wake up," I whispered to the teddy bear I'd settled against the pillow on my father's neatly made berth. "We're at sea." Below us a dull roar echoed along the sides of the ship, and it seemed as if we had already been gone a very long time. I didn't know that we were not yet out of the harbor, still fighting through the slush ice, riding up and backing off, cutting a horse's tail to the lake. My father was not accustomed to dressing me, and he had put my leggings on backward. The wool itched, and the seam pulled against my crotch, but to put them right I would have to take off my boots and Buster Browns. The boots had newfangled zippers, and I had learned to tie and untie my shoelaces, but the rubber fit so snugly over the leather that I was still seated on the berth, struggling with the first one, when there was a knock at the cabin door and then it banged open.

"Sir!" a boy shouted and stopped short as I stood. "Oh." I couldn't see him around the corner of my father's wooden locker, so I stepped forward. He was not so tall as my father, but his face was fuller, his cheeks red beneath his watch cap. Despite the sturdiness of his face, there was something otherwordly about it, an incandescence that made it seem as if his skin might be lined with gold, a rosy flame flickering just behind his dark eyes. I was so young I don't suppose I had ever thought about beauty before, but I was stricken by it now. "I was looking for the captain."

"My father is the captain," I said.

He blinked. The shutters at the windows were closed, and the light in the long walnut-paneled cabin was dim. "There's a row in the pilot-house," he said.

"My name is Fern." After a minute I added, "My father's not here."

"Alv," he offered and stepped inside to hold his hand out. It made me feel quite grown up to shake it, though my bare hand felt small inside his canvas glove. A smell of cold air came off his skin. The coat and mittens I had taken off were lying beside my hat and scarf on my father's berth. The mittens were threaded through the sleeves on a string my mother must have braided. Probably she had knit the patterned mittens too, though I was too young to know to keep them when I outgrew them in a year or so.

"What's a row?" I asked.

"A dustup, you know, an argument." He looked around the cabin. There was a small radiator near the sink in the part where the berth was, and little puddles had formed on the floor where the snow had dripped from my father's big galoshes when he carried me in. "Captain must be below, checking the jacks. Chief engineer thinks everything below deck belongs to him, but it's the captain deals with the rumpus if the cars bust loose." His eyes returned to me. "How did you get here?"

"My mother is sick." I thought of my parents' voices from behind the closed door and turned the terms over in my head. My parents had a dustup, a row, because my mother was sick, and now I was on a big ship headed out to sea. "What did they argue about?"

Alv's eyes quickened. "It's the second wheelsman. The first mate fired him last night, but Odd came back while we were loading, he's at the wheel now, and Mr. Johannessen's mad as a hornet."

Dimly I recalled hearing my father use the same word at the dinner table. He must have been telling my mother that he'd fired someone, and I'd thought he meant burned.

"He's a drunk, Odd is, so Johannessen gave him the boot, but now he's back and won't go." A note of merriment seeped into Alv's voice.

"'Dammit, I fired you,' Johannessen said, and Odd says, 'I like it here. I'll tell you when I'm ready to quit.'"

"My father will make him go."

"Can't. Boat's underway."

"What will they do?" I asked. Someone must have read me a story about pirates, because I imagined my father and all the sailors lining up on deck to watch the drunk man named Odd walk the plank. In the corner, above the sink, there was a wooden rack with an orange life jacket suspended from the ceiling, and I wondered if they would let him wear it. It didn't occur to me that he could simply walk back to Elberta over the ice, as the chief engineer would do that night, when we broke a rudder pin. We would spend our first night on the ice just outside our own harbor while he waited for the blacksmith to forge a new one and the ghost stole out from the compartment where it lived during the day.

"Second mate's already said let him steer, might as well get some use out of him if he has to be fed." The dimples in Alv's cheeks deepened when he smiled. "He says that's the way Captain would see it, but Johannessen doesn't think so. I don't think the mates get along too good."

"Did they holler?"

"You bet."

"I want to see."

"Oh no. I might get in trouble with the captain."

"My father is the captain," I said again. "And Manitou's bored. We want to go upstairs."

"Above," he corrected. "Bosun goes beserk anyone says upstairs or downstairs. Who's Manitou?" he added as his eyes fell on the bear, whose brown silk plush was wearing away along one ear. "Hello, Manitou." To me he added, "I know that story."

"Everyone knows that story." But I was pleased that he knew it, that he understood I had not named my bear for my father's ship. I retreated to my father's berth and sat to give my boot another tug, then frowned. "I can't get these off."

"Might want to leave them on if Captain lets you go on deck."

I didn't want to explain about the scratchy leggings. I didn't want him to know that I hadn't dressed myself. I knew how, but I had still been in my nightgown when my father came in to get me. Alv was my first crush, and I wanted him to think I was more grown up than I was. "I can put them back on when I go outside."

He took off his gloves and knelt on the floor. When he pulled at the first boot, my shoe flew off along with it. He was as tall as some men, but up close I could see he still had the smooth skin of a boy, and his eyelashes were as long and black as a woman's. "There," he said when he had removed the other one. He glanced at Manitou again. "Is Manitou a boy or girl bear?"

"A boy," I said instantly, though until that moment it hadn't occurred to me that Manitou should be one or the other. No one had ever said which the cubs were, and I had never asked. Probably they were a boy *and* a girl, because that's the way a story would work, but Manitou couldn't be both because everyone, even bears, had to be one and whichever one you were meant you couldn't be the other.

"How old are you, Fern?"

"Five." I held up my fingers. "How old are you?"

"Fourteen."

"Is your mother sick too?"

"I'm learning how to be a deckhand." His weight seemed to shift, and his voice seesawed, as if it didn't know yet whether it belonged to a man or a boy. "Well, for now I guess I'm more like an errand boy, but if we get stuck or there's a blow, I'll be a deckhand for sure."

"I think I'd like to be a deckhand," I said.

"You more than me. It's my father's idea."

"Is he one of the mates? How come they don't get along?"

Alv shook his head. "He's an oiler on the *Kewaunee*. He says it's a good living on the boats and with times the way they are I might as well get started. I was in school, but the teacher got sick of me—'Half the time you're not here,' she says, 'and when you are you aren't here anyway.' So my father figured I ought to go to work."

"I'm going to school next year." I fingered my father's blanket and hopped back to my feet, though I still had one shoe off and the other on. "I already know my numbers and my letters. Do you live in Frankfort?" I knew before he answered that he didn't. Only the officers lived in Frankfort. He would live on the other side of the harbor, in Elberta, and if my mother had been there I would have known better than to ask, but I was by myself with this beautiful, almost grown boy who was going to be a deckhand and who was talking to me just like I was almost grown and maybe going to be a deckhand too. I said whatever came into my head. "I live in Frankfort. I live in a big house on the hill on Leelanau Avenue. It has a tower room, I have a swing, we have a car, and the whole end of Fourth Street is our driveway."

"Of course you do." He smiled at me, and his dimples pooled. With his perfect nose, the plump mouth, golden skin, and eyes as big and dark as the whole north woods, he didn't resemble anyone I knew. Though his cap covered his hair, I knew if he took it off, his hair would be as thick and black as his eyelashes. "What it is, a first mate never likes the second mate calling the shots."

"I think this is going to be a very long trip," I said. Already I liked the idea that I was going to sea. I must have known that my destination was Menominee, which was still in Michigan, but on the UP at the very edge of the Wisconsin border. I imagined Wisconsin to be halfway around the world. "And Manitou and I can't see out the window."

"I can fix that." Alv slid a shutter into a pocket below a window. I hadn't known the pocket was there, and I thought it was so clever I asked him to do all the others and then raise them back up just so I could watch him do it again. Then he boosted me to the glass. The sky had paled, and I recognized the white beam inside a fountain of frozen spray way ahead to starboard. It was the north pier light. The south light was red, because a captain was supposed to look for red on the right whenever he came into a harbor in the fog or at night. That was how he knew where to steer. I looked the other way across the ice, and there it was, up ahead to port, the red glow, blinking inside a cage of frozen spray at the end of the icy precipice that was the south pier. In summer, when I played on the beach and hunted for Petoskey stones below the bluff, we sometimes walked out past the diving board on the north pier, past the turn where it narrowed, all the way to the light. So many hours at sea, and I was not yet as far as I had already been. When he set me down I tugged his sleeve and handed him Manitou. Alv pressed the bear's face to the window. "What do you think, Manitou?"

I shook my head. "He's a very nice bear. You can talk to him, but if you want him to talk back you have to make it all up." I liked the idea of such a long trip, but not if I had to spend it all inside my father's cabin. "I want to see the rest of the boat. Why doesn't my father come get me?"

"Because he has a ship to command. But I'll tell you what. If Captain's busy, I'll come back and get you for dinner."

"When?"

"Noon. Bosun says I eat first shift with him."

"Promise?" I asked, even though noon was forever. It was barely time for breakfast, though my father had given me some sweet soup with bread and butter before we left. "Best to fill your belly, Fern," he had said, but noon was half a day, and a day was forever done twice.

When Alv was gone, I sat next to my bear against the pillow on my father's berth and dipped my face to his. "Manitou, this is going to be a long trip, and I do not want you asking if we are there yet. You are going to have to act very grown up."

5

$\mathcal{W}$e were Norwegian, my parents and I, as were most of the people we knew. For a long time when I was young I thought everyone must be Norwegian, or else Swedish. My father's name was Henrik Halvorsen, my mother's Silje, names that make them sound more Norwegian than they were since both of them were born in Michigan, at least I think my mother was. I never learned much about her, only that she was an orphan. She was a great deal younger than my father. It was his parents who came from the old country. His father left Norway to become a sailor at the age of fourteen, the same age as Alv. Eventually he arrived in Frankfort, where he too became a captain, but people didn't live so long back then, and both of my grandparents died before I was born. They're buried in what used to be called the Norwegian Cemetery out beside the highway to Benzonia. Until I was in my teens the Lutheran church in Frankfort still conducted services in Norwegian, but we attended the ones in English, and I don't think my father knew more than a few words in his parents' native tongue. What it meant to be Norwegian to me was Santa Lucia Day with its white lights and fragrant saffron buns, the Christmas *pinnekjøtt*, big marzipan *kransekake*, and buttery *julekake* that even children consumed with strong black coffee, the *lefse* I liked sprinkled with sugar and cinnamon, my stepmother's potato dumplings, and Sunday's *svinestek*, roast pork with pickled cabbage and mashed potatoes. On the occasional evenings when he was home, my father liked to play the old Norsk sea tunes he learned from his father on his accordion and drink a beer brewed the malty Norwegian way, but really we were American, or so I thought until I went away to school and learned that I was not Norwegian or American, either one, but Midwestern.

Alv was Norwegian too, but he was not the same as us. We were a pale people, with blue eyes, blond hair, and thin Nordic noses. His thick dark hair, dark eyes, and full face, maybe even his dimples, came from his Sami mother. I didn't know about the Sami then, those Arctic reindeer herders who migrated from Siberia to the northern coast of Scandinavia thousands of years ago. The notion of herding reindeer would have been as foreign, as exotic, to me as the practice of driving an entire train onto a boat surely would have seemed to the Sami. There were caribou on the Upper Peninsula, but I had never been to the UP. Our house backed on woods and I often saw deer, rabbits, sometimes a fox. In the evenings tourists liked to park their cars at the dump to watch bears come out to forage, but my father had no time for such foolishness, and my acquaintance with reindeer came strictly from "The Night before Christmas."

Yet it was not just Alv's Sami mother who made him different. He had left school to work on the boats because that was what his father wanted, but what he wanted, what he really wanted, was to play the piano. When he told me the first afternoon of our journey, his eyes sparkled in the light of the passenger lounge, as he seemed to see himself playing on a stage or perhaps in a saloon, whatever venue he dreamed, maybe just a room with nothing but himself and a big Steinway, though I don't suppose he would have known what a Steinway was, and the piano where I imagined him was the August Förster upright in our parlor. I was a lonely child, and already I wanted him to come live with us and be my big brother.

"My mother plays the piano," I said, and isn't it strange that I should so clearly remember telling him that when I can't remember my mother playing the piano at all? When I picture that instrument now, it's my stepmother on the stool, picking out "Cheek to Cheek" or "My Blue Heaven" with her right hand and harmonizing with her left. I must have sat down to it a few times myself, though I cannot recall the feel of the keys beneath my fingers; that endless row of ivory teeth looked all too much the same, I had no ear for it, I lacked the patience that would have allowed me to decode the notes spattered across the sheet music on its rack. Even as a small girl I loved the outdoors, the woods, the lake, Betsie Bay, the river that spooled down through the marsh, and the smaller lakes all around us. I wasn't artistic, and my connection to that piano with its candle sconces and burled wood insets was the dustrag.

But isn't it also strange that I should remember nearly every moment of that journey when I have forgotten so much else? Some people say that the distant past comes back to them as if it were yesterday, but those days I spent on the *Manitou* do not come back to me like yesterday, they come back like today, this very minute, the way a book springs back to life and happens all over again, with all its colors and smells, the raw sorrow for each setback and joy in its triumphs, every time you take it off the shelf. That first night we spent on the ice outside the harbor waiting for a new rudder pin, it was so quiet I could hear the crack of the pins in the bowling alley on Main Street. Now, of course, I wonder whether my mother heard them too as she lay in my parents' upstairs bedroom. Did she open her eyes and trace the faint glow of the streetlight on the white curtain, in her grief unable to sleep? Did she think about me, did she wonder where I was, if I was safe, or did she think only that the sound of those pins, that cadence of happy explosions echoing through the frozen silence, was the last cruelty she would have to bear?

I have read somewhere that the memories that seem most familiar to us, the ones we most often visit, are in fact our least accurate, for each time we review them we change them, revisions so subtle we're unaware of making them, until the more we seem to remember, the less we actually do. But what happens to the memories you suppress, the ones you can't bear to visit waking, and so they come to you in dreams? For me it's a moose, a moose with devil's horns, starving, staining the ice red as it dies, looking up at me with its sad, reproachful eyes. I didn't kill it, but awake or asleep, in calling up the past, memory *always* lies.

Yet I have to wonder how a lie could be so fully textured. Surely the true memory is the one that is vivid.

Far more vivid than that of the luncheon I attended at the assisted living out near the airport yesterday, where we all wore party hats like fools to honor a birthday girl much too doddering and weak to blow out the eighty-six candles that should have been on her cake. So many years had passed since we'd last seen each other—though she was two years older, in grade school we'd briefly been friends—she probably wouldn't have recognized me even if her memory was intact, though the truth is I hardly recognize myself, the crepey skin along my arms, web of lines around my mouth, wattled neck, and drooping eyelids. Already I can't pick my voice out of that "Happy Birthday" chorus, don't know any of those cracked, tuneless yaps as mine, only the lilt of a little girl, tucking her hand inside the new apprentice deckhand's as he leads her from her father's cabin, down the ladder to the weather deck and the mess inside the deckhouse and her first dinner aboard ship, and she asks, please, when they are done eating, can she be taken below to see the train?

6

_If_ my father had been captain of a freighter, he would have enjoyed larger quarters, with his own bathroom and an extra bedroom for family visits. But the railroad had designed its ferries for short hauls, never mind that they sometimes stuck in the ice for days or that the sailors spent weeks on board, back and forth across the lake, in order to earn their few days off. My father's cabin was so narrow it was nearly bisected by the wooden locker in the middle, and he had to share a bathroom—which is not called a bathroom on a ship, but the head, and you'd best not let the bosun hear you call it anything else, though later, when I went to school and raised my hand to ask my teacher if I could please go to the head, she stiffened her shoulders as if she'd been struck and said that it was unacceptable for a girl to be so vulgar. But comfort didn't much matter to my father. He was not a complainer—nor, I should add, did he care to hear the complaints of others. As for myself I was glad he didn't have a private bath, because in order to find the head he shared with all the other officers I had to go exploring. And if I couldn't go up to the pilothouse, where a drunk was at the wheel and maybe the two mates were still yelling, I had to do something.

The passageway through the officers' quarters was so tight I braced my hands against both walls until I found my sea legs, even though the ship was just plowing through the slush ice and wasn't rocking like it would in a chop. When I peered up the companionway to the pilothouse, all I could see was a pool of light. The little brass plates above the doors to all the cabins were too high for me to read, not that I knew many words, but what they would say was who slept there, and anyone could figure that out by how many lines there were, because the first mate had his own, but the second and third mates had to share, even though you could tell how small the cabins would be, less than half the size of my father's, so I hoped the second and third mates got along better than the second and the first. I wanted to see a cabin, so I listened outside the doors for a whisper of breath inside. Sure enough, the one I chose was empty, so compact it looked like a child's playhouse, with a sink in the corner like my father's and a little fold-down stool on the wall. At the very back of the officers' quarters, behind the head, there was a compartment for the boatswain, the unlicensed mate in charge of the deck crew and maintenance. All I knew about the bosun was what Alv had told me, that he got mad if you acted like a landlubber and called things by the wrong names, but I knew it had to be his because the word started with B. Later, by way of telling me what a bosun did, one of the watches said it was his job to be a son-of-a-bitch, pardon his French, and that will tell you why the bosun got his own cabin in the officers' quarters away from the crew when even the chief engineer had to bunk off the engineers' hall, along with the cooks and porters and other engineers, in back of the galley, just in front of the cabins for the deck crew.

When I came back my father was waiting for me inside his open door. "Fern?"

"I had to go to the bathroom, Daddy."

He stepped aside to let me in. I had already looked inside the locker that stowed his heavy coat and galoshes. I had opened the drawers beneath his berth and all the drawers of his desk, where I'd found a key that unlocked his wooden trunk, which held only a few books and extra woolen blankets that I had been careful not to unfold. At home I liked to play in the tower room that was fitted out to be his office though he rarely used it, but on the boat I was afraid to disturb his things because he might think that I was snooping, which I was—I wanted to see what kind of things a captain would have with him. I wasn't afraid of him, no more than any child is afraid of her father. I just wanted to please him, though I didn't really know how, except to be good, and that always seemed so very hard.

"Are you warm enough? Are you hungry?" He was not accustomed to tending to my needs, and the questions seemed unfamiliar in his voice. I loved him, and surely he loved me, but I think we didn't know what to expect of each other. He was a tall man with a lanky build and a lean face that was deeply lined from his years on the lake. In his presence, the ceiling of his cabin seemed to lower, but I thought no one in the world was as handsome. He looked so important in his navy blue uniform with its stripes of gold braid on the sleeves and double row of brass buttons, every one of them embossed with the name of the railroad. There was a circle of gold braid around his hat too, just above the shiny brim that had come down over my nose the one time he let me try it on, and the scratchy gray stubble on his cheeks gave him a salty look that seemed just right for a captain. I don't know how he maintained it, because he never shaved it off or let it grow into a beard. He was a gentle man, but he was not demonstrative, and that reticence coupled with the authority of his office often made him seem stern. There was an air of formality about him, a regal loneliness that seemed suited to a man who spent his days in the lofty tower of a pilothouse, staring out at the unbroken line of a watery horizon he preferred to any sight on land.

"I want to see the rest of the boat," I said.

"In a while," my father promised. "The *Kewaunee* couldn't get out last night. Channel's froze up, and there's a west wind pushing all that ice into the harbor, so right now I'm needed on the bridge. Once we get out on the lake we're headed up past Point Betsie to the Passage. The *Ashley*'s stuck off Pyramid Point."

I'd been to Point Betsie. The big lighthouse was there. "Is the *Ashley* going to sink?" I thought it would be something to see a boat sink, especially if there was a man up to his knees in water on the flying bridge

23

waving good-bye. Sometimes men escaped only to freeze to death in their lifeboats. That would be something to see too, a boat full of men turned into icy statues.

"In this ice?" The lines around his eyes crinkled. He always seemed to smile more with his eyes than with his mouth. They were pale but very blue, and the color seemed to soften. "Not hardly, but if the wind stays to the west she could go aground. Wouldn't be the first tub ice pushed ashore. And she's not a good boat."

"What did she do?" It was an interesting notion, that boats might misbehave. Like children. At the time what I knew of the naughtiness of children was so trifling it scarcely bears mention, though I would learn what harm a child can do soon enough. "Keel blocks wouldn't come loose when the Grand Trunk launched her. Then when the Ann Arbor bought her, they changed her name. That's the railroad for you. Any sailor could have told them it's bad luck."

"Is the *Manitou* a good boat?"

"She is." Even the big ships named for men were always *she*, I didn't know why.

"Is she lucky?"

"She is."

"How do you know?"

"A captain always knows." His eyes sparkled the way people's do when they are getting ready to tell a good joke, though I don't remember my father as one to tell jokes. "Boats talk if you know how to listen."

"What do they say?"

He gazed toward the window and beyond, as if he might see what the *Manitou* said printed out the foredeck. "They talk about past journeys. About gales and storms, fog and stinging ice devils."

I listened, but all I could hear was the thunder of ice along the hull. I thought I would like to know about the stinging ice devils.

"Will the *Manitou* tell you how to get the *Ashley* unstuck?"

"She might." It was the longest conversation I'd ever had with my father. True, he felt more at home aboard ship than he ever did on land, but it is also true that we were seldom alone together.

"Can I help?"

"That'd be a mought big a job for such a *liten jente*. Best for you to stay put right now. If ramming doesn't work we're going to have to try backing." Even though my father didn't speak the language, he liked to use Norwegian terms of endearment for me. I didn't know exactly what the words meant, but all the same I thought of them as our secret code.

"But I want something to do." My voice sagged with disappointment. "Are you going to make Odd go home?"

The arch of his eyebrows lifted the brim of his hat.

"There was a row in the pilothouse. Alv told me. The first mate fired Odd, but he came back."

"Well," my father said, and the way he said it made a whole sentence.

"Then the second mate said he could stay, and they started yelling. Odd's a drunk," I added.

My father's face seemed to narrow. He had no ear for gossip, and I would learn that one thing he would not hear were tales about his crew. But then the pinch of lines around his eyes smiled again. "It's all right, *lille*. Odd's a good helmsman. He'll sober up fast enough in this cold. Don't you worry."

"You won't make him go back?" I didn't mind if he sent Odd home. I was afraid that he might change his mind and take me home too.

"We're not going back. Backing's what a ship does when ramming doesn't work, and when we put that port engine in reverse, this boat is going to shake worse than a wet dog. That's why you're best off right here."

"It's boring here," I complained, just as his eyes fell on the drawing I had made in his log.

"What's this?"

"It's for you."

25

"You mustn't draw in the captain's log, Fern." He was frowning, though he didn't seem angry. "I suppose we should have thought to bring some paper and crayons. I daresay there's not much to entertain a girl on a boat, but the boys will have an extra deck of cards and there may be a game or a puzzle in the observation room."

"It's you, me, and Mama."

He turned away. "Yes, I see that."

"We're at the beach. It's summer. See the sun?" Because the house I had drawn was not our house but the big brown log house on Sac Street at the end of Forest Avenue, where it opened to the lake. I loved our house on the hill, where I could walk all the way to the water tower through the woods, but I thought it would be nice to live in a log house at the edge of the lake too. If you lived in a log house you could pretend to be a pioneer girl or even an Indian maiden who'd been captured, but that would be okay because you would like the house so much you wouldn't care.

"It's a very nice picture," he said, though he did not look at it again. His back was still toward me. "I'm sorry that your mother is sick."

"What's a drunk?" I asked.

"She'll perk up." He turned back to me. "A drunk is someone who suffers overfondness. It can be something of a sailor's disease, I'm afraid."

"Is Odd sick like Mama?"

"No, not like Mama."

"What's the matter with her?"

He didn't answer, but I knew. *Female troubles.* It was term I'd heard whispered, though I had no idea what it meant. Something that happened to women that never happened to men, which hardly seemed fair.

He nodded toward the bed where I'd laid my hat and coat. "Berth's a mought narrow for two. If you wouldn't be afraid by yourself, we could put you in one of the passenger cabins. You'd have your own room, just like home."

"Are we going to spend the night at sea?" I asked, then added, just to be sure, "You won't make Odd go back?" I must have known we would spend the night. He had packed a little bag for me. There was a toothbrush and my nightgown, an extra sweater, and some clean underwear.

"Lake's froze near solid, and after we free the *Ashley* I've got thirty-two cars due in Menominee." He patted my shoulder. "Winter runs are never easy, and this is the coldest winter in some time. I'm afraid you're in for a long haul."

"But I want to see the boat."

"In due time. Once we get out of the harbor I'll have one of the boys show you around. Mind, it'll be cold down on the car deck. You'll want to wear your outer things." He looked down. I had put my shoes back on after taking off my leggings, but my boots were lying on the floor with their zippers open. "And your galoshes. The crew's shoveled a path on the weather deck, but it's slippery, and the engine room floor's slick as a whistle. You'll have to be careful."

"Can Alv show me around? He's going to take me to eat dinner with the crew."

"Oh," my father said, as if he were startled to think about something as mundane as meals. "I was figuring to have you eat with the officers."

"But I want to eat with the crew."

"I don't think so, *lille*. The men can get a bit rowdy."

That sealed it. I'd missed the drunk *and* the row in the pilothouse. I didn't intend to miss the rowdy men.

"*Please.*" I waited, but my father seemed to feel the matter was settled. "Alv said I could."

"Oh, did he now?"

I don't remember if I'd ever talked back to my father before, but I pushed my lower lip out. "I want to eat with Alv."

"Last I heard, Alv was not your captain."

"Well, the captain wasn't here!"

To my surprise, my father laughed. It wasn't a sound I often heard, and it seemed unnaturally hearty. "Man's not even out of the harbor, and already he's got a mutineer."

In truth, my father would have felt more capable of putting down a mutiny of men than dealing with a daughter. He was gone so often my mother would have been the one to handle my discipline. And I was a girl quick to sense an advantage. "Please, sir," I said, pulling my lip back in to make nice. "May I eat with Alv?"

My father hesitated. "Well, I'll have a word. If the men behave themselves, I suppose there's no harm. And I was thinking the boy could watch out for you. You don't want to go getting into trouble on a ship."

Oh, but I did. "Thank you, sir." I said.

"Be nice to the boy, *lille*. He's a little bit different."

"He's different from everyone!" I cried.

"Are you hungry? Do you want him to see if the cook has a little something you can eat?"

"Does she have cookies?"

"He." My father paused with his hand on the knob at the door. "I'm afraid you're the only lady on board."

"Does *he* have cookies?"

"I wouldn't be surprised. Second cook does the baking, and he makes some tasty things."

If the second cook did the baking, there would have to be a first. There was a bosun and the mates and a chief engineer, which meant there must be others. Alv was only learning to be a deckhand, so there had to some who already knew how. And Odd, who was only the second wheelsman, was at the helm. "Who's running the engine while you're down here?"

His hand relaxed on the knob. "Oh, I don't run the engines, *lille*. The engineer does that."

On a train the engineer ran the engine, but he didn't have a captain or a wheelsman. I wrinkled up my face in thought. "But if Odd steers and the engineer runs the engine, what do you do?"

"Ah." The question seemed to amuse him. "I keep watch on the bridge so I can tell the helmsman and the engineer what to do."

"You must have to yell awful loud for the engineer to hear you." The engine room was below the car deck. There had to be at least four companionways between it and the pilothouse.

He chuckled, not out loud, just a soft rattle inside his throat. "We use the chadburn. Just remember you're the only lady," he added as he opened the door. "That means you'll have to act like one."

When he left I picked up my bear. "Manitou, do you know what a chadburn is? Because I don't, but Alv is going to come back, and we're going to have cookies and get to see the chadburn and the train and the drunk man all for ourselves." I sat at my father's desk and propped Manitou against the walnut paneling. "Also we are going to have a bed in our own cabinet in the passengers' quarters." But in the meantime there was nothing to do, so I sang to myself. Then I sang "The Cat Came Back" for Odd and every verse of "The Teddy Bear's Picnic" for Manitou, but my father must have forgotten about the cookies, and still it wasn't time for dinner.

I never learned whether the child my mother lost was a boy or a girl, only that it died before it was born and that my mother knew it was dead even before she went to the doctor. I was born at home, but this time my mother had to have an operation, and she went to the new hospital on the hill.

My father was on the lake, and so I was sent to a neighbor's house, where I was put to bed in a baby's crib, even though I was too big. It was parked in a long closet, pressed up against a row of woolens that smelled of camphor. There was a party in the parlor. I could hear the laughter floating up the stairs to the dark closet, where it washed beneath the door on a narrow stripe of yellow light. It was past my bedtime, but the hosts' son, Billy, had been allowed to stay up. He was in the parlor with the grown-ups. I could hear his voice. He sang a song, and everyone clapped, and then they laughed some more. It wasn't fair, he was no older than I was—sometimes we played together in the woods between our houses, only days before we had gone sledding down my long driveway—but his mother let him stay up and put me to bed in a baby's crib in a dark closet. My whole body burned with the injustice, even though I knew it must be my mother's fault, she must have told them that I was to go to bed at eight. But surely she didn't know there would be a party, surely she wouldn't have wanted me to feel so excluded. At eight o'clock in the summertime, when the sky was still light, I often balked at bedtime. In the wintertime I was more compliant, but I hadn't known there would be a party either, everyone in the whole world except me, it seemed, singing and dancing, eating *krumkake*, and having fun. And in the morning, as Billy and I sat poking over our porridge at the kitchen table, no one said anything about it, his mother didn't suddenly slap her forehead and say, "Oh my goodness, we forgot all about you last night, I'm so sorry!" No one offered me a special treat to make it up, and I blistered with rage all over again, but all Mrs. Johnson said was, "Eat your breakfast."

When she wasn't looking, I kicked Billy under the table.

"Ow," he yelled, but his mother didn't turn from the stove. "Fern kicked me!"

"Eat your breakfast," she told him, and I smirked with satisfaction, though it hardly made up for missing the party.

Now of course I wonder why I didn't simply climb out of the crib. I was big enough. I suppose I just didn't think of it, which is odd, because I was a girl who did think of things. Or maybe I wasn't. Maybe I became one only after that night.

My mother came home from the hospital and went to bed, my father came to get me, and no one said a word, no one asked if I had a good time while I was gone or explained why there wasn't any baby, because at some point I must have been told that I was going to have a new brother or sister, surely I would have been curious the way children are, they would have wanted to prepare me. I don't remember. What I remember is wanting to tell my mother what they'd done. I wanted her to kiss me and tell me how sorry she was and how special I was. I wanted her to promise that she loved me and we would have our own party. *I wanted my mother.* But she went to bed and never got up again, and now my memory of that night in the closet has eclipsed any memory I might have kept of her, of those months of her pregnancy, when she must have gone around the house humming in anticipation of the birth. I try to remember her smile or the perfume of her hair, the shape of the baby growing beneath her dress and the way her lap must have felt as her stomach swelled and took more and more of it away from me, until finally it disappeared and I could no longer sit there at all, and maybe then I lay my head against her knees and she sang to me. I listen so hard for the lullaby of her voice, and what I hear instead is the ringing of the guests' laughter inside the crib pressed against those heavy clothes with their suffocating smell of camphor, my body so taut with anger I felt as if I couldn't breathe, couldn't even cry, though I think I screamed, screamed, and screamed, but they were laughing too loud, they were having too much fun, no one heard me. I went home, and no one explained what had happened or why I didn't have the promised brother or sister or why it was my father who fixed my porridge and heated the *fiskesuppe* the neighbors brought while my mother lay upstairs with her face turned to the wall, and my father wondered what to do about his wife and child and next voyage. Because the *Manitou* had first, second, and third mates, there were three wheelsmen and three engineers, but only one captain, and a captain's first duty is to his ship. It's his crew that is a captain's real family.

8

To get to the mess, officers had to go outside, down the ladder from the wing to the weather deck, all the way around to the crew's quarters at the aft end of the deckhouse. It was very cold, we wore our hats and coats and heavy boots, and I tucked my mitten inside Alv's glove. The *Manitou* had cleared the stub piers and was in the basin between the breakwaters. Under the heavy gray sky the bluffs to the north and south of us looked shapeless and dingy. Snow had blown off the sides, and it looked as if the hills themselves were sliding down to the ice that was all around us. Frost rimed the walls of the deckhouse, icicles hung like jagged bones from the boat deck, and when we came out from the overhang there was snow on the deck, but the crew had shoveled a path for us just like it was a sidewalk in Frankfort.

We stomped our feet, and then the rich smell from the galley seemed to suck us inside. It was a smell layered with onions and beef and sweet pillows of yeast, and though the passageway was dim even the yellow lights seemed to exude a warm fragrance, as if the cold outside had mixed our senses up together, and we had walked across the North Pole to a place where warmth wasn't just something you felt but smelled, and you could hear it too, warm spurts of laughter in the stew of voices from the mess, where the crew had gathered at a long table covered with oilcloth in a cheerful red-checkered pattern. It was the jolliest room I'd ever seen. There were stools instead of chairs, like the piano stool in our parlor at home except these were bolted to the table. A blackboard at the end listed the food, but it didn't matter that I couldn't read because it all smelled so very good.

"Who is *this*?" the porter asked, stooping a little, as Alv hung our hats and coats on hooks.

"This is the captain's daughter, Fern," Alv said.

"Well," the porter said with a breath that tickled the top of my head, "pleased to meet you, little lady," and the only man who hadn't looked up laughed, but no one else did, and it seemed as if he wasn't laughing at what the porter said but at some joke he'd told himself. He was hunched at the end of the table, mumbling into his sleeve, and his laugh was so abrupt it sounded more like a bark. "Would you like a glass of milk?"

"Yes, please," I said and picked a stool next to another empty one for Alv. There were six stools on each side, but the only person I knew was Alv, though now of course I remember every one of the crew by name. That first dinner Walter, Holgar, Axel, Red, Slim, Roald, Hans, Odd, Dick Butler, and the bosun were at the table, and that wasn't even half the crew because the men worked and ate in shifts, and the officers had their own dining room, though the bosun and engineers ate with the crew. The porter, Jake Andersen, wore a spotless white apron, because on a boat everything is always kept very clean. The bosun sees to that.

"Coming right up," he said, and the bald man across from me said, "Jaysus!" and helped himself to a salt shaker from one of the wooden boxes that were weighted to the table, because that's another thing about a ship—everything has to be fastened down. Some of the men wore their watch caps, but his bald head was as shiny as a bowling ball though it was shaped more like an egg that seemed a size too small for his thick neck. I put my hand to my scalp and wondered whether my head glistened like that underneath my hair.

Jake brought my milk and asked if I needed something to boost me up, but I liked my stool the way it was. "Wasn't planning on a youngster," he said.

"Wasn't planning on womenfolk," the bald man said. One of his front teeth was gold. I thought that if I had a gold tooth I wouldn't have such a sour tone, but this was Rudy, the bosun, and you wouldn't want a please-and-thank-you voice to boss the deckhands around. "Women's bad luck on a boat."

"Little girl never hurt no one," Walter said. He was the third engineer, and he took a liking to me from the start because he had his own small daughter at home.

"Women and preachers," the bosun said. "You ever hear of the *Hunter Savidge*? Girl just about this size on her when she went down."

"What's the matter with you?" the redheaded fireman asked. His real name was Elmer, but his hair was such a flaming orange they called him Red. Rings of soot were ground into his hands and the skin around eyes. He worked at the very bottom of the ship, in the firehold, where the firemen stoked the fires for the big Scotch boilers and answered to the chief engineer instead of the bosun. "Telling the captain's daughter about ships that gone down."

"Women, preachers, *and* fairies." The bosun aimed a glare at Alv, and that's when I noticed that several of the other men were staring. I thought they probably couldn't help it any more than I could. He was that beautiful.

Holgar made a point of looking away. "So how do you like our tub so far?" he asked me. A little whistle in his voice seemed to come out his nose. He had a face like a mushroom, and his coveralls were spattered with paint. That was how you could tell the deckhands, I learned, because one thing a deckhand never finished was the chipping and scraping and painting that is forever taking place on a ship, that and scrubbing everything down with a kind of soap called soogee that reddened their eyes and turned their hands raw, all except for Alv, whose sweater was as spotless as the porter's apron because this was his first trip, and that was how you could tell a deckhand was new.

"I like it. I think I'll be a sailor when I grow up," I announced.

Bosun rolled his eyes. "Well, if we ain't on the Good Ship Lollipop."

The men began to joke among themselves while the porter brought their orders. "And what can I bring you, little lady?" he asked me.

"I want the meat, please," I said. "And the potatoes and the vegetables and do you have dessert?"

"We got anything you want."

"So Ole died," Axel said. He was the deckhand with a harelip, which was something I had never seen before. It looked like someone had tried to stitch his mouth up to his nose.

"Not another Ole and Lena joke." Slim groaned. He was a watch, and they called him Slim because he was so tall and skinny, almost as tall as my father, but even thinner, and his ears stuck out. He ate with a spindly forefinger planted on the middle of his plate like he was afraid it might fly away. I never did learn his real name. But he had an important job. Every half hour he was supposed to check everything on the boat. Some people thought that the *Pere Marquette 18* went down because a deadlight in the flicker was open and they blamed the watch, though other people blamed the captain for sending the distress call out too late. "We've heard 'em all already."

"Ja, but Alv here hasn't," Hans said, and some of the men gave Alv a sidelong look, like they were peeking and didn't want anyone else to know. A lot of Norwegians and Swedes said *ja* when they meant yes, even the ones born in Michigan, but the word sounded different in Hans's mouth, and that was because he was German. I thought his accent must be the way people in Wisconsin talked. Wisconsin seemed so far away I expected people there would speak another language.

"I haven't heard it either," I said, which seemed to strike most of them as funny as the joke itself, though their laughter didn't take quite the right tone. It didn't occur to me that most of the men, not just the bosun, would prefer not to have the captain's daughter at their table. The porter brought my plate of meat cakes and potatoes fried with onions, and on the side there was a thick, creamy mound of cottage cheese, some coleslaw, big coins of pickled beets the color of rubies, and fat, buttery rolls.

"You just don't like it because Ole and Lena are Norskies."

"Ja, but when a Norskie tells 'em, Lena and Ole are Swedes."

"Well they sure as hell ain't never Finns," Axel said, which seemed to settle it. There was so much paint splattered on his coverall you couldn't tell what color it was. All the deckhands except Alv wore coveralls over their heavy sweaters, which made their arms look so lumpy it was a surprise to see regular-size hands coming out of the sleeves, though the men who worked below just wore shirtsleeves because it was over 100 degrees in the firehold and engine room even on the coldest day of winter.

Holgar put his coffee cup down. "Take it from me. You don't never want to work on a boat run by a Finn. Finns is warlocky."

"Paavo ain't." That was Roald, the deckhand with sloped shoulders and a voice full of gravel. I wasn't sure who Paavo was, except that he wasn't at dinner with us. Anyway I was more interested in Axel. I turned my eyes back to the shiny ruck of skin above his upper lip. The bosun glared at me. "What are you staring at?"

"What happened to your mouth?" I asked.

"Nothin'. It came this way." Then Axel smiled, a big smile, kind of fake, twisted like he wanted to show me the way his mouth worked, and it scared me a little, but I didn't want to let on, so I said, "Well, mine came like this," and the men all snickered, but Axel didn't seem to mind. "Hey, she's a kid. Kids say what they think. Rather that than someone thinkin' but not sayin'." He cleared his throat. "So Ole dies and Lena goes to the paper to put a notice in the obituaries."

"Is this a clean one?" Walter asked with a nod in my direction, and the bosun glared again, which made me think better of asking what obituaries were.

"The man at the counter says he's sorry but what does she want to say about her husband, and Lena says, 'Just put Ole died.' 'That's all?' he asks, but then he gets it, she's worried about the money, because you know that dumb Norskie never made nothin', so he tells her, 'Surely you want to say somethin' more. First five words is free.'"

37

"Know how to tell when a Finn is an extrovert?" Holgar asked. "He stares at *your* shoes while you're talking."

"Do you mind?" Axel said as the men began to titter. "I was the one tellin' a joke here." He leaned forward. "So Lena thinks a minute and finally she says, 'Okay. Put Ole died. Boat for sale.'"

All the men laughed, even the bosun, so I did too. Only the man at the end of the table, who also wore paint-spattered coveralls, who had long, thin fingers coming out from his sleeves and a twitchy rabbit's face, all pink around his eyes and nostrils, didn't laugh. He was still muttering to himself, so I tugged at Alv's sleeve and whispered, "Is that the drunk man Odd?" The men began to laugh again.

"Hey, Odd," Red said to a man on the other side of the table with a sunken chest and little streak of blood in one eye, "you sneak any of that coffin varnish aboard? You know the captain don't allow drink." He winked, and Roald leaned toward me. "That there is Twitches. Don't none of us know what he's jibbering about all day, but doggone if he ain't the strongest hand on the boat."

"He's a teetotaler is his problem," Odd said.

Roald laughed. "Him and this boy that brung the captain's daughter, but he'll learn to take a nip soon enough if he wants to sleep. Matey always makes the new boy bunk with Twitches."

Holgar turned to Alv. "Got your sea legs yet, boy? When we get to Menominee Bosun's going to make you jump the clump first."

"*If*," Dick Butler said.

"What do you mean?" Holgar asked.

"She's leaking. All that ice last run damaged the hull."

"Says who?"

"Paavo. She's leaking in the coal hold. And you can trust a fireman to know."

"Pumps are keeping up," Walter said.

Dick snorted. "For now. It's a long way across the lake. Run into a storm, she's going to need all that coal."

"Wouldn't be the first ship to use fans to dry it out," Walter said. "Captain wouldn't take her out if she wasn't seaworthy."

"Would if the railroad said to."

"Does Captain know she's leaking?" Hans asked.

Dick shrugged. "Ain't my job to tell him."

"Lucky us then. Don't run, you don't get paid. Besides, Larsen calls the shots below." That meant Larsen had to be the chief engineer. Holgar turned back to Alv. "Better get ready for Menominee. That's when we'll see if you know how to earn your keep."

Red rubbed his cheek. "Ain't Menominee got grates?"

Roald guffawed. "Shows what you know down in the firehold all day. Once those pilings ice over, grates don't make no difference at all. Just wait till new boy gets to Green Bay. It's a hell of a lot colder that side of the lake."

"And that's one shallow body of water," Axel added. "Freezes to the bottom, and you never seen a passage so full of rock and narrow. They don't call it Death's Door for nothin'."

"Haunted too." The bosun sat up straighter as if the conversation had suddenly picked up interest. "Storm nights in a north wind that old lightkeeper at St. Martin Island still goes out looking for his kids."

"Did they get lost?" I wanted to know.

Bosun leaned his face across the table toward mine and with a sour spray of breath hissed, "Disappeared in a storm rowing home from school. Lightkeeper's been dead for years, but stormy nights folks still see him out there searching with that green lantern."

"Don't you listen to him, honey." Walter picked up his knife. "He's just trying to scare you and the boy."

"Cap'n's daughter don't look like she scares too easy to me," Red observed as I asked the porter for another plate, because I was hungrier than I had ever been, and everything was so delicious. "She sure as hell ain't seasick."

"Hard to get seasick on an ice rink," Roald said. "Tell the men from the boys when the wind begins to howl."

"She's a *girl*," Walter said.

"Don't know about that." Slim set down his fork. "Looks to me like she might have a bit of the old captain in her."

39

"And a fine captain he is," Walter agreed.

"Wears da suit a bit too much if you ask me," Hans said.

Axel cleared his throat again. It was what he did, I learned, whenever the attention went off him. "You think this is ice? In Green Bay the ice is so thick they used to run stagecoaches from Sturgeon Bay to Menominee twenty miles across the Bay. Marked the road with Christmas trees, even put up a portable hotel halfway across."

"And Odd better hope that hotel has a bar," Red said. The men snorted with laughter.

"Never known you to turn down a drink," Odd shot back. There were little blotches of purple like moss beneath the skin on his nose and cheeks. "Any fool can steer a boat sober. It takes a damn good sailor to navigate drunk."

"Even the captain's daughter'll need a nip when we get to Green Bay." Roald shuddered. "A drunk at the wheel and a crack in the hull. Not to mention the ghost nobody ever sees. Sometimes I wish I'd picked a different line of work."

"And what would that be?" Dick Butler said before I had a chance ask about the ghost. "These days ferries got the only jobs there is."

"That's the truth. New Deal's the same old deal up here, as far as I can see," Odd said.

"Personally I'd rather run 'er through Death's Door on the ice than when the black flies is biting." Holgar took a sip of his coffee.

"Course just because they had a stage don't mean it was safe." Axel turned to Alv. "Your father ever tell you the story of Hansen and Glass?"

"His father wasn't around for Hansen and Glass, and neither were you." Slim scowled. "It's ancient history."

"So's the *Hunter Savidge*," Red said. "And that was Huron."

"What's the difference?" the bosun snapped. "They're both sweetwater seas."

"Wasn't talkin' about the *Hunter Savidge*. I'm talkin' about Hansen and Glass."

"Trouble with history is it gets swoggled every time it gets told," Roald said.

Axel's face darkened, all except the shiny patch of lavender skin above his lip. "Ain't nothin' swoggled about this. Got written up in the paper, that's how true it is. Lars used to tell that story. Pull that paper out and show it whenever anyone disbelieved him."

"Who's Lars?" Alv asked.

Walter shook his head. "Poor sailor. Boxcar jumped the tracks while he was sitting on the apron fence. Fell and broke his neck."

"Keep talking," Odd said. "Scare the pretty new boy off, who knows which of you deck apes'll be bunking with Twitches?"

"Boat's no place for the fainthearted." The bosun nodded at the horseshoe nailed above the door. "Don't catch none of you whistling in the companionways or spitting in the hold. I'm telling you, women and preachers."

"This little girl here don't make half a woman," Walter said.

"Rather bunk with Twitches than a queer," Dick Butler said. He was an oiler, like Alv's father, one of the black gang, the men who worked below deck, and he had a somewhat swarthy look that could have come from the ground-in dirt or the fact that he rarely saw the sun. I didn't like the way he looked at Alv, though later I would learn he was just out of sorts because he'd been passed over for promotion to third engineer. He picked on Alv because Alv was new, just like kids do, or like grown-ups who find an easy target when their real beef is with the world. That was part of it anyway. Years later I would sense something else, but I was much too young to know anything about that then.

"You want to hear this story or not?" Axel didn't wait for an answer. "Winter '03. Hansen's a cigar maker never been to the area before, but he's got business in Menominee, which is where Glass is headed, so the two men hire themselves a horse and cutter in Sturgeon Bay and set out midafternoon. Now that ice is full of cracks, but they get across 'em all till the last one, still four, five miles out from Menominee . . ."

"Menominee!" I cried. "That's where we're going!"

"Jaysus!" Bosun slapped his fork down.

"Nigh on five o'clock, gettin' toward dark, Bay starts foggin' up, and that last crack's a good four-foot wide. Nothin' to do but get that horse to jump, only his hind feet don't make it, and instead of pullin' hisself forward, that dumb horse tries to back up and falls in, two thousand pounds of cement for brains, water cold enough to freeze the balls off a brass monkey, and those men got to haul the damn beast out. Then Glass falls in, so Hansen has to fish him out too, but in those wet clothes he's bound to freeze to death, so Hansen spreads the lap robe on the ice for Glass to stand on, buck naked, while Hansen wrings out his drawers."

The light that came through the windows behind the men across the table had softened to a pale pearl. It had begun to snow, which seemed strange because in town when it snowed it always got so quiet, but here in the crew's mess everything was so jolly, and even when the conversation lulled, you could still hear Twitches muttering to himself and the ice pounding against the hull. It was the best party I'd ever been to, and Billy Johnson didn't get to come.

"Now Hansen's never been on the ice before, he don't know the way, so once Glass is dressed he sets out for Menominee to get help. Course Hansen's own clothes is none too dry, by now it's full dark, there's all this fog, doggone harness busted, and he figures both of 'em are goners since Glass is sure to freeze to death before he ever gets to Menominee, still five miles off if he can even see to walk a straight line. Hansen himself is walkin' in circles just to keep movin' he's so cold, even that dumb horse is shiverin', walkin' circles right behind him like he's hitched to a grindstone. But, whaddaya know, Glass makes it and gets two stage men from Menominee who know the route to go back out. There was icicles half a foot long hanging from Hansen's moustache when they found him, but they took him back to the Menominee Hotel and gave him some brandy and that perked him right up, though he said he'd never cross the bay again unless someone come along to invent a flyin' machine."

Odd turned to Alv. "Imagine icicles half a foot long hanging from your moustache."

"You think that boy can grow a moustache?" Holgar asked, and most of the men laughed.

"But what happened to the horse?" I wanted to know, which made them laugh even harder.

"Don't you worry about that horse, honey," Walter said. "That horse survived just fine."

"Never went anywhere near water again though," Axel said. "Not even to take a drink."

I pondered that as Jake brought a platter of cookies to the table and eyed my plate. "I believe this little girl likes Sam's cooking."

"Thank you for my dinner. It was delicious," I said, remembering my manners.

"Glad someone does," Odd said. "He serving that bilgewater for supper again?"

The men began to guffaw. "Oh, thank you for our vittles, they was ever so good" several of them chanted in falsetto.

"That's *fiskesuppe* to you," Sam said as he appeared in the door to the galley. "Made with the finest lake perch."

"Finest lake perch is fried," Bosun said. "You going ice-fishing this afternoon or serving last week's stew?"

"Matey, you're skating on thin ice." Sam had big, square, yellow teeth and freckles, even on his hands. He was dressed all in white with a white apron over his white shirt and pants and a funny little white hat that looked like it was made out of paper on top of his crinkly ginger-colored hair. "It's a risky business, insulting the cook." I didn't understand because everyone had seconds and seemed to like the food as much as I did, and Alv had to explain to me later that they were just having fun.

"You ought to wish it was thin ice," Red grumbled. "Ice this thick we'll be lucky to get back before opening day."

"*If*," Dick repeated. "I'm telling you, she's leaking."

43

"Don't be such a sad apple," Sam said. "What do you think, Walter? You're the engineer." Which was a sore point, because it was Walter who'd been promoted instead of Dick.

"Pumps are working." Walter turned to Red. "You think the Hebrew Hammer's wrist is healed back up?"

"Counting on it. I want to see the Tigers take two in a row."

"What do you care?" Roald said. "You ain't going to see or hear it. You're going to be down in the firehold, and the whole season's going to pass you by."

"Doesn't matter whether I see it. World champs are world champs whether I'm there or not."

Axel cleared his throat. "I got another joke. Sailor meets a pirate in a bar."

Bosun stood. "Chow's over. Time for you whores to get back to work." Everyone else worked two four-hour shifts a day, but the deckhands worked eight, though whenever a ship docked all the deckhands went to work no matter whose shift it was.

"I want to hear about the pirate," I said.

Walter pushed his cup aside. "Aw, let her hear about the pirate."

"You too, new boy," Bosun said.

"Captain says I'm supposed to move his daughter to one of the passenger cabins," Alv said.

"Oh, I see. We ain't got one woman aboard, we got two. Captain's daughter and her nursemaid."

"It's snowing. Go ahead and take her through the galley," Jake offered.

"Inside, outside, don't make no difference on a ship," Slim said.

"Does to me," Holgar said with that little whistle in his nose again.

Bosun glared at Alv. "Five minutes, and I want you down in the engine room with a paintbrush in your hand. I don't like your sweater."

"Yes, sir."

"But I want to hear about the pirate," I said. "*And* about the ghost that no one sees."

"Well, that's the thing," Axel answered. "Don't nobody know 'cause nobody ever sees."

"But if I could get a picture . . ." Holgar said.

"You and your camera. You think a ghost is goin' to sit down and pose all pretty?" Axel turned his profile to Holgar and primped a hand along his cheek. "Say cheese."

"That's okay," Alv promised me. "I know that joke. I'll tell you later."

9

*M*y stepmother was a gay woman. I hesitate to use
that word because it has such a different meaning now, yet none of the
other words I might choose—*cheerful, lively, happy*, though she was
all of those things—convey quite so precisely her zest. I don't know
what my mother was like, but I imagine they were quite different. My
stepmother liked to sing, she was a noisy woman, always banging on the
piano. When she raised a window or put one down it thumped, in her
kitchen pots and pans rang out, her scrub brush rasped, her footsteps
echoed. When my father was gone, she kept company with her women
friends, and they seemed to have a jolly time of it, chattering their after-
noons away, playing *spardam* and gin. At the end of July, when the
cherries ripened, they got together to can, and the house filled with
the sound of glass jars rattling in big enamel pots. It was my job to pick
the stems, then they had to dig the pits, and when they boiled the fruit
down, the fragrant steam seemed to carry their gossip back and forth
like the cartoon clouds in *The Captain and the Kids* and *Little Orphan
Annie*. Driving was not something many women did in Frankfort in the
1930s, but she did, and on the occasions when she drove us up to the
Elberta bluff to watch my father's ship depart, she packed a picnic.
"Now, Fern," she would say, "we are going to have a good time,"
though to me it always sounded less like a wish or a prediction than a
decree, something that was going to happen whether I liked it or not,

and I did not. I wanted to be aboard the ship, listening to the men's jokes in the mess, up in the pilothouse at the helm, down on the car deck fastening the clamps and turnbuckles, in the engine room wiping down the crankshaft, playing cards in the flicker, or even in the uneasy dark of my cabin waiting on a ghost. The only place I didn't want to be was where I was, up on the bluff watching.

She was different from my father, but it was that difference that made her so well suited to him. She was the ideal captain's wife—she never seemed to mind that he was gone, though she was equally merry when he was there. I should have taken to her, but I didn't. She was nice to me, but there was something relentless about her cheer. She was a woman who made the best of things, not out of effort but because she was incapable of doing otherwise. There was something simple about her, and she was admirable in that particular way that simple people sometimes are. Do not misunderstand me: I don't mean that she was simpleminded. Nor did I dislike her. I accepted her, I just did not take to her. This was not out of loyalty to my mother. Already I could scarcely remember my mother. Yet there was some part of me that I withheld. She did not try to kiss or hug me, and I did not kiss or hug her. I called her Mother because I was supposed to. Her name was Lene.

She was older than my mother but still a good bit younger than my father, a widow I believe, though I never heard mention of her first husband, and she brought no children to the marriage with my father, nor did they have children together. It may have been that she was what they used to call barren, though if she wanted children of her own, if it pained her not to have them, she did not let on. She would have been over forty when they married, and I suppose it's possible that it was simply getting past her time. In any case, I suspect she did not show disappointments because she felt none. She was a woman of enormous energy but no passion. It was all the same to her, children or not, my father home or not, winter or summer, fair weather or foul.

They married a year after my mother died. I don't know if he loved her. As I say, my father was not a demonstrative man. And perhaps

47

love didn't matter. It was not unheard of for a widower to remarry in order to give his children a mother. My father was gone so much, and in the time between my mother's death and their marriage I was often cared for by this or that neighbor, the women of the West Side, those blocks of Forest and Leelanau Avenues closest to the lake. There was a woman who came in once a week to clean and do some cooking, and he might have hired her or someone else to stay with me, but I suspect they wouldn't hear of it. Norwegians, and they were primarily Norwegian, are a hospitable people who help each other out. Another mouth to feed or child to tend would not have troubled them. Or perhaps they were wary that a live-in woman might set her sights on my father. Either way their generosity, which I did not perceive to be generosity because children take for granted whatever they are given, was not extended out of fondness for my mother. They said little about her to me, so little I think they must have made a point of it. I'm not saying they disliked her—because she was my father's wife, they would have accepted her— but I never had the feeling that they embraced her, not in the way they did Lene. It was one of those West Side women who introduced Lene to my father. She came from Beulah, otherwise he would have known her already, and once she married him they took her in completely. It's quite possible that they chose her for him as a way of choosing her for themselves. My father wasn't the only captain or mate from the West Side, and they set great store on the friendships that sustained them while their husbands were away.

   She was a large woman, not fat but dense, thick through the middle, big boned, and tall, taller than my mother. It was as if her personality required a larger presence, took up more space. I sometimes wonder if the reason I don't remember my mother is that she took up no space at all. I have always imagined her to be a quiet woman, somewhat solitary, much like my father, but without his sustaining passion for the lake.

   Certainly she was smaller. That much I know from the few photographs I possess. I never saw a picture of her as a girl—she was an orphan, and it's possible no one ever thought to take one. How she came to be orphaned I don't know. I liked to imagine her parents both died on one of those many ships that sailed through a crack in the lake, as sailors say of those ships that disappear without a trace, that sail from fair weather into the sharp teeth of a storm and simply vanish, or maybe they went down with Captain Kilty, perhaps her father was a mate on the *Pere Marquette 18* and her mother the cabin maid, though I knew it wasn't so, for if it was we would have known it.

The earliest of those pictures is my parents' wedding portrait, in which she wears a simple drop-waist dress of white or cream with a V-neck, long sleeves, and a soft hem that falls below her knees, what appear to be pale, silk stockings, and white or cream-colored Mary Jane heels with pointed toes. The long flap on her matching cloche hat conceals her forehead and all but a few wisps of blonde hair. In one hand she holds a small bouquet; the other is linked inside my father's arm. He wears his uniform, and they both look very formal. Neither smile, though I think that is less a comment on their union than a convention of the wedding portraits of the time. The photograph is so stylized it seems to say more about the era than either of my parents. With that hat I can't even tell whether she was pretty or if I might resemble her, only that like all of us she was fair.

There is another picture of her holding me as a baby, but the print is so small inside its wide, white crenellated border, the camera so far away, you cannot read her expression. It would have been taken in late afternoon, for the shadow of the photographer stretches toward her across the grass. Her dress appears to have some sort of subtle pattern, tiny flowers perhaps, or maybe it's geometric, and the light-colored Mary Jane heels look to be the same ones she wore to marry. I want to believe that she is smiling, though a magnifying glass yields only blur. The wind is blowing her hair, which is neither long nor short, across her mouth, and in her arms I am no more than a lump in a blanket.

In the last picture I am three or four. She is seated on the top step of the front porch of the house on Leelanau Avenue, and I am standing on the second, our heads nearly level. We are facing each other, her arms are clasped around my knees, one of mine reaches around her shoulder, and the other rests against her collarbone. I am wearing a pale, short-sleeved shift that might be organdy with a starched white cotton collar, and my outstretched arms have lifted the hem to expose the edge of my underpants. Her dress drapes around her calves. It too is a light color, though hers has a waist, and both of us wear Mary Janes, hers the same white or ivory heels, mine black with rounded toes and a sheen that must be patent leather, the sort of shoes a little girl would get for Easter, though it is clearly summer, for on Easter in Frankfort we were often still picking our way up the walk to church in boots. Her hair is swept back from her forehead, mine is cut short, bobbed in the back, with bangs like a little Dutch girl's, and though my face is in shadow, I am surely smiling. She is. Her lips are parted, she is not looking at the camera, but at me, and her face is so radiant she may be laughing. It's not much to tell me who we were, but it does promise that in that moment we were happy. She wasn't always the woman who came home from the hospital and turned her face to the wall.

I think my father must have loved her. Why else would he have married after all those years spent single? He was near fifty when they wed, and she was not yet twenty. Moreover, he sailed a perilous inland sea. He could not have expected to be widowed. On that day he or whoever took that picture of us on our porch could not have imagined she would leave us so soon. But what's to be made of that, what's to be said? That we never know what will happen? True enough if trite.

But it is also true that sometimes you know exactly what will happen, or to be more precise, you know what cannot. That was my problem. And I held it against my stepmother, whose only crime was to accept things as they are.

10

We couldn't just pass through the galley to the passenger quarters because Sam had to show me how everything worked, the cupboard that opened from the top so nothing could fall out in rough weather, the plates that were stacked in wooden cages to keep them from flying off the shelves, the rail across the front of the stove. Even the shelves for the cups slanted backward. But all he said about the tall metal urns with spigots for hot water and coffee was that I was never to touch them lest I get burned. Down the passageway a walk-in refrigerator let off a chill breath of air, and on our way I peeked inside the officers' mess, where the first and third mates were still at the table drinking coffee, not even talking. It was fancier than the crew's, with a white linen cloth and chairs instead of stools, and the passenger dining room was fancier still, with curtains on the bottom windows and that soft, even, white light coming through the windows of its clerestory just like it did in the galley and the extra room for preparation and washing dishes.

The *Manitou* was ticketed as a freight boat, which meant it couldn't carry more than twelve passengers, though even in summer it rarely carried that many, just the occasional railroad official or family of tourists taking a shortcut across the lake. I couldn't see why the whole, wide forward part of the deckhouse should belong to them while the crew was packed into the narrow aft space.

My father had told Alv that I was to choose whichever cabin I wanted and entrusted him with the key to the purser's office, where the keys for the whole ship hung from a rack above the desk. The purser was the officer in charge of money and supplies, but he was sick, and my father had put his third mate, Casper Strom, in charge of supplies, though he still had to bunk in the cabin he shared with the second mate instead of the bigger cabin behind the purser's office. I wanted to choose it, but Alv said I couldn't, just one of the regular passenger cabins, though he let me look around the office while he fetched the keys. There was a wavy glass window that opened in the door so the purser could take the passengers' money, and I raised it up and down until Alv told me to quit because he had to get below and I still hadn't picked my cabin, but first I had to look at the safe beside the purser's desk. That was where the purser kept all the ship's money and if they wanted, the passengers could give him their valuables for safekeeping. I liked the word *valuables*, so I tried it out a few times to see how it felt in my mouth, and then I said, "What kind of valuables?"

"If they had lots of money or jewelry or something," Alv said, but the way he said it made me know he couldn't imagine having lots of money or jewelry. I wanted him to open the safe so we could see the jewels, but it didn't have the kind of lock he could open with a key, you had to know the combination, and anyway there wouldn't be any jewelry inside now, though I still wished he had the combination because I wanted to see what the inside of a safe looked like, if it was lined in velvet or fur, but even when it was empty it had to be locked because . . .

"I *know*," I said. "In case the ship begins to roll."

There was more, but Alv said for me to hurry up, and even though the cabins were all the same, I had to inspect every one, along with the smoking room, where he said no women were allowed, and neither was the crew. Even when it was below zero they had to go out to the weather deck because it was dangerous to smoke below. The only thing the crew ever got to do in the passenger quarters was clean, though every two weeks they lined up in the passageway to collect their pay. Then Alv showed me the ladies' head, which had wooden stall doors for the big square camp toilets like the one in the officer's quarters, though I hoped this one wouldn't be quite so stinky, and a shower that I would have all to myself when even my father had to share. At home we took baths in our big clawfoot tub. I had never taken a shower, but thought it would probably be like standing in the rain.

"What would you do if the ship began to roll?" I asked him but didn't wait for an answer. "I like to roll down the hill where I live. Do you have a hill to roll down?"

"There's too many trees on the one at the end of my street." A memory that wasn't quite a smile flickered at his mouth. "What we liked to do, us boys, we used to take a big piece of cardboard and slide down the dunes."

That sounded like fun. The dunes were way steeper than my hill.

"It's a short ride down and a long climb up" was what he said, though the way he said it made me know he thought the climb worth it.

"Maybe you could find a piece of cardboard and take me when we get back." I had forgotten he would be working on the ship while I had time to play. Already I imagined us doing everything together. "Dick Butler says the ship is leaking. He said we'll be in trouble if we hit a storm."

"I guess you're always in trouble when you hit a storm."

I couldn't decide if I hoped we did or not. It would be an *adventure*. "Maybe he's wrong."

"I hope so. But he's no dummy. He knows his way around an engine room."

"He's mean to you."

"Everybody's mean to me."

"How come?"

"Because. Anyway, it's not going to storm. Before you know it we'll be across the lake and back."

That left me even more undecided. I wanted to be on my journey, but I didn't want it to be over before I knew it.

"What's that?" I pointed to a narrow door that had a hole where a knob or a handle should be. It looked as if my hand would just fit, but Alv said not to try it in case my hand got stuck.

"A closet," he guessed, because the ship had to have someplace to keep all the linens. There was another door he hadn't opened at the back of the lounge, but I couldn't choose it either, though he unlocked it to let me see, because that was the special room for the managers from the railroad whenever they crossed the lake, and it was bigger than the purser's and fancier than any of them. It had a big double bed in case a manager wanted to bring his wife, and there was a blanket with stripes that matched the rug on the floor and a built-in leather sofa, when my father didn't have a rug or a sofa. The managers' compartment was where the ghost lived, that's what the men said. Bosun claimed that people saw the ghost's face in the wood paneling at the back, but I didn't see it, so I called, but it didn't answer, and Alv said again to hurry up and choose my cabin because he had to lock the managers' room back up before the bosun came looking to see what was taking so long.

"And don't you be calling the ghost out anymore," he told me. "Because ghosts can walk through walls, and I don't want to see one."

"I do." I wanted to know what a ghost looked like and if you could see through them like people said.

I chose the first cabin behind the smoking room even though they were all alike, small as the mates', with the same dark-wood paneling, but dressed up for company with bright green wool blankets instead of gray. And the top berth folded up like a Pullman car on a train, so a passenger could use the bottom berth as a sofa, though there wasn't any need, because the wide, wood-paneled lounge that ran down the middle of the passenger quarters had all the seating anyone could want, little divans with side tables and leather armchairs that all had brass eyes on the back, where long hooks attached to the baseboard could secure them when seas got rough. Two square wooden columns ran straight up the middle, a fat one that enclosed the escape hatch that Alv was going to show me when we went below and a thinner one for the forward spar, and though there weren't any windows and the ceilings were very low like they were everywhere on the ship except in the galley and passenger dining room, there were lights overhead, and at the front of the lounge, just below my father's cabin, an observation room was fitted out like a sunroom with lots of windows and hemp chairs.

When Alv returned the keys to the purser's office, I spotted a rack on the wall that held a row of little brass tubes that I hadn't noticed before because I'd been so interested in the safe. "What's that?"

But Alv said he was done answering my questions, the bosun wanted him below.

"Ask your father," he said and had me put my coat in the wooden locker in my cabin while he went up to my father's cabin to fetch Manitou and the little bag my father had packed. I thought Manitou would like the observation room because all the shutters were down inside their pockets and we could see out on three sides, plus there was a big brass compass that would tell us where we were going. I wondered if he would like the top berth, which is where I wanted to sleep because you got to climb a ladder that was hooked to the side. That was the rack I'd decided on, which is what sailors called their beds. When they went to sleep they said they were going to rack out. Even though it was his first trip, Alv knew a lot about ships from listening to his father talk; he just didn't have any practice. Also there was a hitch in his gait, which I hadn't noticed at first because everyone walks a little funny on a ship, but now when I asked he told me he'd had polio, but even so he was lucky because a lot of people with polio had to live inside an iron lung, and he just barely limped.

I didn't know anyone with polio, so I thought maybe it was something you got from living in Elberta, but that wasn't nice, and anyway I was more interested in the ship. I hadn't thought when I decided on the upper berth, because what if Manitou fell out? He would get hurt, and it would be my fault, so I decided to climb up there by myself to look around but sleep with him on the bottom. I expected he would be impressed with all the new words I was learning. The handles on the doors were called dogs, and when you secured a door you were supposed to dog it down. I had wrapped a cookie in a napkin for him, though Alv told me that Billy Cooke—that was the second cook's name, which was a big joke among the crew—got up in the middle of the night to make sure there were baked goods on hand all day, and whenever I wanted I could get a glass of milk or a cookie or even a sandwich because there was always meat and cheese in the big refrigerator. But what I wanted to know was how the refrigerator worked. At home there were electric wires, that's how we had lights and why we didn't have to buy ice from the icehouse.

"There's generators." His almond-shaped eyes lit. "Wait till you get a look at the engine room. You've never seen so much equipment."

"Yes, please." I tugged his hand. "Let's go see it now."

"When my shift's over," he said. "*If* Captain says it's okay."

"And the train," I reminded him. "Don't forget the train."

"I won't," he promised, and then I was by myself in the big lounge, where I sat first in one chair and then another and pretended I was a grown-up lady on a grand tour, even though I didn't really want to be a lady, until he came back with Manitou and my bag and I remembered that he was supposed to tell me about the pirate, but because I wanted to see everything and asked so many questions, he'd been gone too long already, though I knew if he had his choice he'd rather stay and tell me about the pirate. *I* would.

After he left I looked at the jigsaw puzzle that someone had left on the wood shelf beneath one of the hemp tables, along with a couple of books, and a game of checkers. The puzzle was a picture of mountains, but it had a *lot* of pieces. So I ate Manitou's cookie, and we played checkers, but it wasn't that much fun because I had to move his pieces for him, and when you play that way it doesn't matter who wins. I pressed his face to the window. Snow was piled on the foredeck, and even though it wasn't falling very hard, it made everything look a little blurry. The north and south pier lights had come on, or maybe because the day was so gray they had never gone off. And even though I was learning so much, I wished the ship could go faster because I wanted to see the other side of the lake where the mother bear and her two cubs escaped the fire. There were no pictures in the books, Alv wouldn't be back anytime soon, and my father was probably talking to the engineer on the chadburn that I hadn't seen yet, so I sat in the dark-paneled smoking room where ladies and the crew weren't allowed. It had a big humidor and smelled like tobacco even though no one had used it in a long time. A drawer held a row of cigars. I pretended to smoke one, but it tasted bad, like wet, moldy leaves stuck to the bottom of a shoe, and then I couldn't decide whether to throw it in the dented brass spittoon or put it back, because if I threw it in the spittoon whoever found it would know I'd been there and maybe tell the bosun, so I put it back even though it was all slimy at the end, and then, because there was nothing else to do, I decided I would just have to explore the ship for myself.

11

*C*hildren are animals. They want what they want. And all the unwanting in the world can never undo the damage.

12

*T*he hatch to the car deck was behind the aft deckhouse, and because Alv had said that I could get a snack whenever I wanted, I went back through the galley, where Jake was washing dishes with his back to me in the prep room. From the crew's quarters it was just steps across the deck to the doghouse, the big metal hood over the steep companionway we'd come up that morning when we boarded. I held the rail, which dipped at the top. The railcars blocked most of the light that came through the portholes strung like pearls high along the hull and over the top of the massive seagate that was supposed to keep waves from washing over the car deck, though sometimes seagates bent or even tore off, and the first Ann Arbor ferries didn't have seagates at all. From the top I could see that the boxcars had a little peak to let ice and snow slide off. Then I was at the bottom, and the peaks disappeared, the cars looked flat on top. Down here the rasping thunder of the ice was much louder, along with the thumping of the boilers. The chains that held the cars creaked and seemed to echo inside the big metal cavern despite all the racket. I could have shouted, and no one would hear. A thrill of goosebumps rose along my arms. In the whole world there was no one who knew where I was. I could do anything I wanted.

The metal car deck pulsed through my feet, not the movement of the ice or the water (the higher you go the more you feel a ship's sway), but the steady vibration of the engine. It was like something alive, and I liked the idea that the ship might be a living creature.

A row of white stanchions ran down the middle of the deck, but the train wasn't like I thought it would be, because they had to park the cars on four rows of tracks that gleamed faintly in the shadowy light, so it was more like four short trains, which I would have known if I had thought about it or remembered from the loading, would have known even a ship as big as the *Manitou* wasn't long enough for a whole train to stretch out like I was at a crossing watching it go by. Also the weight of the cars had to balance or else the ship would capsize and sink, which had happened to the *Ann Arbor 4*. Everything happened to the *Ann Arbor 4*. It seemed to be even unluckier than the *Ashley*. There were eight cars on each track, fastened in place with chains, big heavy side-jacks, blocks, clamps, and turnbuckles, because cars that broke loose in a storm could do worse than bend up the companionway rail, they could tear a hole in the hull, the engine room and flicker would flood, and the ship would go down, though sometimes if a ship was sinking the crew would raise the seagate and push cars over the stern into the lake to try to make the ship lighter. That's what they did on the *Pere Marquette 18*, but Peter Kilty went down anyway. And before the *Ann Arbor 4* sank at our south pier there was such a terrible storm that a brand new load of Buicks tore off the seagate and rolled into the lake. That happened before I was born, but to the crew it must have seemed like yesterday because the retired chief engineer still buttonholed anyone he could to show off his watch.

A tiny orange light flickered at the end of one track, and I pressed myself against the car so no one could see me, then when nothing happened, I peeked my head out. It was one of the men from below, from the black gang, because he was in his shirtsleeves and even in the dim light I could see rivulets of sweat and grime on his face. After a minute I recognized Dick Butler, the oiler who said the hull was leaking. He was smoking a cigarette, and when he was done, he dropped it to the deck, squashed it with his boot, then picked it up and dropped it into his shirt pocket. Then he disappeared through the hatch to the companionway that went below. The crew wasn't supposed to smoke anywhere but the weather deck, but it was snowing, and I guessed it was warmer on the car deck even though I was cold. I hadn't put my coat on because I wanted to pretend I was just looking for a snack, and I shivered in my sweater, but I wasn't done exploring.

There was no reason to look for an engine, because the engine was too heavy for the apron. They only used it to push the cars on board, and in Menominee there would be another engine waiting to pull them off. What I wanted to see was the caboose. Sometimes when you watched a freight train go by, the man in the caboose would come out on the little platform in back and wave, and I thought I would like to stand on that platform and wave too. I could wave good-bye to all of the people in Frankfort who were going about their business just like always on a cold winter day, trying to dig their cars out or shoveling their steps or walking to the butcher or grocer or maybe just visiting. Billy Johnson might be making a snowman in the yard that was just the other side of the big wooded lot between our houses. Or maybe he was coming through the woods with his sled so he could could ride down our long, steep driveway, and he might wonder where I was and why I didn't come out to play, and he wouldn't know that I was on a boat, that I was on a boat and a train both at the same time, and that I was going to sail all the way across the lake just as soon as we got out of the frozen harbor, and even Manitou, whom I had left in the observation room, got to go, and Billy didn't. The tracks were so close together I had to be careful not to bang myself up on the jacks as I walked the length of the deck between each row. I had to climb over because you couldn't go under, and there wasn't enough room to go around, but I walked up and down the tracks between the cars, wondering what was inside them, and never once thought about my mother.

13

*I*n school, the first thing we learned about the Great Lakes was that HOMES was the way to remember all their names, and we should have no trouble remembering HOMES because the Great Lakes region was our HOME. But the problem with remembering them that way was that it put them all out of order. They were not in an order in which one might sail from one to the others, not in alphabetical order or any other order that would have made sense to me. And anyway our home was Michigan. You might as well say you were from the world as from a region so big it included eight states and two countries.

It came as a disappointment to learn that Michigan was only the third largest of the five lakes, though I was glad to know it was the sixth largest freshwater lake on earth. Sailors called the Great Lakes our inland seas, the sweetwater seas, and I wanted to be a sailor, I wanted to talk like one, but my teacher talked like a book, which meant that she was forever correcting me. I don't mean she punished me for cursing—there was less of that among my father's crew than you might imagine, and not just because they watched their tongues around me but because blasphemy is bad luck on a boat, along with cats, women, and preachers. No, it was my names for things that she objected to. An ice devil was not an ice devil but a waterspout, and they were fairly rare on the Great Lakes, I couldn't possibly have seen one. Nor had I seen the wooden ghost steamer *Chicora* blowing distress signals and should not tell my classmates that I had because there was no such thing as ghosts, and South Manitou Island was not haunted by cholera victims who had been dropped off by immigrant ships enroute to Chicago and buried alive, though every sailor on the lake has heard their cries, and it was the coast guard that showed us a picture of the *Chicora* and asked if that was the ship we had seen, because other ships had reported seeing it too. There was also no such thing as a snow wasset, but I knew there was, because Bosun had encountered it on Lake Superior. It was as big as the *Chicora*, a cross between a whale and a giant snake, with scales on a belly that was bulging with blubber and you didn't want to think about what else, because it could swallow a man as big as my father in one gulp and would follow a ship for days in a blow, just waiting for a chance to eat the crew, and even though it lived in the frigid waters above the UP, I kept an eye out, because if a ship could sail from Lake Superior to Lake Michigan, a giant snow wasset could get there too. For all she knew it could be the monster people kept seeing in Grand Traverse Bay, and that was in the newspaper so it had to be true. My problem, she told me, was that I had an overactive imagination. On my report card she wrote that I told lies.

She liked numbers. Lake Michigan, she said, had 3,200 miles of coastline, but I thought she meant the lake was 3,200 miles long, and so I put my hand up to tell her that it was actually 307 miles from top to bottom, with a width that varied from 118 miles at its widest to 63 between Frankfort and Kewaunee, which was a regular run for our ferries, but she didn't care, and anyway it was not the distances but the difficulties, the weather, the harbors, the channels, the passages, the currents, the reefs, the shoals. That was how a sailor knew the lake.

She had her own stories. Once upon a time where we lived had been ocean. That was in the Paleozoic era, the time my teacher called the age of ancient life, six hundred million years before any of us were born, and there were no people then, only corals, mollusks, brachiopods, and trilobites, so many that when they died and sank to the bottom of that sea their own weight smooshed them into limestone. The Petoskey stones I liked to hunt along the shore each summer were not stones at all but prehistoric animals, fragments of fossilized coral polished by the waves until they looked like honeycombs.

And even longer ago than that, before the ancient sea, there were volcanoes. The volcanoes erupted, and then the molten rock cooled and hardened, and plates beneath the surface of the earth collided and pushed up mountains, but by the time she finished her next sentence those mountains had already eroded, they weren't mountains anymore but a low region of exposed bedrock she called the Canadian Shield. I liked picturing the volcanoes and the mountains and then a big shield like a knight might carry into battle, but the millions and billions of years were impossible to grasp, and so I imagined the land riding up and down like the waves in a steep storm on the sweetwater sea. This shield still bordered the northern shore of Lake Superior, she said, but around the rest of the Great Lakes that bedrock lay buried beneath sediment from the ancient ocean and debris from the glaciers that came later, that she hadn't told us about yet, because her story was all out of order, like the lakes she called HOMES. In the middle of the shield there was a circular bed of shale that eroded to form river valleys that were surrounded by escarpments of hard limestone made from the skeletons of all those dead sea creatures. *Then* she told us about how it got very cold, and the glaciers came, pushing down from Hudson Bay in sheets that were hundreds of miles across and a mile high or even higher. I liked thinking about the glaciers, because I felt that I had traveled one the year I went across the lake, though I didn't see how she could tell me there was no such thing as ghosts when according to her the very ground beneath our feet wasn't ground at all but a bunch of dead animals and no one really knows what happens after you die, if you keep on thinking, and if you do then I guess you would be a ghost. That's the problem with ghosts, they're dead but they can't stop thinking, and I thought that I would probably be that way too. As for the glaciers, they were so dense the ice was like a bulldozer, a giant tank smashing up slate and other soft rock, pushing it along in front and to the sides until it built up walls that separated the ice into lobes that plowed through the river valleys, making them deeper and deeper, thirteen hundred feet in the basin that became Lake Superior, nine hundred feet in Michigan. When a ship went to the bottom of one of those lakes, it went a long way down.

That was nearly two million years ago, she said, but then it warmed up again, the glaciers went away, the plants and animals came back. The way she told the story it was like a Frankfort winter, longer than anything you could imagine, but then it was summer again, and then winter, everything died, and the glaciers came back, and this happened over and over, and I didn't see what was to prevent it from happening again, any more than the Soo locks would prevent a snow wasset from swimming from Lake Superior to Grand Traverse Bay, and so all the while she talked about the glaciers I kept looking out the window to make sure the snow and ice weren't piled any higher than they had been that morning, but it was so cold there was no one out, I couldn't see if there were any people or if everyone had died and the minute we left the heated brick schoolhouse we would all die too and have to wait a million years and then turn into rocks.

"Pay attention, Fern," she said.

Finally the weight of the ice made those valleys so deep that when the glaciers melted for the last time—I took another look out the window—they filled with water and turned into our Great Lakes. But even then, she said, sometimes winter ice still blocked the water farther north, so Lake Superior found a narrow valley in the Upper Peninsula and poured into Lake Michigan through the little Whitefish River, and Lake Michigan found the Chicago River and drained into the Mississippi, all the way to the Gulf of Mexico, which worried me, because if all the water drained out of the lake what would happen to my father's ferry? I couldn't imagine him working in a tailor's shop or standing behind a counter wrapping meat up in brown paper like other fathers did. But there was more, because a mere seven to ten thousand years ago, she added as if it were yesterday, the St. Mary's River opened, connecting

Lake Superior to Lake Huron, and it became possible to sail all five of the lakes without ever crossing land, and on up the Erie Canal to the Hudson River and Atlantic Ocean.

"And that," she said, "is the story of our special lakes."

HOMES, she had us repeat. Because this region and its history were our HOME.

It was an interesting story, but it wouldn't get you through the Manitou Passage or the Straits, wouldn't help you navigate Gray's Reef or the Wobbleshanks ("Waugoshance," she corrected, though all the sailors I knew called it Wobbleshanks), that graveyard of wrecks between the mainland and Hog and Beaver Islands, wouldn't teach you never to put your boat broadside to the waves in a storm or how to quarter them in a heavy north or south wind until the ship could turn and run downwind, didn't tell you that the lead line was useful only in calm waters or that iron and steel throw the magnetic compass off its marks. It didn't tell you that anything sent overboard should go leeward, which you would think only common sense, but more than one ship has burned because someone flung a bucket of coals into the wind. It didn't show you how to load a ferry to balance the weight, how to place idlers, empty flat cars, between the cars to be loaded and the locomotive, wouldn't warn you never to board a ship if the rats were leaving, wouldn't teach you how to clear the limber holes in the bulkheads and clean the scuppers when they clogged, how to rig and fit a steering tiller to the end of the rudder stock if the pin in the steering quadrant broke or how to steer with the engines if the quadrant came loose, how to back and how to spud, didn't caution you never to christen a ship with water, change its name or choose one with too many *a*'s and especially never a name with thirteen letters, didn't tell you never to start a trip on Friday or use gear salvaged from a wreck or let you know that a starboard list coming out of port forebodes an unlucky trip or that whistling aboard ship will bring on a gale, and it was important to know these things, because for all her knowledge about how the lakes formed, she failed to tell us what all sailors on the Great Lakes know, which is the most important geological feature of all, because when the lakes formed they shaped themselves into a horseshoe, but the horseshoe's upside down, its prongs at the bottom, where all the luck runs out, and that's why most ships carry a horseshoe nailed right side up, and the *Manitou* was no exception. And when you set out on any of the lakes you'd best keep these things in mind, because what you need to know is not about brachiopods and glaciers but that a halo around the sun means rain and so does a red sky at dawn, that most storms take three days to blow in and another three to blow themselves out but there are other storms that come up without warning, and even without looking at the barometer you know a storm is coming by the pressure in your ears and the way your voice seems to echo inside your head, you need to know that in a storm waves come in sevens and the seventh is always higher than the previous six, that when a ship is going down lifeboats aren't really of much use because they take too long to launch and any storm furious enough to sink a ship is going to break up a lifeboat anyway, you need to know how to call for a breeches buoy just before you scuttle a ship to keep it from smashing against the shore, but most of all you need to know when to call Mayday and fly the flag upside down.

She knew a lot, my teacher, but the sailors knew more, because they also knew that no matter how much you know, your ship can still go down. And land is just as dangerous to navigate, I learned, because while you are at sea, back on land your mother can drown.

14

The Annies were stern-loaders, and in the early days of the ferries, after the railroad removed fifty feet of the aft deck to accommodate bigger railcars, captains had to stand atop a boxcar with lines to the port and starboard whistles in each hand as the boats turned around to back up to the dock. One of those captains was my grandfather, and everyone said he was lucky because he died of a heart attack at home in his bed before he could fall off and break his neck, but if my grandfather was anything like my father I'm sure he would have preferred to fall off a boxcar and break his neck. A captain would always rather die on his ship than at home in his bed.

Though the newer ships had been built with an aft pilothouse and more clearance, I thought it would be fun to stand on top of one of the boxcars and pretend to be one of the old captains, so I hoisted myself to the ladder of the nearest car. My mittens were with my coat, back in my locker, and my fingers numbed on the metal rungs. Then, when I swung myself over, there wasn't enough room to stand up. I wanted to see what the world looked like from up there, but all I could make out was a slice of pewter sky above the seagate.

I lay on my stomach next to the little peak those captains would have had to straddle, but slivers of ice soaked through my dress and sweater, so I rose to a squat, taking the invisible lines in my hands and hollering out orders. "Full speed ahead! Whoa, starboard, no to port, easy does it!" I wasn't sure what kind of directions a captain would give, but I knew what his crew would say, "Aye aye, sir," because that was the first rule on a boat, never argue with the captain. The ice rumbled and scraped along the sides of the hull. Wind out of the west had pushed more and more slush ice into the basin, and the narrow passage had closed up overnight because the *Ashley* was stuck up at Pyramid Point and hadn't docked yesterday.

When I got tired of playing captain, I climbed down. My sleeve had caught on something, my shoelaces had come undone, my dress was wet, and I knew without looking that I was dirty, so I was glad my mother wasn't there to scold me, but if she wasn't sick I wouldn't be there, so then I was glad she was sick, because otherwise I would be at home with nothing to do but build a snowman and sled down our hill. Here maybe I'd get to play captain some more, maybe up in the pilot-house standing at the wheel and talking on the chadburn, because if I was the captain that was what I would do, I would stand at the wheel and steer the ship instead of letting the wheelsman do it. I would steer the ship *and* tell everyone else what to do.

When I jumped from the bottom rung I landed so hard my teeth hurt and I lost my balance, gouging my knee against one of the heavy jacks. Something scurried away, and I scrambled to my feet. I squeezed along the arcade of white stanchions that stretched down the middle of the deck, then along the starboard rail, hoping to find a car that was open, even though I'd already looked. The doors had to be shut tight to keep the cargo from spilling out in big seas, and there were metal seals on the doors that the watch checked every shift so the railroad would know if any of the cars were broken into, but I wanted to see what was inside, maybe valuables like the ones passengers stored in the purser's safe, gold or something like diamonds and rubies, because it was a lot of trouble to take all these cars across the lake on a boat and whatever was inside had to be worth a lot of money. Anyway maybe the watch had missed a door, there was always a chance for the watch to miss something like an open deadlight or broken seal, and if a watch could miss a seal, then I might have missed a door that was cracked. It didn't occur to me that it would be too dark to make out what was inside. I was fixed on the idea that the cargo would be diamonds or gold and all sparkly.

It was funny how I could hear little things like the rat beneath the explosions of ice, the hiss of the steam, and throb of the engines. Somehow I seemed to hear everything more acutely through the din, as if each sound was a little thought inside the ship's language, and I was starting to hear it talk like my father said, and even though I didn't know the words yet, I loved its music, so I listened very hard. Near the end of the row there was a mewing that grew louder as I reached the last car, but before I could check the door, footsteps rang on the companionway below, the one that came up from the engine room, and a shadow moved into the square of light that was the open hatch, so I ducked beneath the car to hide. Even though everything on a ship is kept very clean the deck was wet and gritty, and instead of the mewing now I heard the scrabbling claws again. I thought the footsteps might belong to Dick Butler, come back to smoke another cigarette, which he really shouldn't do, because what if he set the ship on fire? A fire was one of the worst things that could happen aboard a ship, though a leak could be bad too if it was big enough, and I didn't want to think about that. There wasn't any water on the car deck, just some melting ice, but Dick had said the leak was in the coal hold below. I wondered if one of the engineers had sent word up to my father in the pilothouse, maybe on the chadburn. It seemed like something he should know, but already I had learned that the engineers regarded everything below deck as their realm. It wasn't just the first and second mates who didn't get along. The engineers resented the captain, and the captain didn't always trust his engineers, even though they had to work together because everyone had a job to do.

Whoever it was started up the companionway to the weather deck. I popped back out the minute he was gone, but then he was back, starting down the ladder that was bent at the top because at some point in a storm the railcars must have busted loose, and I had to crawl behind the wheel underneath the car again. I was good at hiding. Once when Billy and I were playing hide-and-seek I crawled into the space beneath his back steps, which was the best place because he was afraid of snakes and I never told him there weren't any.

A beam of light crossed the track.

"Fern? Fern, are you down here?"

It was Alv, so I crawled out and said, "Surprise!"

"You scared me!" He turned his flashlight on me, careful not to shine it in my eyes. I looked down. My dress was torn, one sock had fallen down, my shoes had come untied, my knee was scraped, there were rats, and maybe I had crawled through rat poop, which I had also maybe done underneath Billy Johnson's back porch, but that was different because I hadn't thought about it, and now that I had maybe my knee would fester up and I would get gangrene, which was something I had heard about, it was something sailors got when their fingers and toes froze and had to be cut off, but even though I might already have gangrene and my leg would have to be cut off, I hadn't cried. "Captain called. I went above to check on you and you weren't there."

"I wanted to see the train." We weren't shouting exactly, but we had to stand close and talk very loud. "Did he call you on the chadburn?"

"You're not supposed to be down here by yourself. It's *dangerous*."

"Want to play hide-and-seek?"

His silence was full of frowns.

"There isn't any caboose," I said sadly. "And the cars are all closed up. I can't see what's inside." His light flickered between the rails. "What's that?"

"The hatch where they load the coal."

"Open it." I wanted to see the leak.

"I can't. Anyway there's nothing to see. It's dark down there."

"But if the coal's wet it won't burn." I listened for the mewing inside the boxcar. "Do you hear that?"

"It's probably a rat."

"There *is* a rat," I said. "It ran across my foot." That wasn't quite true, but it had come close.

"Captain would have my hide if he knew you were down here. How come you left your compartment?" He was looking at me sternly now.

"I'm not afraid of rats. I'm not afraid of snakes or spiders either, and if you don't believe me you can ask Billy Johnson. Boost me up. There's an animal inside the car."

"Maybe it's Manitou." I couldn't tell whether he meant for me to laugh, but I didn't think so.

"Manitou's above. And anyway bears don't mew, they growl."

"*Why* are you so much trouble?" The elongated first word sounded like a grown-up's sigh. "Anyway the door is sealed. I couldn't open it even if I wanted to."

I put my hands on my hips and pressed my lips together, the way Mrs. Johnson did when she meant business.

"I'd lose my job, and then what's my father going to say?"

It took a while, but you couldn't budge, or people wouldn't do what you wanted. Finally he said, "*All right*, but right after that you have to go above."

"There's nothing to do up there."

"I'll get you some paper and a pencil. You can draw a picture."

"I did that already."

"There's paper in the purser's office. If I unlock it and tell you what the little tubes are for, will you go up?"

I did want to know. "How come you didn't tell me before?"

"They're for sending notes when a ship is going down." And before I could ask what kind of notes or what they said he put his hand on the car, and the moment he did, something dark leapt to the deck and disappeared beneath another car, so close I felt a soft kiss of fur across my leg.

"It's a squirrel!" I cried, because we had black squirrels in Frankfort.

"It's a kitten," he said.

A kitten was even better.

"It wasn't inside the car. It was up underneath the axle."

"I want to keep it! Catch it for me, please. Please?" I was so excited I was hopping in place. "Catch the kitty, Alv, pretty please, oh pretty please with sugar on it!"

"A black cat." His voice flattened. "You better hope it stays up under the cars so Bosun doesn't find it."

"But I want it. It's dark under there, the poor kitty doesn't have anything to eat, the harbor's all froze, it's going to take forever to get to Menominee, and by then my kitty's going to die."

"It'll catch mice."

I made a face. I didn't want my kitten eating mice. "What if it doesn't find any?"

"A cat can always find a mouse," he said, but there was a thread of uncertainty in his voice. "It looks to be pretty young though. Maybe we could find a box or something. I could hide it in the closet off the flicker where they keep the mops and paint and cleaning supplies. Bosun never goes in there, but . . ." He seemed to be thinking. "Watch out!" he yelled as the kitten reappeared, and he dove for it, but the cat leapt past him, then turned and stood looking at us with yellow eyes that glowed in the dark.

"See, it's hungry," I said. "And Sam said I could have a glass of milk whenever I wanted. Please."

"Here, kitty-kitty-kitty." Alv crouched, and the kitten slowly approached, but instead of going to Alv it came to me, arching its back and rubbing all around my ankles.

I stroked its back. The fur was very soft, and I could see now that it wasn't all black, there was a little triangle of white on its chest and some white hairs at the very tips of its paws, and it was much smaller than Billy Johnson's cat, which was orange. "See, it's lonely. We can take it above, and Sam will give us some milk and maybe even some *fiskesuppe*."

Gingerly Alv reached out.

"My father would let me keep it." I didn't know about that. We didn't have a cat at home, a cat or a dog or even a canary. "It can sleep in my rack with me and Manitou."

"Not on your life. Bosun finds out, he'll pitch it overboard. This *has* to be our secret. You and me."

"But I haven't ever had a pet, and Sam has all that food." My mouth began to tremble. "You said you'd hide it in the closet."

"I changed my mind. The deckhands go in there, and what if one of them told?" All the while he seemed to think, the cat kept arching around my ankles and I petted its back. "I like cats," he conceded. "We have a cat named Ashes at home. My mother found her on our doorstep."

I kept quiet, because I could tell that he was going to give in, and when you know that's going to happen the best way to argue is not to say anything at all.

"What's my father going to say if I don't get to be a deckhand?"

We were standing very close because it was the only way to hear each other. I could feel the warmth of his body inside the coverall someone had loaned him. "I'll tell you what. We'll leave it to hide down here, but you can ask Sam for a glass of milk, and later I'll come down and feed it and hope Bosun doesn't throw *me* overboard. He hates me."

"Why?"

"Bosun never likes the new boy." He looked away. "Anyway my father says I'm not right."

"But I like you. I *love* you," I cried. Because that's the way children are, they choose to love, and the choice takes no longer than an instant. It's their power, because love is the only thing they possess, the one thing they have to bestow. "Don't you love me?"

"You're going to get me in trouble."

I was so crushed, I bit my lip and looked down at the deck, afraid I would cry.

"*Okay*," he said. "I like you. But you're still going to get me in trouble."

I tucked my hand in his. "Well, I'm going to make the bosun like me, and when I do I'll tell him he has to like you too." I hurried on in case he might change his mind. "What about the watch?"

"It'll hide," Alv said. "Kittens are always getting up under stuff or inside."

"You said you'd find a box and put it in the closet with the mops."

He shook his head. "I told you. It wasn't a good idea."

"But how are we going to feed it?"

"*Me*," Alv said. "You're not supposed to be down here."

"Okay. How will *you* feed it then?"

"If I bring food it'll come out, and then it'll know to expect me."

I didn't tell him that I planned to sneak down too, because if it was going to be *my* cat, it needed to know me too. "We have to name it. Is it a boy or girl cat?"

"I couldn't see."

I wondered if the ghost no one ever saw was a boy ghost or a girl ghost. Billy Johnson had shown me how to tell, but if nobody ever saw it, how would anyone know?

I tried to think of a name that would work for either. Manitou was a good one, and I hadn't even thought about that when I named him. Sleeping Bear was a girl, Ashley was a boy, because James Ashley was the man who started the ferries and now the railroad had given his name to an unlucky ship, which didn't seem right because if you were the man who thought it all up it seemed like they ought to name the best ship for you, but *Manitou* was the best ship, and I was proud that it belonged to my father. Elberta sounded like a girl, Frankfort a boy, and anyway I wouldn't want Alv to think I picked my town over his. "I know. Let's call it Whispers. Because it's our secret, you and me." I bent down again to pet the cat, which rolled onto its back, but the instant Alv reached out it sprang up, twisting in the air as it struck.

"Upstairs," he said, clutching his hand to the front of his coverall as he led me to the foot of the companionway. Already Whispers had disappeared beneath one of the cars. "We need to put some iodine on your knee."

75

"Will it hurt? Above," I added, because he forgot and said upstairs.
"Probably."

He stepped aside for me to go first. It wasn't until we reached the
light at the top that I saw blood where he was holding his hand against
the coverall. He washed it in the sink in my cabin and wrapped it with a
towel, then knelt to wash my knee.

"Whispers bit you!" I said.

The overhead lamp seemed to burnish the top of his face. "Captain's
not going to be happy when he sees your clothes."

"It's okay to tear your dress on a ship." I thought about my mother
then, because our mothers always told us to keep our Sunday clothes
nice, but there was a tree to climb right outside the church, and no
matter how many times the Sunday school teacher warned us not to,
the boys always ripped the knees of their pants and the girls tore out
their hems, and when their mothers saw them they would say, "What
did I tell you?" But maybe my father wouldn't notice.

"Do *not* leave this compartment," he said as he went off to find the
first aid kit.

"I did what you said. I stayed right here," I said as soon as he came
back. The towel he'd wrapped around his hand was sopped red. "You
promised to tell me about the pirate." I winced as he applied the iodine,
and he recapped the bottle. "Aren't you going use some?"

"That's okay."

I took the bottle, but when I poured it over his hand he yelped. "A
pirate meets a sailor in a bar," I prompted, adding, "You yelled and I
didn't. I must be braver than you."

"You used too much." He took another towel, staining it with iodine,
and that never came out in the wash.

"What's a bar?"

"It's where men go to drink."

"Is that where Odd goes?"

"Of course it's where Odd goes."

"Have you ever been to one?"

"Not yet."

"Are the pirate and the sailor drunk?"

"I don't know. Maybe. They're at a bar. What they do, they tell each other stories."

"What kind of stories?"

"About their adventures at sea."

"Do you think we'll see pirates?"

"I doubt it."

"Does this pirate have a parrot?"

"He has a peg leg, an eyepatch, and a hook."

"He should have a parrot," I said.

"*Okay.* He has a parrot."

"What's the parrot's name?"

"I don't know!"

"Is your hand still bleeding?"

He peeked beneath the towel. "I think it's stopped."

"Tell me the story."

"It's a joke, not a story. The sailor asks the pirate how he got his wooden leg, and the pirate says, 'We was caught in this monster storm around Cape Horn, and I got swept overboard, and just as they're pulling me out, a big shark swims up and bites off me leg.'" Alv made his voice all funny like the pirate, then leaned toward me to chomp his teeth.

I felt my eyes widen. "Do you think we'll see sharks?"

"No."

"Why not?"

"Because sharks live in the ocean."

"Sturgeon," I said. "I bet we see big sturgeon."

"Through this ice? About the pirate and the sailor"—Alv pitched his voice again—"'Blimey,' the sailor says. 'And what about the hook?' So the pirate says, 'See, we was boardin' a trader ship, pistols blastin', swords a-swingin', and in the ruckus me hand got chopped off.'"

I hugged my hand to my chest. "Does your hand hurt? Do you think you'll get gangrene? You might have to get a hook."

"I hope not."

"Then you could be a pirate."

"I don't want to be a pirate."

"Where is Cape Horn?"

"I don't know where it is," he admitted.

"But why do they call it Cape Horn?"

"I don't *know*. 'Zounds,' the sailor says, and then . . ."

"What's the difference between a joke and a story?"

"Stories aren't always funny."

"Are jokes always funny?"

He thought a minute. "Depends on who's listening."

"Is this one funny?"

His mouth twitched. "If you'd let me finish, you could decide for yourself. Sailor asks, 'How came ye by the eye patch?'"

"Do you think the bosun might throw me overboard?"

"No."

"You said he'd throw Whispers."

"Cat's not the same as the captain's daughter."

"You said he'd throw *you* overboard."

"I told you, he doesn't like me."

But I was going to make the bosun like him. "Tell me about the eyepatch."

So he did the voices again. "'Seagull dropping fell in me eye,' the pirate says, and the sailor says, 'You gotta be joking. You mean to tell me you lost an eye just because . . .'"

"A seagull pooped in it!" I shouted, but the joke wasn't over.

"'Well,' the pirate says, 'it was me first day with the hook.'"

I clapped my hands and laughed. "That's a funny joke. Tell it again."

"Bosun needs me below. When I finish painting, I've got to practice knots. Anyway, you interrupt too much."

I followed him into the passengers' lounge. "Well, I don't care if he doesn't like you, because I'm going to grow up and be a sailor, and you and I can work on the same boat, and we'll have a different bosun, or maybe you can be the bosun. What would you rather be, a bosun or the captain? I think I'd like to be the person who gets to steer."

We were standing near the wooden column that enclosed the forward spar, and that's when he said, "See, what I like—what I want—I like to play the piano." And I knew then he didn't want to be a bosun or a captain and that he didn't care about hearing the ship talk and didn't hear its music, because the music he liked was different, but his father wanted him to be a deckhand, and maybe that was why he said Alv wasn't right, because he wanted Alv to be different than he was, like the bosun wanted everyone to be different than they were, and I was glad my father was the captain and not the bosun or my father would want me to be different than I was too, but I didn't think Alv could help the way he was any more than I could help the way I was, whatever that was, somebody who was too much trouble and interrupted too much.

"My mother plays the piano," I said.

15

*Y*ou may want to know what I looked like back then, but I can't tell you. There are no pictures except the ones Holgar took, and who knows what became of those? I had a narrow face, blonde hair, and blue eyes, and was small for my age, my ribs a thin cage of bones. Kids are supposed to be cute. And maybe I was, but my hair was snarled, my clothes were torn, my knees were scraped, my fingernails were dirty. I wasn't pretty.

16

*D*espite everything that happened, I remember my childhood as happy.

I loved where I lived.

The lake stretched so far it often appeared to be a world without limits, the horizon seamless, no edge between sea and sky at all, though other times the line was as sharp as the blade of a knife, still others a single stitch of silver thread. Some days the water turned so blue it looked almost navy, or else it was a pale aquamarine, delicate as crystal. On those days you could stand on the breakwater looking down at veins of sunlight dancing on the mossy boulders piled around its base, then when you raised your head, there across the great shimmering bowl of clear, green water was our bluff with its crown of trees and steep, sand-streaked face. At the north end, where our beach met the bluff, the shore narrowed and turned stony, and I used to walk along collecting pebbles as the waves washed up over the sand only to slide back into the lake, a rush of cold water over my bare feet. The shallow surf swirled around the larger rocks, and I pretended they were islands inhabited by creatures so tiny no one could see them but me. Most years there was a strip of beach below the bluff, though the year before I left, the water was so high the lake lapped right up against it, toppling trees and shearing off little cliffs. That frightened me, because what if the whole bluff tumbled in and disappeared? I didn't know that was just the way lake levels cycled. Nor could I imagine how many of those cycles I would miss because I never intended to leave. I was sent away.

Sometimes a cloud would pass over the sun where I was standing on shore while the same sun still shown farther out, and then there would be a spangled patch on the rolling quilt of water like a sparkling far-off land. Late in the day, if you turned your eyes west the water looked cold as crumpled steel beneath a sun so blinding it flattened all the boats to silhouettes, though all you had to do was turn your head back for the world to warm, the same sun melting like butter across the sand. Often on summer evenings after supper we strolled down to the breakwater or beach to watch the sunset. On clear nights the sun turned into a huge red ball that dropped behind the lake in a way that made you understand why people used to think the earth was flat, the way its waist lost shape and seemed to puddle on top of the great shelf of water, but then it would pull itself back together and sink behind the edge as if the snow wasset had swallowed it. Always I begged to go, and when my father wasn't home my stepmother frequently relented, because on partly cloudy evenings no one could predict. Sometimes the whole sky would catch fire, or else the sun might lurk behind the clouds, edging them with gold while they turned to smoldering pink and purple ashes inside, and we would wait until the last ember died, lingering as those purple-gray clouds took the shape of dinosaurs and long-nosed fish, not turning toward home until the sky deepened to cobalt and the lights at the ends of the piers came on. "It's a sight," my stepmother would admit as we walked home in step, acknowledging the world we shared in a way we never did at other times.

But even better I liked early morning, when the lake was such a lovely pastel blue, the sand pink and amber, and I wasn't coming up on bedtime but had a whole new day stretched out before me. If the wind was still, the outer harbor, that pool between the breakwaters, was smooth as glass, while outside the embrace of those arms the lake kept lap-lapping to shore, and overhead the gulls wheeled and cried. Other mornings a gauzy silver mist rose from the inner harbor, and the small fishing boats coming through the channel between the stub piers seemed to appear out of nowhere like ghosts. On blustery days the waves thrashed, exploding over the breakwaters in enormous white plumes that trailed off into veils as they slid down the other side. You didn't dare walk out then, lest you be swept off and drowned. Sometimes storms turned the morning sky black, lightning forked, and the roar was so ferocious you couldn't tell the thunder from the tumult of lake and wind, but every now and then the sun would come out before the sky caught up, and that was magic, a rainbow arcing over the shining white spear of the lighthouse against a wall of black sky. And once I saw a seiche, one of those giant waves that slosh all the way from one shore to the other and back. It emptied our harbor like a bathtub and then surged back up past the beach.

It was never the same. Not the sight, not the sound. What I mean to say is that when you grow up on the shore of a great lake you learn its moods, and observing those you begin to learn the inconstancy of the world.

In the old days, before the lights were electrified, the keepers had to go out no matter how perilous the weather, and so some of the lighthouses, like the one at Manistee, had catwalks built on stilts above the piers. There must have been one intended for Frankfort too, because the north pier light has a second-story door with nowhere to go, like the doorway to the hayloft above our carriage house, except the hayloft didn't have a door, just an opening that I liked to jump out of, so it was a good thing the lighthouse was locked up tight because otherwise boys would have been hurling themselves from that second floor and shattering their skulls on the rocks.

We called Lake Michigan the big lake because there were so many others. To the south there were the Upper and Lower Herrings, Portage, and Bear, to the north Long Lake, Rush, Loon, and the two Plattes. Benzie State Park was on the Platte River, and there was a little store where you could rent rowboats to go down the Platte, across Loon Lake, all the way to Platte Bay. The Empire Bluff was right across from where you came out, and it was so lofty, so rich in color, it would take your breath away just to know there could be that much beauty in the world. And if the day was clear you could even see the bald, white flank of Sleeping Bear in the distance. Once we took inner tubes down the Platte, which you weren't supposed to do unless you were a good swimmer, because Loon Lake is so deep and the bottom so mucky if you fell out you would sink into it and never come up, but I was a good swimmer, all of the children were because we had been jumping off the diving board on the breakwater since we were tots, though I don't think Mrs. Johnson could swim at all, and she had the funniest old-fashioned bathing suit, but nobody tipped over, nobody drowned, and we all had the best time.

The biggest of the inland lakes was the closest, only a couple of miles north. That was Crystal. Once, a long time before I was born, they tried to dig a channel to connect it to Lake Michigan, but the plan backfired and nearly drained the smaller lake, which never did get back up to its previous level. A flat, sandy beach appeared all around it, and then people rushed in and built so many vacation houses and camps they boxed it all in. It's still a popular tourist destination, though as a child I couldn't see why. I loved the big lake, my father's lake, *mine*, so much I couldn't see why anyone would prefer Crystal. Only when I came back did I realize how pretty Crystal really is.

North of the Plattes are the two Glens. When you climb Sleeping Bear Dune you can see them set into the land like two sapphires with a platinum band that is the road in between them. I liked to say their names. Big Platte, Little Platte, Big Glen, Little Glen, Otter, the Bars, School, Bass, Lime, Lake Leelanau, Little Traverse, and some so small they didn't even have names. Plus Lake Michigan had all those bays, Platte, Sleeping Bear at Glen Haven, and Good Harbor up past Pyramid Point. On a still day the water in those bays might be nearly as smooth as our harbor, not at all the way the lake was at Frankfort and especially Point Betsie, though even the smallest lakes could rage in a storm.

Our inner harbor was called Betsie Bay, but before the sandbar at its mouth was dredged it was Betsie Lake, and even before that it was called

Aux Becs Scies, which was French, because back then French fur traders came down from Canada, but Leelanau, which was not just the name of my street but also the county to the north of us, was an Indian word, Ojibwe for Land of Delight, or so we were told, and even though it turned out to be just a made-up word and not Indian at all it seemed appropriate because I felt I lived in a land of delight. The ferries docked near the front of the bay, in Elberta, but at the back where the Betsie River curled in, there was a marsh where fish came to spawn, and when you went canoeing back there in the summer you would often flush a great blue heron or an egret hunting in the shallows. I don't think there is anything quite so pure as the sight of an egret taking flight on a clear morning, like a clean, white handkerchief flung against the bright-blue sky. It makes the day seem so buoyant and full of promise.

It was beautiful, where I lived.

My house was set back from the street on a hill so steep there were four separate flights of stairs between it and our front porch. We didn't have a backyard, but it didn't matter because the woods were right behind us and our side yard was so big. I had a tire swing, and at the top of our driveway was the carriage house with its hayloft that wasn't a hayloft anymore and downstairs beside my father's car there was an old sleigh. My bedroom was in the back of the house, overlooking the woods, and in the fall my window filled with crimson, yellow, and orange, and after the maple leaves fell, little apricot flags still fluttered from the beech trees, pale against the deep green of the hemlocks, cedars, and firs. My favorites were the birch trees with their peeling, papery white bark. One of my father's mates brought me a little canoe made out of birch bark from St. Ignace, and I put a clothespin in it and pretended the pin was an Indian maiden paddling around one of the little lakes tucked into the woods, but I guess it was the kind of toy you were just supposed to look at because when I put it in our bathtub it sank.

Officially Frankfort is a city. It became one the year I was four, but it wasn't really a city, not like Chicago or Detroit, which is where a lot of the people who spent their summers at Crystal Lake lived. In a city you would get lost, but it would be impossible to get lost in Frankfort, because you could walk from one end to the other. And it's not that much bigger now than it was then. At the west end, along Forest and Leelanau Avenues, hardly anything has changed, from the outside anyway, the same houses with their big front porches wearing fresh coats of paint. The grandest houses, the ones with turrets and tower rooms, are on the north side of Leelanau, where I lived. The house where I grew up has been painted a paler shade of gray, but it has the same clean, white trim—cornices above the tall windows, dentil molding, ornate brackets beneath the eaves, and pierced bargeboard along the carriage house roof. Even the woods between the house where Billy Johnson grew up and mine are intact. His didn't have a tower room, just three steep gables across the front, and some of the other tower rooms were only second-floor bays with tall, pointy roofs like witches' hats, but ours really was a tower, a small third-floor room reached by a steep ladder, with a dormer on each of its four sides and a mansard roof covered with shingles shaped like fish scales, though after my trip across the lake I always imagined them on the belly of the snow wasset instead.

Even most of the buildings on Main Street remain, though the businesses have changed. The Civil War cannon is still there in a little park at the end of the street behind the beach where the bicycle path ends. No one knows who put it there or even when. It's simply been there as long as I can remember, unlike the cross on Second Street that marks where Father Jacques Marquette was supposed to have died and been buried, though a few years after his death his bones were dug up and taken to the mission in St. Ignace, and now no one knows where he died for sure because Roald was right—history gets swoggled. There's an art center in the old coast guard station and a new coast guard station next door, but half the Coasties don't remember the old station, even though it was decommissioned only a decade ago. That's the way it is when anything changes. I remember though.

My house was only two blocks from Main Street, but even so the simplest errand took half a day, there were so many greetings and conversations, and you had to stop in all of the shops whether you had business or not, because if you didn't the owners would wonder why. At Collins Drugstore Mr. Porter always gave me a new penny for the gumball machine. There's still a drugstore, though it's not Collins anymore, and what it sells more than anything else now is toys. About the only business that hasn't changed names is the Garden Theater, where I went on Saturdays to see *Our Gang* and Shirley Temple and *Snow White*. For a nickel you got a cartoon and a short plus the feature. I liked all of the cartoons, but *Popeye* was my favorite. The welcome gate stood at Seventh and Main, and between that part of Main Street and the harbor there was a park called Mineral Springs where people brought jugs to fill with the healing water. You can still drink the water, though not long after the year I crossed the lake the welcome gate was moved to the top of the hill on the highway, so people coming into Frankfort from Benzonia go through the gate and get a view of the town and glittering blue lake below like a preview of coming attractions.

On the Fourth of July we always had a parade down Main Street with a band and floats and kids on bicycles with crepe paper streamers. Afterward Mineral Springs Park turned into a carnival with tents for food and games in front of the spur line that ran to the passenger station on what they used to call "the island," where the Royal Frontenac Hotel once stood. We drank lemonade and ate hot dogs and cotton candy and Cracker Jack, which was the best because there was a sailor on the outside of the box and inside was a prize. My favorite was a little tin whistle shaped like a bird. It had painted-on feathers, and when you blew, it didn't shriek like most whistles do but went tweet like a bird.

At Christmas there was an enormous tree in the intersection of Fourth Street and Main, twenty feet high at least, so tall they had to anchor it in the manhole, but up the hill on Leelanau Avenue I could stand in the hayloft or peek out the window of our tower room and look down on all the sparkling white lights, like stars that had fallen. The lights were always white because the tree was lit for the first time on Santa Lucia Day. The whole town came out for the lighting, and then afterward we went to the church for coffee and saffron buns. The girls wore white dresses and evergreen crowns, and the girl who was chosen to be Santa Lucia got to wear candles in her hair and carry the basket full of buns. I always hoped it would be me, but it never was because by the time I was old enough I was gone. The party was at the old church, which is where they put the new church, though the old wooden altar is still there, on a table in the fellowship hall. It looks more like a whole church than an altar, with spires and a little stained-glass window and its own tiny altar inside, like a church from the Old Country, and that's probably why it was built that way, to remind people where they were from.

The new elementary school is in the same place where the old school was too, at the corner of Leelanau and Seventh, but they didn't keep anything, and it looks like a school that could be anywhere with its flat roof and fluorescent lights and cement-block walls, which is sad, because the old school was so grand, a big, brick, three-story building with stone around its base and a tall tower above the entrance, and the sidewalk that led up to it was flanked by trees that made you feel as if you were a bride walking down a canopied aisle, and then when you opened the door beneath the tower you turned into a princess stepping inside a castle, but now there's nothing left, the trees are gone, and you can't even tell where the old sidewalk was.

On Christmas Eve the town gathered again at the big tree on Main, and then we walked up and down Forest and Leelanau singing carols, and the people who stayed home would open their doors and offer us hot chocolate while the yellow lights from their porches spilled out across the snow. And in the daytime cardinals and waxwings fluttered in and out of the big tree, which was strung with garlands of popcorn and cranberries, and the birds were so pretty against the greenery it seemed as if they were part of the decorations. It was such a festive time.

What I am saying is that winter in Michigan is not the unendurable runny-nosed, aching shiver people elsewhere in the country imagine, all goose bumps and an extended huddle around a woodstove, drinking toddies from cups that chatter on their saucers and pining for spring. We got outside. We explored the woods on snowshoes and cross-country skis. We skated on the harbor and went sledding down our hill. Sometimes we even got up a party to go tobogganing at Sleeping Bear Dune, near Glen Haven, where we rode the Dunesmobiles in summer. We took the train to Thompsonville and went skiing, we built snow forts, there were sleigh rides. Later, after I was grown, there was snowmobiling. You would be surprised at the number of seniors who pass on the palm trees and endless summer to retire back to Frankfort, no matter where they have spent their adult years or how long they've been gone.

Someone else now lives in the house where I grew up, of course. The open door in the loft above the carriage house is boarded up, and the double front doors with their gingerbread screens are painted a soft mulberry instead of green, though I know that if I wanted I could knock and say I used to live there and the owners would invite me inside and offer me a refreshment. But I don't have to see it to know that the wallpaper with the little brown stain in the upstairs hall would be gone, maybe the sconce, and probably one of the bedrooms has been turned into a master bath and walk-in closet, the kitchen would have granite countertops and stainless steel appliances, and maybe the wall where the butler's pantry was has been knocked out—these days people seem to like what they call an open concept—though perhaps they've fitted it out as a laundry room instead, with a set of those steam washers and dryers with windows on the doors that look like portholes on a ship. Who knows what became of the wringer washer on our back porch or the baroque August Förster piano in our front parlor? It's not that I disapprove or wouldn't have made the same updates myself, only that I like to imagine somewhere in the room where I slept, in the back of the closet perhaps, slipped through a crack between the woodwork and wall, there is still a little tin whistle shaped like a bird.

I insist: despite everything that happened, I remember my childhood as happy.

17

*L*ater that afternoon my father took me up to the pilothouse to see the wheel that steered the ship. It was the biggest wheel I'd ever seen, and the helmsman, who wasn't Odd now, but someone named Pete with a big nose that took a sharp hook down, stood on a thick mat of latticed wood to keep him in place in bad weather, though it had stopped snowing, the sun had come out, and there were so many windows it was brighter than the galley, so bright I felt as if I was on top of the clouds. Out past the bow the ice looked like a map with all the cracks dividing it up into different countries, and when I saw it I said, "This is the world!" and Pete laughed and said, "Well, it's a right frozen part of it, that's for sure, miss." Up in the pilothouse you could barely hear the hum of the engine, and the grinding of the ice against the sides of the ship was muted, but it was harder to keep your balance, and we weren't even in the tallest place—that was the crow's nest, which looked like a nest it was so high up the forward spar. If you were up there you really would be standing in the sky. I wanted to climb up to see how that would feel, but my father said I couldn't, couldn't ever, only the most experienced watch got to do that, and never in heavy seas, because in a gale the ship would pitch so much a man might fall out and be smashed to pieces on the deck. My father didn't say the part about being smashed, but you could see what would happen, and even though I didn't want it to happen to me I did think it would be fun to see what the world looked like from up there. So that was another thing I would have to think about.

There was a lot of brass for the deckhands to polish—because that would be their job, along with all the painting and soogeeing that never ended—the shiny heating pipes in front of the windows that curved so tightly against each other they looked like a musical instrument, the binnacle that housed the big magnetic compass, the tall brass tube with a ring on top, and more. On the floor to the left of the wheel was the courtesy whistle, the one they used when they were docking or leaving port in the middle of the night so they didn't wake up the whole town, but to blow the big steam whistle, according to my father, you just pulled the cords that ran across the ceiling on each side of the front-most window.

I wanted to blow all the whistles, but my father said I couldn't. I had washed my face like Alv said, and I dangled Manitou at my knees to hide where I'd torn out the hem of my dress. I had brought my bear up so he could see the chadburns, but he didn't care about them once he heard about the whistles. He wanted to blow them all too, and I had to tell him to be quiet so that I could hear how the chadburns worked.

You didn't talk into them like I thought, though on the wall there was a telephone the captain could use to talk to the engine room if he wanted the lights turned on or someone sent up on an errand, and there was even a voice tube to the car deck in case he wanted to say something to the hands down there. But the chadburns were topped by dials instead of speakers, which made them look like big brass lollipops, and there wasn't just one, there were three, one each for the port and starboard engines, and another smaller one that could be used to communicate with the aft pilothouse when the ship was backing up to dock. That one told the wheelsman how to steer, but on the engine chadburns each position on the dial rang a bell for different speeds, with one side for forward and the other for reverse, so the engineer would know what the captain wanted him to do.

"What happens if he doesn't hear the bell?" I asked.

The wheelsman had been staring out at the ice, but now he glanced at me with an amused smile that made his big hawk's nose look even bigger.

"It's happened." The lines around my father's eyes crinkled. "That's why one of the boys sits on a stool beneath the bell and never moves, to make sure the engineer gets the captain's orders. If he doesn't move his needle to signal that he's understood, I sound the general alarm." My father pointed to a metal box near the tall chart table built into the back of the pilothouse. There was a little gold star made out of braid just above the stripes on the sleeve of his uniform, and I thought I would like to have a star on my arm. I couldn't know that only a few years later there would be little Norwegian girls who would have to wear gold stars on their arms, Norwegian girls, German, Polish, Danish, Dutch, even French girls. I was too young to understand how much intentional evil this world holds, too young even to follow my father's explanation of the cavitate bell and all the other things in the pilothouse, like the sign above the windows that told the wheelsman which way the ship would go when he turned the wheel, because even if he knew left from right, some posts had the rudder in front and others had the rudder in back, and that changed the directions around. I hugged Manitou to my chest and wondered if I was on a ship where left was right and right was left would my shoes be on backward.

"There sure is a lot of stuff on a ship," I said.

My father and the wheelsman smiled. "Wait until you get to the engine room."

"Got so much stuff down there you can't hear yourself think," Pete added. "We like it up here. Nice and quiet."

"Well, I guess I know everything now," I said.

Pete laughed. "Girl's ready to write for her captain's." That's what sailors called taking the exam to move up in rank. Mr. Johannessen had written for his captain's, but he was still my father's first mate because the Ann Arbor didn't have a ship for him. And Dick Butler had written for his engineer's, but the railroad passed over him for Walter because

Walter had more hours at sea, but the rest of the black gang teased him that it was because he didn't have the right temperament, and even though they were just kidding, they got under his skin and reminded him to be sore.

"When do you get to steer?" I asked my father.

"Captain's not allowed to touch the wheel," he said.

I thought a captain ought to be able to do whatever he wanted, but no, each man had his own job, and steering was the helmsman's. And the job I'd set myself was to make the bosun like me so that I could make him like Alv. Pete's profile was turned, and I stared at his nose, which seemed to grow more grotesque the longer I looked.

"What if the wheelsman died?"

"Ho!" Pete said in a voice so big and round he sounded like Santa Claus, and just then the deckwatch named Loke, who had been on the bridge, came inside with a stomp of his feet and cold breath of air. "Captain's daughter's trying to kill me off."

"Now there's an idea," Loke said, and they both laughed. The watch studied me for a minute. "I think she likes your nose," he said to Pete.

Pete winked at me, then reached up to rub the crook. "Tell you a secret. Keeping your nose out of other people's business gives it a chance to grow."

I reached up to my own. I didn't want it to look like his, so I guessed I would have to go around sticking it in other people's business, even though I knew neither my mother nor father would approve.

"What if the wheelsman's drunk?"

"Hah!" the watch said.

My father patted my head. "Don't you worry about Odd. He's sober enough when he takes the helm."

I wasn't worried. Not about that anyway. I just didn't think it was fair that the captain never got to steer. I blew a little puff of air out my mouth, like a sigh. "What if the ship was going down?"

"Ship's going down it's all hands on deck," Loke said. "Job description don't much matter then."

Pete winked at me again. "Well, missy, captain's not allowed to touch the wheel, but if the first wheelsman died, second wheelsman was drunk, third wheelsman nowhere to be found, and the ship was going down, maybe we'd make an exception for your father."

My father looked out the window. "Steady as she goes," he said as he picked up a newspaper from the chair beside the wheel chadburn and sat.

"Steady as she goes," Pete repeated and turned the wheel a quarter spoke to port even though we were making such slow progress.

"Let her take it for a minute," my father said, and Pete bent to whisper in my ear.

"Steady as she goes," I repeated in my best sailor's voice as Pete placed my hands on the satin-smooth wood, and even though he stood right behind me and never took his own hands off, for a minute anyway I got to steer, and my father didn't.

When Pete took the wheel back, I looked at the chart desk. There was a book on top and behind that a radio, which was how the captain called the radio shack on the Elberta bluff, so the railroad could call the coast guard. The Ann Arbor was among the first to equip their ships with radios, though the connections were so bad mostly all you could hear were pops and crackles of static.

My father was reading, so I asked the watch, "Is that the ship's log?"

"Yes, ma'am."

"Do you write in it?"

"Captain and mates keep the log." I climbed on the tall stool beside the desk to see. It looked a lot like the one in my father's cabin, except bigger, and my father must have had the same thought, because he said to Loke, "Look in the drawer and see if you can find her some paper and a pencil before she starts drawing on the log."

"Does the bosun write in it?"

Pete snorted.

"You're in the head shed," Loke said. "Up here's where Captain and his mates plot the boat's course and decide on everyone's job."

"I thought the bosun did that."

The watch and Pete exchanged glances. "Now there's a good position for a bully. Never met one didn't train for it on the playground."

"But does he get to write in the log?" I didn't want Bosun to write something bad about Alv.

"Bosun comes up to get his orders." Loke handed me a sheet of paper and a pencil. He had taken off his gloves, and there was a fleece of blond hair across his knuckles. "That's it."

"Can I draw up here?" I asked my father.

"If you're quiet." Briefly my father rose to look out the window again. "Steady as she goes."

"Steady as she goes," Pete responded. I set Manitou beside the radio. There was a blotter with four corners that held the marked-up chart in place. Except for the ice and the faint thrum of the engines it was quiet. My father's paper rustled, and steam hissed in the curvy brass pipes below the windows. The watch and the wheelsman stared out at the ice as if they were hypnotized, which was something I had heard about. Sometimes at home I would close my eyes and walk around bumping into things and pretend I was hypnotized. But up here in the pilothouse I could see how the endless horizon, nodding warmth, and slow drain of hours might hypnotize you for real. And what would happen if you were hypnotized when the pumps stopped working and the hold filled up with water and the coal got so wet it wouldn't burn and the engines quit and you couldn't see land on any side?

I wanted to ask my father about the leak but was afraid to bring it up. He didn't like it when people repeated everything they heard.

I drew a boat with two big stacks, though the vibration of the ship made my lines a little shaky. I thought maybe my picture could go into one of the waterproof brass tubes in the purser's office that were for sending messages when a ship was going down and someone would find it, and even though they didn't know me they would be sad because they would know that I was just a little girl and had drowned on a ship that sank and could never, ever come back again. Or maybe I should write a note from Manitou. I wondered what he would want to say if he knew he was going down, and I thought it would probably be about me because he loved me so much, and the person who found it would be even sadder because my bear drowned with me even though he tried—that's what he would say in his message, he would say how very hard he tried to save me before he drowned too—and thinking about how sad it all was, I almost began to cry.

"Daddy?" I said, and my voice sounded very loud because no one had said anything for such a long time. "What do the messages in the little brass tubes say?"

My father looked up.

"The tubes in the purser's office where they write notes to send overboard when the ship is sinking."

He set his newspaper aside. "I thought you were drawing pictures."

"I am." I showed him my drawing of the boat, which he seemed to like, but said I couldn't put it in a canister or send it overboard.

"But what do they say?" I persisted.

"Well." He cleared his throat. "Sometimes they're a message to a sailor's wife or parents to say that he loves them. Usually they say what's happening so the railroad can try to figure out what went wrong."

"But the sailors are going to drown."

"I suppose they are, but they're sailors, they do their duty and don't complain."

"What kind of things?"

My father ran his hand along the stubble on his cheek. "Well, when the *Milwaukee* went down the purser wrote she was taking water fast and they had turned around to try to make a run back to shore." He glanced out at the ice. "Pumps were working, but the seagate was bent in, flicker was flooded, seas were tremendous, things looked bad. It was eight thirty—that's important, to say what time it is. The first body they found had a watch that stopped at nine forty-five, so the old girl must have put up quite a struggle."

"What would you write?" I asked Pete.

96

"Don't know," he said. "Might curse the fates if it was me."

"You'd do no such thing," Loke said. "You'd tell your mother you loved her and go down like a man."

"That's enough, boys." My father's voice stiffened. "No use calling on disaster."

"You want to know about disaster, talk to Bosun." Pete shifted his eyes. "That sailor's more superstitious than Ahab."

My father stood. "Who told you about the message tubes?"

"I saw them when Alv unlocked the purser's office to get the key to my cabinet. There's a ghost in the managers' compartment."

"Did you see it?" Loke asked.

"No," I said sadly.

"Ghost never hurt anyone," my father promised. "Don't you worry about that. It's a rare boat doesn't have a haunt."

"Keeps us boys on our toes, eh, Captain?" Pete said.

"That's right," my father said.

I looked down at their feet. My father wore shiny black shoes with his navy-blue dress uniform, but the wheelsman had scuffed, brown lace-up shoes, and the watch had on galoshes that were unbuckled down the front. I didn't think you would want to be wearing galoshes if you escaped a sinking ship because water would get inside them and you wouldn't be able to swim. I thought about the purser's note from the *Milwaukee*. I liked the part about the seagate because I had been where it was. Whispers was down there, and what if since I'd left, our seagate had bent and the flicker I hadn't seen yet was flooded because the pumps had quit and up in the head shed I didn't know that my kitten and everyone else was swimming around the lower decks, trying to keep afloat. I would just have to write a note to my mother, I decided. I would tell her I loved her, and I would ask my father what time it was so I could put that in my note, and then go ahead and drown like a man.

Bells rang. I looked at the chadburn, and scrambled off the stool. "Daddy?"

"Eight bells. Shift's over," my father explained.

I had been certain it was the general alarm. "Does that mean Alv is done working for the bosun?"

"Doesn't anybody ever get done working for the bosun," Loke said, adding to no one in particular, "Don't know why the boy didn't start as a coal passer." A coal passer, I would learn, was the lowest position on the ship, the poorest paid, but he didn't work for the bosun, he worked for the chief engineer.

My father seemed to stand a little taller. "I'll not put a lad of fourteen without papers in the firehold is why. Not that it's any business of a watch."

"Just reporting what the black gang has to say. And the men . . ." Loke gave a surreptitious look at me. "Some of the men think . . ."

"Did you see a captain in the black gang?"

"No, sir." Loke took a breath as if he was about to say something more, but my father cut him off.

"Well then." A lot of captains wore their uniforms only to pose for pictures, but I think my father liked the way it reminded his men who was in charge.

They seemed to have forgotten me, so I said, "Alv promised to show me the engine room when he gets off, and then I'll get to see the man who sits on the stool." I almost added that maybe Alv would take me to visit Whispers, but then I remembered my father wasn't to know, which was too bad because I'd never had a pet before and I wanted to tell someone. For a minute I wished Billy Johnson was there so I could tell him, but then I thought maybe I could write a message and put it in one of the little brass tubes when Alv opened the purser's office again. I could draw a cat and print my name, and as soon as the ice melted the message would wash up on the beach, and if Billy was playing there he would find it, and even if he didn't, someone would be walking, there was always someone taking a walk on the beach even in winter if the ice wasn't too slippery or the wind too raw, and they would find it, they would tell him how I was at sea and had a cat named Whispers, and I would be sure to have Alv say in my note that I was okay so Billy wouldn't think I'd drowned. It would be like a postal card that people on vacation send home to say what a good time they are having so that everyone else who isn't on vacation will be jealous.

"Depends on the bosun." My father's face softened. "You seem to have taken a shine to the lad. That's good. He'll be able to look out for you."

"Oh yes, please," I said, and my father picked up the telephone and asked the engine room to send Alv up to the pilothouse to get me. He gave a pointed look to Loke. "The men say a lot of things. Best to stick to your own business."

18

*T*he first legal plat from Benzie County was the "Plat of Frankfort City," filed in 1867, though the area that was mapped was not the old part of Frankfort where I would live, but Elberta. Legend has it that the name came from a fur trapper named Frank Martin, who ran his operation from the beach to the north of what was then Lac Aux Becs Scies, trading with the Indians and the French in the mid-nineteenth century. In their bitterness about a business that excluded them, the trappers on the other side of Aux Becs Scies dubbed it "Frank's Fort." No one knows what happened to Frank Martin, but there's no record of the early German settlers who supposedly named the town after their native Frankfurt either. A more recent version of the Frank Martin legend places him at the mouth of the Betsie River in a cabin so buffeted by the winds off the lake that he built a fortlike fence around it. This is the version the Frankfort Chamber of Commerce offers tourists, with no mention of the disgruntled trappers. Take your pick, though I can tell you anyone who's ever lived in Benzie County would put money on number one.

As a settlement Frankfort preceded Elberta. Seventeen years before the plat was filed, a schooner caught in a storm on Lake Michigan rode a wave over the shallow bar to safe harbor in Lac Aux Becs Scies. When the weather cleared, the captain explored the region while his crew dug an opening in the bar. As a result of his report the ship's owner purchased more than a thousand acres, which he sold to a company from Detroit that brought in a sawmill and dredged a channel to transform Betsie Lake into a harbor. By the time the Civil War brought construction to a halt, the town extended all the way to Fourth Street. The post office closed, and the channel disappeared, but the sandy lane that ran uphill to end at our carriage house was already in place.

After the war, the federal government dredged a new channel at the south end of the strip of land between the lakes, and the lumber barons arrived to build their houses in the town already established on the north side of the harbor and their mills on the south, where the Bestie River offered a way to float logs to Lake Michigan. The Frankfort Iron Works opened in what was then known as South Frankfort the same year the plat was filed. And by 1892, when the first ferry steamed out of South Frankfort, loaded with four coal cars and bound for Kewaunee, the town that would soon cut its ties and change its name to Elberta had become the industrial hub of Benzie County. The roundhouse and railyard, grain elevators, cannery, and warehouses have vanished, but the road behind the ruins of the Iron Works, where wildflowers bloom through the collapsing walls and cracked cement floors, is still called Furnace Avenue.

Somewhere behind Furnace Avenue is the house where Alv would have grown up. It would not have been that far from mine, less than a mile as a gull flies and no more than two if you drove around the harbor. He would have gone to my school, for in those days one school served both towns. It was three blocks from my house, and much of the winter I picked my way over paths shoveled through the snow and ice, my face wrapped in a scarf that grew so stiff with my breath it cracked when I took it off. All winter there were little puddles on the floors of the coatrooms outside our classrooms. The first thing we did when we sat down at our desks was to break the skin of ice that formed across our inkwells.

Stop me here, if you will. My children would—five miles to school, uphill both ways, one of those dreary stories parents tell the children they have worked hard to overprivilege, though the gratitude such stories are meant to inspire seldom comes, something I must have sensed, because I rarely spoke of my childhood to my children, rarely spoke of it even to my husband, who was an engineer, more interested in how things worked than the inner lives of people. How could my children have appreciated the challenges of a Michigan winter growing up as they did in North Carolina? In their world the least hint of snow stripped the stores of bread and milk and canceled school.

But there it is, because Alv would have had to walk those two frozen miles around the harbor. Perhaps in early fall or late spring, when the harbor wasn't iced over, some of the Elberta children crossed in boats, though most of the waterfront belonged to the railroad, crisscrossed by tracks and the trains waiting to be loaded. In winter they may have skated. Certainly there were no school buses, no public transportation, and few of their families would have owned cars. What *did* those children from Elberta do? I suppose I am hazy about this not just because so much time has passed but because the truth is we didn't pay much attention to difficulties that were not ours.

Did we make fun of our schoolmates from Elberta? Probably, yes, I'm sure we did. Children are cruel. They take privilege for granted, and if we were heirs to the lumber barons whose mansions we lived in, the children of Elberta were the spawn of those disgruntled trappers, the shanty boys and mill hands whose drab little houses lined the streets behind the blighted waterfront, though no one would have used the word *blighted* then. The railroad, those warehouses, and factories were food on the table. But either way, eyesore or boon, it's all gone now. When the ferries stopped running in 1982, Elberta's economy collapsed. Even the gas tanks, those four asphalt storage tanks near the beach that gave the town its distinctive odor, have finally been removed. Thirty years later the village is sprucing up. There is a park along part of Betsie Bay, and the restored lifesaving station is now rented out for weddings, though the houses will never rival those on the other side of the harbor and the old railyard is just a weedy lot with locked chain link fence where the trains once lined up to be loaded.

Of course the children of Frankfort tormented their classmates from Elberta. More than anything else it was those gas tanks that marked them. Whenever one walked by, the children of Frankfort would hold their noses and hiss, "You stink."

I would like to say it was because of Alv that I never took part in that schoolyard teasing. More likely I was not invited to. I was an odd child—not unpopular, though I was certainly unpopular among my teachers, who felt I had too many ideas, "more ideas than you can shake a stick at," one of them wrote by way of requesting a meeting with my stepmother. To her credit, Lene did not tell my father—although this was perhaps less a kindness to me than a wish not to disturb him—and only said, more than once, "Fern, you have to do better, do you promise?" and I would promise, knowing that I not only would not do better but wouldn't even try, and so instead of creating a bond between us our secret only opened more distance. My schoolmates liked me well enough—children are drawn to rebels and troublemakers, though I would not say that I was actually either, at least not by intention, and it's useless to speculate on what kind of girl I might have been if my mother hadn't died and I hadn't gone across the lake that winter with my father. I was too young to remember or even know what kind of girl I'd been before, and anyway what is the point of that sort of navel-gazing? I have no patience for people who prattle on about themselves, listing for anyone who will listen their virtues and special quirks, a call best left to others, if you ask me. I had playmates, but I didn't make close friends, I was not a joiner, there was a wildness inside me that was not driven by peers who might long to see how far I would go, to hear what story I would tell next, or what disturbance I might cause. It was more private than that. Always, as far back as I can remember, I held myself apart. I preferred the outdoors, which was hardly unusual up north, but my habits tended to the solitary and make-believe even when I was snowshoeing through the woods.

It's possible that Alv actually fit in at school better than I did, though I doubt it. The children would have taunted him, wrinkled their noses, and called him "crip" or "gimp." Or maybe they too called him a fairy. Was he gay? I don't know. Maybe at fourteen he didn't either. I'm not even sure why some of the men aboard the *Manitou* assumed he was, unless it was his uncanny beauty. I blame the rumor on Dick Butler, Dick and the bosun, though the bosun called all the deckhands faggots and pussies and whores. It was years before I understood what any of this meant, even longer before I sensed that Dick's animosity to Alv might have been a response to his own attraction. How else to explain his obsession? It's not the sexuality of others people fear nearly as much as their own. Perhaps my father sensed as much, and that's why he started Alv on deck instead of with the black gang below.

In any case Alv's classmates would have been all too aware of the slight limp I didn't notice at first because, as I say, on a ship everyone walks a little funny. Sailors barely touch the steps when they come down a companionway—they grab the rails and skim their feet along the edges, and once he mastered it Alv must have loved that trick because it gave him an agility he'd never had. On land he would have shuffled up that tree-flanked walk to the tower that always made me feel like I was entering a castle but would have left him wanting nothing more than to hobble back out, because he too would have been something of a loner. He was artistic in a world dominated by the physical pursuit of the outdoors, and I suppose I appreciate that all the more because I wasn't. I picture him in a dark parlor in one of those dingy Elberta houses, which one I never knew. There is a piano, not so fine as ours, perhaps it's a bit scratched, perhaps its yellowed keys are chipped, though I'm certain it's in tune. He would have seen to that, or perhaps his mother did, perhaps she played, perhaps he learned from her, and maybe in the evenings while his father tended the crankpins in the engine room at the very bottom of the *Kewaunee* Alv played for her, she who came from that line of reindeer herders, though she had no memory of the herd's gamey scent or the midnight sun and midsummer snow, or of the native tongue that was forbidden to the children who were sent to boarding school under the Norwegianization policy, just like the Native American children who were taken away from their parents and stripped of their language and traditions here. All that would have been prehistory to her, and yet she would have understood how her son felt, what it was like to be different, to be lonely. That's what I imagine anyway, Alv's mother in the parlor, tipping her head as she listens to him play and thinks that maybe he will grow up to be a pianist, as she once dreamed that she would do, a girl who had come so far from the land her ancestors once wandered that she could aspire to a music other than the pounding of hooves and barking of dogs, but then she married an oiler for the ferries who couldn't see the point, not for her, and especially not for his son, not when there was a living to be had from the boats, and even by his own account the boy wasn't much of a student, so why wait? What kind of money did she think he had, talking about the music camp at Interlochen, just a few miles away? As far as they were concerned, it might as well have been on the other side of the world. It was enough that he had bought the secondhand piano she insisted on. Too much in fact. Because the boy was different, not just crippled, and to his father that meant not right. And it is one thing to be different if your father is a captain and you live in a big house on the north side of Leelanau Avenue and quite another if you live behind Furnace Avenue in a dreary little house with a toilet seat perched over a bucket, even if those houses are no more than a mile apart.

Or maybe it wasn't that way at all. For all I know he might have loved where he lived. The steep face of the bluffs, the cries of the gulls, the songs of the orioles and grosbeaks courting in the woods, the smell of lilacs through an open window and blush of cherry blossoms in the orchards come spring, summer's flash of goldfinches or an egret sailing the bright-blue sky, the wind licking through the trees and cattails soughing in the marsh beyond the gaudy splashes of spotted knapweed, goldenrod, and Queen Anne's lace along the tracks, the veils of morning mist that married lake to heaven, the many colors of sand and sky and that transcendent stretch of sweetwater sea that lay between us and the edge of our world, most of all the rhythm of the waves coming home day after day, night after night, all that would have been there for him just as it was for me. For all I know he too might have remembered his childhood as happy.

19

$\mathcal{T}$he ghost came that night, after supper, after Alv coaxed Whispers out of hiding with a saucer of milk, after my tour of the engine room and the firehold, where I stood in a corner to watch the fireman feeding the big furnaces that glowed such a bright red-orange inside the doors it was like the sun exploded—you couldn't see anything except the silhouettes of the fireman with his long-handled shovel and the coal passer removing the clinkers. And even though I did what they said and didn't move, the heat scorched my skin, and then when we came out into the big two-story engine room, because that's how tall the engines were, we were covered with coal dust. Alv's face was as black as a minstrel's in a show, and mine must have been too because he said I would have to take a shower before bed and leave my clothes out on a chair in the lounge so that he could take them below and wash them in the wringer washing machine that was just like the one on our back porch, except ours was a General Electric, but on a ship it had to be a Maytag because that was the only kind that could run on direct current, that's what Amund, the Yooper who was playing cards at a long, red table in the flicker, said. Manitou was above, and I was glad I hadn't brought him down with me, because his fur would be all burnt and he would have to take a shower too, and it's not easy to dry a stuffed bear.

Dick Butler, who was playing cards with Amund and Nils, glanced up at Alv. "Looks like a new boy ought. Ain't right startin' the little faggot above."

Nils looked up. "Takes one to know one."

Dick scowled. "Said it yourself, if you recall. Boy should have started at the bottom."

"So I did," Nils acknowledged. "But I'm not the one all worked up about it."

"You want to be captain, start out as a deck ape," Amund said. His sleeves were rolled up, and I could see the bottom of his tattoo. My father had one of those blue anchors on his arm too, though I rarely saw it, only when he was coming out of our bathroom at home in his undershirt. "Me, I like it down here. Do my job and don't owe Bosun shit."

Like Dick Butler, Nils was an oiler, one step above fireman, but I was confused because I didn't know what a Yooper did on a ship, and Amund had to explain that he was a water tender, that was his job, but he was also a Yooper because he was from the UP. Supposedly the term is new, but sailors used it even before the Mackinac Bridge was built and the Yoopers started calling everyone who lived below the bridge, on the Lower Peninsula, trolls. Sitting at a table in the flicker playing cards the men called each other a lot of names, though no one seemed to mind. Nils picked me up and set me on his lap even though I was all sooty, but no one in the black gang cared about that, not as long as you washed your hands at one of the sinks along the bulwark between the flicker and the hold before you picked up your cards, because even after they washed up there was coal dust ground into the creases around their eyes and in the back of their necks and their wrists and knuckles. Nils showed me his cards and even let me hold them, making sure I pointed them straight up so no one else could see, and that's how I learned to play poker. One of his fingernails was black and sort of bubbled up, but it wasn't from the coal dust, it was from catching his hand in a hatch. Malley, the other water tender, was at the end of the table playing a sad song on his harmonica instead of cards. That was because his girlfriend wouldn't marry him, Amund said, she didn't want to marry a man who was at sea all the time. Nils, Malley, and Amund, all of the men in fact except Bosun and Twitches, would explain a lot of things and tell all kinds of stories as we crossed the lake. They seemed so eager to explain how things worked it was like a contest, who got to tell me most, probably because there wasn't anyone else to tell what they knew because the other men knew the same things and when they came home the people who hadn't been to sea didn't care. Or maybe it was just because I listened so hard. I wanted to learn everything so that I could grow up to work on a ship too.

Amund and Dick Butler each threw another penny in the middle of the table, but Nils took his cards back and laid them facedown. "I'm out."

"I want to keep playing," I protested, so Dick explained that when you folded it meant you knew you couldn't win and if you couldn't win and you were smart you got out of the game. He said it so nice I wondered if he knew I'd seen him smoking on the car deck. Not that I'd tell. Because that was the second rule on a ship. Though they might quarrel among themselves, sailors didn't rat each other out.

But one thing no one explained was the shower. It was like I thought it would be, but in the shower you had to turn the faucets just right or else the water was ice cold, and then it was so hot I jumped back and fell, with scalding water pouring down all over my backside. I wanted someone to come, but my father didn't know I needed help because at home the person who always helped me was my mother. So I had to get up by myself and reach around to the faucets, but finally I found the place that was like a warm summer rain, and after that I cheered up and sang a song because I had heard about singing in the shower. Later I would wonder if the ghost knew about the faucets, because if it did it could have helped me, though I guessed ghosts didn't care to go around assisting people. What they wanted was some kind of help themselves, but ghosts can't say what they want, and that's why people are so afraid of them, though all that was something I thought about later, after I was used to it. That first night I wasn't used to it at all.

When it came, it was after the rudder pin broke and the engineer began his walk across the ice, after the bowling alley closed and I could no longer hear the crack of the ball and explosions of the pins, and I began to hear the ship speak in a way you don't hear it in the daytime, maybe because the way you listen in the dark is different. There was still the grinding of ice against the hull, though not as loud because we weren't trying to push through it anymore. Instead the ship itself was groaning and creaking, moaning and carrying on like it was a ghost, or like you think a ghost might do, but it wasn't the ghost, it was just the night air making the steel hull contract. A ship is built to flex or else the hull will break apart, so I knew what I heard was the ship and not a ghost, but even so I clutched Manitou tight against my neck and kept my eyes open. The snow had stopped hours before, and the air outside was colder now not just because it was night but because the sky had cleared, and before I went to bed I knelt in one of the hemp chairs in the observation room and saw all the stars like a sky full up with diamonds, the way you only ever see them from the beach on a winter night because up on Leelanau Avenue there were too many trees, and so I tipped my head up and looked until I was dizzy, and then I went back to my cabin and closed the door and got in bed and the ship started making all that night noise.

But even though my eyes were open I never saw the ghost, because no matter what some people say about glimpsing apparitions, figures you can see through or shadows without anyone to cast them, the main thing about ghosts is not what you see. Holgar, who was one of the deckhands, the one who didn't like Finns and was always taking pictures with his Brownie camera, was forever asking to see the special compartment because he'd heard you could see the ghost's face in the wood paneling, and he said that sometimes ghosts will show in pictures even when you can't see them in real life, but the crew wasn't allowed to hang around the passenger quarters, except Alv, who came and got my clothes and washed them and hung them to dry on the line strung across the flicker, so I don't know whether this ghost would have showed in a picture or not. Also when the ghost came it was dark. Outside, all around the deckhouse and the aft pilothouse there are lights. On a platform on the forward spar below the crow's nest, red and green port and starboard lights keep ships from running into each other in the fog or at night, and from the passenger lounge you can see the light that's kept on all night in the galley, but inside my cabin with the door and shutters closed up tight it was what they call pitch black.

And what happened when it came, it wasn't the way you would think, because it didn't make any noise at all, and the way I knew it was there was how quiet the ship got. All of a sudden you couldn't hear the ice or the flexing steel plates on the hull, all the moaning and groaning and shrieking just stopped. Some ghosts are supposed to weep, and the ghosts of the cholera victims buried alive on South Manitou Island cry out for help, their voices echoing over the water, trying to hail the passing ships. People hear footsteps on the stairs, the thump of an empty chair set to rocking, or the slamming of a door, though the only reason a ghost could have to slam a door would be to get your attention, because they don't need doors or windows to go from room to room, not that they travel much—they don't wander the earth like some people say, only a very little part of it where something terrible happened. I didn't know what happened to the ghost on the *Manitou* or even who it was, nobody seemed to, only that in the daytime it lived in the special room the managers used when they crossed the lake. I'm not sure the men even knew that it came out at night and moved around the passenger quarters because it never went anywhere else on the ship, not down to the flicker, where the black gang bunked, or up to the pilothouse, not even to the galley or messes nearby, because if it had, the men would have talked about it, but they never did, not even the bosun, and he was not one to keep a ghost to himself.

So that was how I knew it was there, because everything got so quiet, and at the same time I felt it, because you don't have to see or hear a ghost to know one's there. You feel it the same way you feel a storm is coming, there's a change in pressure, a heaviness in the air, you can't breathe, and what you hear isn't the ghost but your own blood pounding inside your ears and what you feel is that same blood beating in your throat, but a ghost doesn't warn you like a storm will, it just comes all of a sudden and then it's there. And what this ghost did, it reached down and took hold of my big toe. I can't say whether it lifted the scratchy wool blanket, reached through it, or what, because I couldn't feel anything but the pressure of its hand on my foot, not the nib of a fingernail or warmth of a palm, because the ghost didn't have surface, only weight, a heaviness that was not like anything else, and all night long it gripped my toe and never said what it wanted or why it was there, and I wanted to be the girl I bragged I was, but I wasn't, because that first night when the ghost came into my compartment and clasped my foot in its hand I was so scared I couldn't even scream, and in the morning when I woke and the ghost was gone, my eyes were all crusty in the corners, and both Manitou and my pillowcase were wet, and I realized that I had cried all night long without ever making so much sound as a sniffle.

·

20

I am wrong. Alv wouldn't have gone to my school, he had his own, for there on the wall of the Benzie Area Historical Museum in Benzonia is a picture of the Elberta schoolhouse, a white frame building near the bottom of Betsie Lake at the corner of George Street and Frankfort Avenue. It even had a tower entrance, though not so tall or grand as ours. In the picture, the harbor seems to open out behind it, and in the distance you can see the rise of the Frankfort hill, though my house is much too far away to pick out. You can't even locate the water tower that crowned our hill because the three-story school in the foreground eclipses all the Frankfort landmarks. Once, before I was born, the water tower burst and sent a flood coursing down the hill—it was something people still talked about when I was a girl, and I was disappointed to have missed it, because I liked the idea of sailing down Fourth Street with Manitou, like a couple on Noah's ark. That was the old wooden water tower, which has long since been replaced. At one time Elberta too had a wooden water tower atop its bluff. The railroad built it to fill the boilers on the ships, so it must have been there when I was a girl, though I have no more recollection of it than I do of Alv's school. There is no tower on the Elberta bluff now, just as there is no longer a railroad or a school, only the rotting dock where the ferries once tied up. If it weren't for the picture in the museum I wouldn't know the school ever existed.

But it did, whether I remember it or not. What does it mean, I wonder, that I've invented that cold morning trek around the harbor through drifts of snow and Alv's numbing dread of the walk up to Frankfort's school? He never hung his jacket on the iron hooks of any of those coatrooms I later used, where I can still summon the dull light that filtered through the transoms from the classrooms, the way it gleamed on the waxed floor of the long hall, can still smell the mixture of melting snow, rubber boots, and wet wool. He never stood on the fringes of our playground, longing to be chosen for dodgeball or included in a game of tag. He had his own playground, his own playmates, on the other side of the harbor, a schoolhouse whose light and smells he would have known as well as I knew mine. It's an understandable error, I suppose. The children of Elberta do attend the Frankfort schools these days, the two districts having long since been consolidated. But the truth is I was long gone by 1956, the date the museum lists for the consolidation, and I have no reason to know where the local children go to school now. My children grew up elsewhere, as have theirs, and those days when they were bringing home report cards and permission slips, when I was checking homework, baking cupcakes, and chaperoning field trips seem a lifetime ago, somehow more distant than my own report cards, first readers, and minutes counted till recess.

Memory is a notoriously faulty tool, of course, and at such a span of years it is easy to put the bank where the butcher was and the drugstore on the wrong corner, to lay out a map of the past with the streets transposed and sweet breezes wafting through windows that were walls, to remember a second-grade teacher with a blue dress and red curls when the redhead was Sunday school and your second-grade teacher wore rolled stockings and old-fashioned tortoise-shell combs in gray hair pinched into a bun, easier still to forget a school I may never have been aware of in the first place. It is not what I've forgotten that disturbs me, rather what I remember, those children from Elberta huddled at the edges of our playground, noses running, eyes cast down, as we chose sides for the games they were never asked to join, the ugly chords of insults we never delivered. Why would I remember something so false? More important, why would I remember that cruelty so vividly and yet claim I stood apart? What does it mean to remember crimes that never happened only to insist that you are not to blame?

The more I relive that trip across the lake with my father that mercilessly cold winter, the less I seem to know who I am, the little girl I was then or the old woman I've become. They're mixed up together, I see, after so many years of wanting to believe that any connection between them would be the slightest of threads, as if we were distant relatives who had heard of each other but never met. And now their thoughts seem so jumbled I can't even tell you which is speaking when. Fortunately my children are far away, one in California, the other in France. Otherwise they might assume I've gone senile, though no one uses that word anymore. Back when I was a girl, people tiptoed around the elderly's habits of mind, spoke of them, of their non sequiturs and lapses, as entering their second childhoods, but no one is allowed a repeat of childhood anymore, old age is no longer a phase of life but a disease caused by too much plaque in the brain, Alzheimer's or some other fancy kind of dementia, syndromes with names like Korsakoff or Lewy body, and at the first sign, off you go to the nursing home.

No thank you. I didn't even move to the new senior center on the hill when I came back to Frankfort, though my children think coming back at all is evidence of dementia enough. "Mother," my daughter, Ellen, said over the phone, and I started at the word, it seemed so strange you'd think I'd never been one, though I blame that on her intonation, that exaggerated patience grafted onto exasperation that turns daughter into mother and you the child. "Have you lost your mind? What about winter? What happens when you fall on the ice and break your hip? Who's going to take care of you?" "I want to go home," I said, and Ellen sniffed. "Home? You haven't lived there in more than seventy years. What makes you think you'd even recognize the place?"

What she doesn't know is how little has changed, at least to the eye. And it's not as if I proposed to buy one of the big, beautiful old houses like the one I lived in as a girl. I'm not that foolish. My children grew up in an old house in Raleigh. I've had enough of the maintenance that kind of charm requires. What I wanted was simply to wander the same streets, to walk out along the breakwater come sunset, to stroll the beach up past the bluff and feel the cold rush of water over my feet again, and though the senior center offers spectacular views from its lofty perch on the bluff, they're like looking at a postcard, a picture on the wall, a landscape you see but cannot enter, can't smell or touch. I wanted to be a part of the town again, not to have to search out a parking space as if I were a tourist. So here I am in a condo on that spit of land old-timers called "the island," not far from the cross that marks where Father Marquette ended his earthly journey. Perhaps it's only hard for Ellen to accept that I would call a place she's never seen home, but I think my husband would like it if he were still alive, though he *would* be surprised, for we never traveled to Michigan, there was no reason to, I never expressed a desire to come back, even though the mere sight of a Michigan license plate in a parking lot could cause such a pang I would stumble, and each time the Tigers won the World Series I became the sports fan I never was, remembering the voices of Walter, Red, and Roald so clearly they might have been cheering along with me in my den. But only since Ed—his name was Edmund, Edmund Fitzgerald if you can believe it, how that's for irony?—only since he passed and that part of my life ended did I begin to think so much about it. Things that happen in your childhood come back to haunt you more and more as you get older, and once you are alone you no longer need pretend that the life at hand is where you live. So, yes, he would be surprised, yet I think he would like the view of the lighthouse and outer harbor, in the evening he would enjoy walking along the breakwater or the beach or even sitting on our porch to watch the sun set over the great lake beyond, so much bluer and more beautiful than the Atlantic Ocean at Wrightsville, where we took the children every summer. Ed always wanted to take a cruise, but I demurred, and he was such a kind man, so considerate, much more thoughtful than I deserved, he would murmur, "Of course.

Your father . . ." and I never told him that wasn't it at all. I haven't set foot on a boat larger than a canoe since my father called for us to abandon the *Manitou*. I simply could not bear to board a ship as a passenger.

In the picture at the Benzie Area Historical Museum it is winter, perhaps the very same winter I crossed the lake, for the cars lined up beside the school look to be of that era, though I am certainly no expert on cars. Children cluster on the hard-packed street, some with sleds in hand, and perhaps just beyond the frame there are others dangling skates. School has apparently just let out—they are leaving, not coming, the joy on their faces belongs to afternoon, to the unencumbered fun of the remaining daylight hours. Across the harbor Frankfort's children would have been leaving school in just the same way, gathering merrily at the corner of Leelanau and Seventh with sleds and skates, eyes just as bright, cheeks just as flushed, but they are not pictured.

And though it is surely true that if the children of Elberta had been there on the north side of the harbor outside the brick schoolhouse at Leelanau and Seventh, the children of Frankfort would have been holding their noses, blowing raspberries, and hurling names, the fact is they are not. Those other children are secure in Elberta, about to belly down on their sleds, lace skates, and sling snowballs, faces chapped with cold, their breath little clouds in the air, as unaware of the children on the other side of the harbor as those children are of them. They're much too far away to hear anything the arrogant sons and daughters of Frankfort have to say. They don't care whether my voice is among them, they blame me for nothing. They don't know I exist.

21

*T*he ghost disappeared the same way it appeared—first it was there, then the air got thinner and lighter, I could no longer feel the pressure of its hand against my foot, and so I knew it had gone. That must have been when I fell asleep, though I didn't sleep very long because as soon as Sam started breakfast the smell of coffee and bacon seeped into the passenger quarters and I woke up. Alv had returned my clothes, folded and dry, to the chair outside my cabin, so I got up and brushed my teeth and tucked my nightgown underneath my pillow just like I always did at home and tried to make up my rack. In the crew's mess Alv was drinking orange juice and eating flapjacks, and I wondered when he had brought my clothes, if it was before or after the ghost left, because I hadn't heard him. Bosun was sitting right across from him with a cup of coffee, baring his gold tooth and grousing about all the things Alv needed to do that should have been done yesterday or even before that, to hear him talk you'd think they should have been done a hundred years before Alv was ever born. He was so mean I began to worry that if he found Whispers he really would throw my cat overboard, and he would do something terrible to Alv, I knew. I had failed to make him like me, so I would never make him like Alv the way I'd promised.

At the end of the table Twitches was muttering to himself, and Roald and Red were arguing about baseball again. Axel wasn't there, but the rest of the men were all talking about the new rudder pin and how long it would take to install, how soon we might get underway, and when we might hope to reach the *Ashley*, which had been on her way back to Frankfort from the Straits, where she had been leased by the Mackinac Transportation Company while the *Chief Wawatam* was in dry dock for repair. That was why we had to go through the Passage instead of heading out into the lake for Menominee, which was something the men had plenty to say about, and I could see how things were on a ship. It was like a parade, which was the best thing ever, but if you've been to one you know how they go, a little bit of parading and a whole lot of standing around. Everyone except Bosun seemed a bit sleepy, and I was about to announce that the ghost from the managers' cabin had visited me last night—maybe I meant to liven things up or perhaps I thought that saying it out loud would put a little daylight on the long, terrifying shadow of the night—but just then Alv's sleeve brushed my arm, and I remembered that he had told me not to go calling the ghost out and maybe he would think I'd called it and that's why it came, he would think it was my fault and be mad. His canvas coverall had white paint streaked down one arm, which made him seem more like a regular deckhand instead of a boy, and that was good, because maybe the bosun would lay off, he wouldn't be the new kid anymore, and everyone would stop picking on him. Except it made me feel a bit bereft too, like maybe he'd get to be so friendly with the crew he'd forget me.

On the other hand I thought if Bosun knew I had spent my whole night with a ghost and never once screamed or called out for help maybe *that* would make him start to like me. At the least he would be interested since he liked to talk about haunts, being more superstitious than Ahab, that's what Loke had said. But the new rudder pin wasn't in place yet, and we were still within walking distance to Frankfort, and if my father knew the ghost had come to me he might make me go back, maybe he would make Alv take me back, and then neither one of us would get to go across the lake and see Menominee and Death's Door and maybe even the old lightkeeper still looking for his children on St. Martin Island, which wouldn't scare me a bit because a phantom green lamp bobbing along in the distance was nothing compared to having an actual ghost reach out and touch you.

So I kept very quiet, which gave me time to think. And that brought me to the ghost itself. Because I hadn't considered the ghost, and what if it got angry with me for telling? I didn't know what a ghost might do if it got angry, but I was pretty sure I didn't want to find out, so that settled it, and I decided that what I would do instead was listen, because if I listened hard enough the men might let on who the ghost was and where it came from and what it wanted. And maybe Holgar would get a picture with his Brownie camera, and that would answer all my questions, so I drank my milk and ate my flapjacks and bacon and eggs and the apple Jake brought me, but all the men talked about was the rudder pin and the *Ashley* and how soon we might get to Pyramid Point until Bosun aimed a stare at Alv and said, "What happened to your hand, boy?"

Alv dropped it from the table to his lap so fast I couldn't see, but it was his right hand, the one Whispers had bitten. "Nothing," he said.

"Better be."

I wondered if his hand had festered up like the time I fell and cut my knee and the cut got infected. Or maybe the iodine hadn't washed off in the shower, and what Bosun saw was a big orange stain. And maybe Alv's hand was why he hadn't learned to go down a companionway like a real sailor yet, which was another thing the men rode him about. I had no trouble with it once I saw how it was done, because that's the way kids would always go down steps if grown-ups let them. And Alv would remember that, because even with the new paint on his coverall and a paycheck to come he would remember how it was to be a boy. So now I had two secrets, Whispers and the ghost, but no one asked about either one, because little girls weren't supposed to have secrets. They were supposed to wear hair bows and pretty dresses and sweet smiles and never talk back.

Instead the men were still grumbling about the *Ashley* and having to go through the Passage, and before I knew it the first bell rang and breakfast was over.

22

*I*t was in the Manitou Passage that we sighted the *Chicora*. The watch saw it first, in the early afternoon, when the light that had been so clear all night and early morning suddenly turned gauzy. It was off to port, and we were just done with noon dinner, some of the men lingering over their coffee, when the watch burst into the mess, yelling, "Holy smokes, you gotta see this!" And we all rushed out to the deck without bothering to put on our coats, and there it was like an apparition coming out of a mist that wasn't mist but that strange, webby light, like the air was made out of curtains, a big wooden vessel with a single stack and two broken masts that somehow gave her the appearance of an old sailing ship even though she was clearly a steamer, but the way the spars were broken over they looked like what was left of a skeleton rigging, not a sail hoisted, the ship just drifting in a way that seemed impossible in the ice. No one ever saw ships like that, which is why the watch called us and we raced out just in time to see her before she disappeared inside the filmy air.

"It's the *Chicora*," Bosun said.

"Can't be," Walter said. "She's too far off course."

"It's the *Chicora*, I tell you. Ship comes up from the bottom can go anywhere she likes."

"What's she doing in the Passage then?" Odd asked. "I could go anywhere I wanted, I'd head for the South Seas."

"Go on home," Red suggested. "There's people waitin'."

"Not anymore. Even the people waitin's all dead."

Everyone was talking at once, words streaming from their mouths in white plumes.

Roald snorted. "South Seas! You want those balmy breezes, whyn't you sign on a saltie?"

"Next time maybe I will."

"Says who? You're like a bad penny. Captain himself can't get rid of you."

"Wish I'd had my camera," Holgar said.

Walter shook his head. "I don't like it."

"Course you don't," Bosun said. "Going to be a hell of a blow."

"It's too cold for a blow," Walter said.

"Ain't never too cold for a blow. It's an omen, I tell you."

Alv was still standing at the rail, staring off to where the ship disappeared. Though it was below zero, none of us seemed in any hurry to go back inside. "How do you know it's the *Chicora*?"

Bosun glared. "What do you think, it's the *Griffon*? Can't tell a barque from a steamer. Little fairy thinks he sees La Salle himself walking around on deck."

"I didn't see anybody." Something in Alv's face steeled when he turned.

"First trip out, already solved all the mysteries of the deep."

"It was just a question," Alv said, and I was proud of him for talking back, but the bosun must have sensed it because he turned his glare on me.

"Course he didn't," Roald said. "Crew's been dead for forty years."

Dick Butler chortled. "Guess that's what you call a *real* skeleton crew."

"It's what you call a bunch of pussies standing around gawking when they're supposed to be working." Bosun included everyone in his glare now. "Any of you ladies hear eight bells?"

"No, sir," Axel and Alv said in unison.

"Ghost stories," Walter said like he meant to dismiss them, even though he looked shaken because he'd seen the ship too, broken masts and listing until it disappeared, as if behind a windrow, but there wasn't any windrow, and despite what Bosun said, despite the cold, we were all lingering on deck to see if it would reappear, but it didn't, and finally the men began to disperse back to their posts. Then there was a windrow, out of nowhere it seemed, just like the ghost in my cabin and the *Chicora*, but the windrow wasn't any ghost, we were face to face with it, solid ice, and I knew that up in the pilothouse my father would be instructing the wheelsman to change course and go around, there was room even in the narrow Passage, there had to be because we couldn't see South Manitou or North Manitou, not the new crib light that marked the North Manitou shoal or the mainland either, just the wall of ice and filmy air, and because I was the captain's daughter I climbed the steps to the bridge to get a better view, and from where I was the veil seemed to lift, I was standing in full sun, and beyond the mountain of the windrow it was just plains and plains of ice as far as I could see, plains strewn with so many white boulders I had never seen anything like it, and I sucked in my breath and said, this time to myself, "This *is* the world!"

We were stuck, but the ice in the passage was different from the slush ice in the harbor, and when my father had the engineer fill the aft ballasts and empty the forward ones, which I knew he was doing because I saw the prow rise, we backed up, then sped toward the ice until we ran the prow right up on it, and I felt as if I was standing on top of a mountain, but then we crashed down through that mountain of ice with a huge roar that sent big chunks of ice flying up around the hull like an explosion, and I grabbed onto the rail because it felt like we were falling through the bottom of the world. I was standing on the bridge with a sweater buttoned over my dress because my coat was in my locker, but for the moment I didn't feel cold, it was too exciting, all those big chunks of ice boiling up into the sunlight, bobbing and heaving like toy blocks, except the blocks were as big as refrigerators, almost as wide as I was tall, and Holgar, who was supposed to be on duty, ran up the steps with his camera to snap a picture, so I knew I was seeing something you didn't get to see every day. Then he ran back down and around the deckhouse, and I realized that my fingers were so stiff I couldn't straighten them enough to let go of the rail. They hurt, but they weren't red, they were white, so white they looked blue, and when I yanked them away I jammed them up beneath my wool sweater. I was shivering, but still I couldn't stop watching until finally a taller windrow rose before us, a dam of ice that stretched as far as I could see, all the way across the Passage it seemed. As we backed up to ram it I imagined the bells ringing in the engine room and the man dozing on the stool beneath the chadburn. He had missed the *Chicora* because he was down where he missed the whole show and it was hot down there, warm enough to fall asleep, and I imagined him sitting up with a start and yelling for the engineer to reverse the engines, and that happened three times, and then we stopped.

I opened the heavy door to the pilothouse. "Why are we stopping?" I asked because I wanted to keep hitting the wall of ice and watch the pieces fly up.

"Can't risk peeling the hull," my father said. My eyes widened as I imagined the hull splitting open like the skin of a banana. No pump would be able to keep up with that. "Did you see the ghost ship?"

I nodded. "Bosun says it's the *Chicora*."

"First time I've seen it," my father said, "but I daresay it is."

"They say there's always a blow after you see it." Ebbe, the wheelsman on duty, glanced at my father.

"Have you seen it before?" I asked.

He shook his head. "Can't say I have."

"Bosun says there'll be a blow," I said.

"Maybe," my father said. "But I wouldn't put too much stock in his stories."

"What'll we do if there is?" It felt good to be inside the warm space, even with a million fiery needles pushing up beneath my numb skin, but I was thinking again about what Dick had said, that we'd better not run into a storm because we'd need all the coal we had and even with fans it would be too wet to burn.

"Well for now there isn't," my father said. "And for now what we do is wait."

"But we have to free the *Ashley.*"

My father chuckled inside his throat. "Looks like the *Ashley* waits too. Right now we could use another boat to free us."

While we waited, a smaller boat tried to come through the Passage, and then it was the two of us stuck out there in the world of ice together, both with all our deck lights on because the light had suddenly turned dingy again, it was almost like night coming on, and even though the other boat was much smaller with all our lights it looked like we had a built a little city out there on the ice, just like the hotel Axel talked about on Green Bay.

The ice looked solid, but underneath the surface it was pushed by the northwesterly winds that had built up the windrows even inside the Passage. There were waves beneath the ice, and all that movement brought so much pressure against the sides of the ship the *Manitou* was moaning and shrieking almost like it had in the night. You could hear it even up in the pilothouse, which meant that down below in the flicker and the cabins where the engine crew slept it would be so loud the men wouldn't be able to hear each other talk. Even with the engines standing by it was the noisiest place on the ship because there were the big boilers, the generators, the crankshaft and screw, steam hissing through all those pipes, and the gush of water from the hoses used to flush them. I didn't know if it was the heat or the noise or just so much to see, but my first time my eyes seemed to come loose, as if they were rolling around in their sockets, I couldn't focus, and my head got so light I was afraid I would faint and then I wouldn't get to see everything, but I didn't faint, I didn't even throw up, and after a few minutes everything came back into focus. And right now besides all the other noise down there maybe someone was doing laundry, with the soap swishing and metal buttons clinking against the sides of the tub, and someone might be shouting, "Watch out," if someone else got too close to the big electrical panel, and every now and then the big wooden cane they used to rescue anyone who touched it by accident would fall over and clatter to the floor.

It was the busiest place on the ship, and it would be the best except that you couldn't see out, because there weren't any ports down there below the water line, no ports in the engine room or the quarters off the flicker where the black gang bunked. I thought about the spring on the UP that people talked about. It had an Indian name I liked to say out loud, Kitch-iti-kipi, and it was supposed to be forty feet deep with an emerald bottom and water so clear you could read the date off a penny if you dropped one in, and there was a raft with a window in the floor that visitors could pole out to the middle and look down. I thought maybe people cheated and memorized the dates before they tossed their pennies in, but that wasn't so according to the second mate's brother, who owned the tailor shop on Main Street. It was a state park like Benzie State Park on the Platte River, and he had been there and ridden on the glass-bottom raft where people took turns looking through to see all the coins and the fish, and I thought there should be a window like that on the *Manitou*, because then I could lie on the floor of the engine room and watch all the fish swimming around below the ice, the big sturgeon and muskies and the pike and all the little perches that got fried up in the restaurants every Friday, but that was silly, because no window would be strong enough to withstand all the action that was beneath the surface of such a great lake.

It was almost too much to think about, the ghost that came to my cabin at night, the ghost ship, and all the fish and the movement of the wind and the waves beneath the surface, and somewhere down there would be the crew of the *Chicora*, the skeleton crew, Dick Butler called them, and the crews of all the other ships that went down, Captain Peter Kilty himself, maybe all walking around, and I wondered if the *Chicora* and the *Griffon* and all the other ghost ships mostly stayed on the bottom and just sometimes came up and if that was so was it because they wanted to warn the ships that hadn't gone down yet a blow was in store or did they just come up when they felt like it, and it was such a lot to think about—what if there really could be a ship with a window on the bottom like the Kitch-iti-kipi raft, what would you see when you lay on the bottom of the ship and looked down?

23

$\mathcal{I}$ didn't go to the Benzie Area Historical Museum to find the picture of Alv's school, of course. I made the short trip up M-115 to see the car ferry exhibit. When the museum moved into the Benzonia Congregational Church that is its home, I'm not sure. I don't know if it even existed when I was a girl, though Benzie County had plenty of history even back then, from the prehistory of the corals and brachiopods on up through the Indians to the white man's exploration, Father Marquette, the fur trade, the lumber mills, commercial fisheries, a peach industry that failed after an especially hard winter, the heyday of the railroad and grand opening of the Royal Frontenac Hotel, the summer Frankfort's streets were paved, the year electric streetlights went up, and so on. But children never think about history. Oh, they're aware of some of its significant moments, like the night the Royal Frontenac caught fire. That was emblazoned into the collective memory at least in part because it was such a shame on the town, upright citizens having joined the looting once they realized that the building would burn to the ground and nothing would be saved. People remember shipwrecks and fires. But children cannot see the past as a timeline, a road from the brachiopods and the glaciers that runs past the Potawatomi and Ojibwe, fur traders and timber barons, and if they did they would think the line ended with them, they wouldn't see how they too were only a small station, no more than a spark from the wheel of an express rocketing past, destination unknown. If children think of the past at all it is as a still life, a curiosity, a tableau. It is too much to ask a child to comprehend that the world went about its business moment by disappearing moment for billions of years without her. It's the sad shock of adulthood to realize what a short blip of time we inhabit.

One person's lifetime, give or take a few years: that's how long the railroad car ferries lasted. An historical marker near the site of the old railyard in Elberta offers up the dates, 1892–1982, though if you were to ask someone when they stopped running, a waitress at Dinghy's, say, a drugstore clerk, or the cashier at the BP, he or she would most likely frown, give a little shrug, and respond, "I don't know, five or six years ago maybe?" Even for adults the line of the past contracts, years run together, sequences blur. No doubt there are many citizens, not just transplants but young people born right here in Benzie County who no longer remember or perhaps never knew that for ninety years, not a single day or night passed without the blast of the steam whistle or wail of the foghorn. I was long gone when the *Viking* docked in the harbor for the last time, but I imagine that to the people who were here, the people who would crowd the breakwaters a year later to watch the once proud ship be towed away, the town must have seemed as eerily silent as a forest suddenly abandoned by birds. But then another day would have passed without horn or whistle, and another and another, until everyone forgot what Frankfort used to sound like.

I have said that little has changed to the eye, but that's not entirely true. Though what is here hasn't changed that much, so much is gone. If it weren't for the bike path it would be hard to picture where the railroad tracks once were.

I can't say exactly why I went to see the exhibit on the car ferries when I haven't gone to visit the S.S. *City of Milwaukee*, the only railroad car ferry left, which is permanently docked in Manistee and open to the public for guided tours in season. I haven't been because I don't think I could stand to climb the companionways or file through the passageways and silent engine room, where I once got so hot and dizzy, to visit the crew's mess with its table sitting empty or the flicker without the black gang and deckhands playing cards, to see the vacant passenger cabins so like the one where I once spent a night weeping because a ghost got hold of my foot.

A museum is different. You enter a museum expecting the dimensions of the past to be flattened. It wasn't a space where I would look for Holgar or Nils or even the bosun, though I wouldn't have minded one of those interactive exhibits, a button you could press just to hear the whistle again, that sound that was not a moan, not a shriek, not a wail or a cry, rather a deep-throated call that contained all of those things, but I suppose such technology is beyond the budget of a county museum, one that recalls the history of a sparsely populated county at that. Still, I was surprised by the museum's scope, by the size of the upstairs corner devoted to the ferries and how much it holds, so many photographs and paintings, along with lanterns, life preservers, seaman's papers, nameplates, union cards, binnacle and compass. All of the Annies are pictured, the *Manitou* looking just as I remember in the black-and-white photograph on the wall.

The glass cases held even more, including the yellowed newspaper clipping from the year the ill-fated *Ann Arbor 4* sank at the south pier. There is a copy of the mural in the new Frankfort post office that depicts the derailed cars plunging overboard, the desperate men, the icicles hanging from the deck. I say new because it was new the year I left. The post office I remember is the one where I used to stare at the wanted posters for the Barker Gang and Al Brady. And of course there's that other yellowed clipping, the one that tells what happened to the *Manitou*, but I didn't need to read that. Because the paper would tell only half the story. I alone ever knew the whole.

The objects are all so familiar and yet out of place, behind glass or hung from the vaulted ceiling and walls there on the second floor of the old church that opens out to a dormer with an arched stained-glass window, just one of the four corners of a vast second-floor room in a museum devoted to everything bygone, railroads, vintage kitchens, doctor's offices, summer camps, schools. In the middle of the car ferry display a dressmaker's dummy sports a double-breasted, navy-blue, wool, twill captain's jacket with its gold star and four gold stripes on the sleeves, each button embossed with the name Ann Arbor. It is topped by a red silk scarf such as my father never wore and a captain's hat like the one he once let me try on. The scarf covers the upholstered stump of the neck that holds the hat, but that crimson-covered space is so short the hat looks as if it belongs to a headless horseman, and I wanted to snatch it off, never mind that it belongs to a museum and is not to be touched. I wanted to lift it, to make room for that long, grizzled face with its pale but intensely blue eyes set in a crinkle of lines above the gray stubble along his cheeks and chin, a face I have waited for, waited and waited, because the ghosts I want will not come, they will not tell me what they want. I should say I'm not a woman much given to tears. Perhaps I suffered too many losses early on, I didn't dwell, I made the best of it, as my stepmother said. I was a child after all. The world might have ended, and still I skated on the harbor and ran through the woods, sledded, had snowball fights, played tag, sassed my teachers, told stories, exchanged penny Valentines, and passed notes in school. But the sight of that legless uniform with its empty arms and headless hat assailed me like a blow. My knees buckled, and there, on the second floor of the Benzie Area Historical Museum under the watchful eye of the stained-glass Jesus with his staff and flock of lambs—a Jesus whose eyes don't actually look watchful at all, whose face is nearly as blank as the tumble of white clouds behind his head—there, in the room with what is left of everything I once desired, I let loose a sob so loud the docent came flying up the stairs.

"What's the matter?" she cried. "Are you ill? Is there someone we should call, something I can do?"

I struggled to my feet and said, stupidly, "Your captain needs a face."

I would like to say I left it at that and walked away, dignity intact, but no, I am an old woman, she had to help me to a seat on the long pew that faced that indifferent Congregational shepherd, obviously uncertain whether she should stay with me or go summon the director.

"Can I get you a glass of water?"

"Your Jesus," I answered, "he needs a face too."

24

*O*nce when my father was home we found ourselves alone together in the back parlor. This would have been in 1937, late spring I think, because there was a slight prickle to the air, a damp chill, but no fire in the hearth. My stepmother had already come to live with us. I would have been nearing the end of my first year of school, and I was sprawled on the rug practicing my printing. My father had been reading the paper and listening to the radio. He often did both at the same time, as if the two things somehow enhanced each other. On the radio he liked to tune to Father Coughlin. As I understood it at the time, Father Coughlin was on the side of the downtrodden, an early supporter of President Roosevelt and the New Deal. Whether he had yet soured on the president as he became more vehemently anticommunist and anti-Semitic, more outspoken in his approval of the fascist governments in Europe and his opposition to American involvement in the coming war, I don't remember, likely because I was too young to understand what he was saying in the first place, any more than I understood the labor unrest that had boiled over in Detroit and Chicago. I just knew his voice, along with the president's, because my father listened to FDR's fireside chats when he was home, and so I believe he must have approved of the president, though what he felt about the labor unions and growing tension overseas I can't say, only that he followed the news. He was a thoughtful man, he listened and seemed to weigh things but seldom voiced his opinion, unlike my stepmother, who listened less and spoke more. She preferred *Your Hit Parade* and *Moon River*, which came on after I went to bed, and variety shows like *The Fleischmann's Yeast Hour*, a name I can't recall now without picturing the show rising from the speaker like dough.

My favorites were *Little Orphan Annie, Buck Rogers,* and *The Green Hornet.* We had an old-fashioned radio, old-fashioned even at the time, I think, since it was a big wooden console that sat on the floor with a top that was arched like a church window and wooden fretwork over the nubby beige fabric that covered the speaker, an instrument as grand in its way as the upright piano in the front parlor. And that's what I see first when I remember this scene, the handsome radio, the cold fireplace, the newspaper folded on an end table with a fretwork rim, and my wide-ruled tablet on the Persian rug. The rug had a slightly musty smell, though perhaps it was just the smell of that chilly in-between air. I knew every figure and whorl because sometimes I lay on the floor to do up its fringe in little braids, though some of the fringe was worn away and too short. That day I was copying a story from my primer, and I can still see my uneven block letters on the page: "A ball was in the basket. It was a big red ball. It was a pretty ball." I suppose we hadn't learned the beauty of compound and complex sentences yet. No models of style, those early readers. No one I knew, not even children, talked like that.

My stepmother was out, perhaps at the grocer's since it would have been unusual for her to be visiting one of her friends on an occasion when my father was home. They were newlyweds, married no more than a few months, but there he was seated alone on the sofa, which must have been an antique even then, maroon with wood trim, all tufts and buttons, and not at all comfortable, but then my father was not comfortable anywhere except in his pilothouse high above the lake. He had turned off the radio and was tamping the bowl of his pipe, and I suppose it was that sound that caused me to look up from my tablet.

"Daddy," I said. "Why did my mother die?"

He continued to tamp the pipe. "Lene is your mother now."

"But why did my mother die?" For some reason the matter must have seemed particularly urgent to me that morning because I don't remember asking before, though why that should be so I can't say. Perhaps it was simply an opportunity that had not presented itself.

"Lene is your mother now," he repeated. Abruptly he set the unlit pipe on top of the newspaper beside the flowered glass lamp, rose, and left the room, but then he must have thought better, must have weighed out an answer, because he came back, though not until I had copied two more lines. *Spot said, "Mew, mew. I see a big red ball."* My children would correct me here, silly me, remembering a dog who mewed, or perhaps even worse, they would say nothing and just exchange glances, poor old mom, what to do now with her memory going, though the truth is I remember things they never knew. For them Spot was a dog and Puff the cat, but in those Elson-Gray primers of the thirties Spot was a kitten, and I recall the image of that gray cat on the arm of the overstuffed blue chair so clearly I can still see my crooked letters on the lines of my tablet and through the lens of all these years realize I have failed to capitalize the naughty feline's name.

"It was complications," he said, standing stiffly in the wide doorway between the two parlors.

"What kind of complications?" I asked.

He seemed at such a loss that I thought the conversation was over and bent to copy the next lines. *I want it. I want the big red ball.*

"The kind of complications you'll understand later." His hand did a little half circle in the air.

"When?"

"When you're a woman," he said.

"When will that be?" I asked, and perhaps I sighed, or maybe there was a high note of panic in my voice. Did I sigh because I thought it would be such a long time, or was I terrified that the time was already too short?

He smiled at me then. "Not for a while yet, *lille.*"

There was a short silence.

"I don't want to be a woman," I said.

I don't recall that he looked alarmed. I think he assumed that I simply wanted to remain a child, and that would have been partially right, though already I envisioned myself as a grown-up, not one stirring pots in a kitchen and gossiping in parlors, but a sailor steering a great ship across the big lake.

"Lene will tell you all about it when it's time," he said, as if that concluded our commerce. He crouched beside me. "What do we have here?"

So I showed him my tablet and the book so that he could see for himself the red ball of yarn in the basket and the cat, and then I turned the page so he could see how it all came out, the pounce, the overturned basket and table, the kitten tangled up in yarn, because I must have wanted him to know I was just copying from my book, it wasn't my story, it wasn't my fault, and I didn't want it, I didn't want that big red ball of yarn at all.

25

I was six years old that year, a schoolgirl, a big girl, my father said. Why didn't the naughty kitten make me think of Whispers and Alv? Or did they? Did I think of them and then go on with my childhood anyway? How could I? I loved where I lived, it's true, but maybe nothing I remember is quite right.

26

$\mathcal{A}$lv had cat scratch fever. At first it was just a bruise and a bump that began to fester up where Whispers bit him. Then he said he was tired, he had a headache, one minute he was hot, the next he had chills, but he wore his gloves as much as he could and in the mess he kept his right hand in his lap, even though he wasn't used to eating with his left, but he wasn't hungry anyway, and maybe no one would have noticed if he hadn't spilled his coffee. "Don't anybody sit next to new boy when this ark starts to rock," Axel said. Then the bosun was all over Alv because he didn't work fast enough and hadn't learned some of his knots, but that was because his hand was swollen. When Alv left the mess, he vomited over the rail, and Bosun was right behind him, jabbing his fist into Alv's ribs. "Ship ain't even moving. What kind of sailor you going to make, boy?"

It was my fault, because I'd made him catch Whispers, but all Alv would say was that he'd scratched his hand on a rusty nail and it must have got infected.

"Where'd you find a rusty nail?" Bosun drew his lip back as he turned his mean face from Alv to the rest. "Unless some of you deck apes ain't doing your job." So Alv said it happened before, before he ever got on the *Manitou*.

"Step on a rusty nail you get lockjaw." Axel offered a pantomime of the victim's death throes that went on until Dick Butler noted, "Looks more like a case of cat scratch fever to me," but still Alv didn't tell, even though he could have said he had a cat at home, and that was true, he could say that Ashes scratched him, but he'd already said it was a nail, so he stuck to his story. "It was a nail come loose out back in the crap-house," he said. But later when we went below to give Whispers a little fish mushed up in milk he let me see.

"I'm sorry." My throat closed, and a hot mist of tears stung my eyes. "Are you mad? Because I'm the one made you get bit, but if I tell Bosun he'll yell at me instead of you."

"Fat chance." I tried to swallow. "Anyway you can't tell. He hates cats. You know what he'd do."

My mouth trembled. The noise of the engines and the ice swallowed up my answer, and now I can't remember what I said or if I said anything at all.

Alv's face softened. "You would really do that? Take the blame for me?"

I nodded.

"Aw, Fern. I'm not going to let Bosun throw your pet overboard."

I didn't want that to happen. Even if Whispers landed on his feet, which he might, he would never find his way back to land over all the ice, and what if he fell through one of the cracks? Cats couldn't swim, they didn't like water. I knew, because once Billy Johnson threw his cat in the bathtub, and it jumped out so fast it was like the bathtub blew apart, and then it shot all over the house, hissing and spitting, and Mrs. Johnson took a belt to Billy's behind, saying once again he would be the death of her. But even more than I didn't want Whispers to drown, I didn't want Alv to get lockjaw and die.

"It's just a scratch," he promised, pressing on the festered-up bump and grimacing, mashing down on the pain, making it sharper as a way of perceiving it as pleasure. I knew because sometimes I did the same thing. "I'll put some more iodine on it and take an aspirin. It'll be fine in a day or two.

By then Whispers had smelled the fish and crept out from his hiding place, and all the while my kitty ate I talked to him, telling how we were stuck behind a big windrow right now but were going to break loose and then we were going to free the *Ashley* and cross the lake and back and after that he could come home and live with me and Manitou and there would be another cat for him to play with next door, but I would never let Billy throw him in the bathtub even if he tried, which he might, because Billy was that way. "If you're nice you can sleep in my bed with me and Manitou," I promised, "but you can't bite me or my bear and if you ever bite Alv again I'll tell the bosun where to find you, and let me tell you Billy Johnson is nothing compared to him."

As soon as I stopped, Alv burst out, "I hate this boat, I hate everyone on it but you. You're my best friend here."

A rill of joy opened inside my heart. "You're my best friend in the whole world!"

"They all think I'm queer."

"Well, that's okay," I said, because I thought queer just meant a little bit odd, and if that was the case then I was queer too. And so maybe because we had settled that I crouched beside the saucer and said to Whispers, "Alv's my first best friend, and Manitou's my second, but you can be my third, only you can't come sleep with me in my cabinet because the bosun might find out, and anyway there's a ghost comes at night."

So I guessed I'd told after all, because Alv was standing right there, and he said, "What did you say?" And because he didn't blame me about Whispers and had let me come down to feed him after he said he wouldn't and was going to keep our secret, I said, "The ghost comes into my cabinet at night."

Even in the shadows of the car deck I saw his eyes widen.

"Were you scared?" he asked and didn't even scold me for calling it out, and because of that and because he was my best friend and friends always tell each other the truth, I said, "I was very scared."

"I would be," he admitted.

"Would you cry?"

"I might."

"I did."

He reached down to take my hand with his good one. "Poor little Fern, all by yourself with a ghost."

"Manitou was there. But I think he was scared too."

"What did it do?"

"Nothing," I said, but it wasn't the same way he'd said "nothing" to Bosun. It was a surprised kind of *nothing* instead of the sullen *nothing* that means something but I'm not going to tell you.

"Did you see it?"

I shook my head. "It grabbed my foot."

He shuddered.

"Maybe Holgar could take a picture. Then we'd know what it looks like. Except if he did it wouldn't be our secret anymore."

Another shiver rippled down his back. "I don't want to know what it looks like."

Whispers mewed and rubbed against my ankle, but scampered off when I picked up the empty saucer, because we couldn't leave it for the watch to find. When I straightened, Alv clasped my shoulder. "It's okay to be scared. If it comes again, I mean. I would have cried too. But if it tries to hurt you, yell."

"Nobody would hear me," I said matter-of-factly.

"I'll hear you," he promised. "Because I am not going to let anyone or anything hurt you. Not ever." He stooped to look me in the eyes. And even though he'd thrown up, his breath was as fresh and light as feathers. "Promise."

I nodded. "Well, I am never going to let anyone hurt you either," I said, even though I had yet to make the bosun like him.

The ghost did come back. It came every night, and I can't say I liked it, but I got used to it. Once I even said, "What do you want?" But it never answered, and after Alv told me he would hear me if I yelled— even though I knew he couldn't possibly, not all the way at the aft end of the deckhouse where he bunked with Twitches—I wasn't quite so scared anymore. And because he was my best friend, someone who kept his promises, I thought I'd never have to be afraid of anything again.

27

$\mathcal{M}$y stepmother liked to visit her sister, Inger, in
Beulah, at the eastern end of Crystal Lake. Before Lene married my
father she and Inger had lived in a dark, little, two-story house on Clark
Street in the shadow of the Granary, not far from the railroad track and
the highway overpass, across the street from an empty field with a drainage ditch. The house was so dreary it looked like it belonged in Elberta,
but that's where they grew up, and where Inger, who never married,
kept house for their father until he died. I don't remember whether
Inger had a job. She couldn't have been a schoolteacher because she
didn't like children, or perhaps she was just unaccustomed to them and
didn't know what to say or how to act. Mostly Inger ignored me, and
while she and Lene revisited old times I was left to my own devices,
which would have been fine with me, but the field was hemmed in by
the highway and the ditch, the ground was always muddy, and in the
summer it was so buggy I would come home covered with red welts. I
didn't know any children to play with, and who wanted to swim in
Crystal Lake? You had to walk halfway across before the water got deep,
and there weren't any big waves to dive into for the thrill of the cold
water rushing over your head. The beach was so narrow it was just a
strip of sand, and on the other side of the bathhouse there wasn't any
beach at all because the railroad tracks ran right along the lake's edge.
There was nothing to explore, no woods, no bluffs to hike around and

see what surprises they might hide. Next to the beach there was a little park with a drinking fountain the children loved, you would have thought it was the circus come to town they made such a fuss, trip after trip to spray one another and drink from the spout. I didn't get it. I considered those Beulah children bumpkins. But I was a snob. I thought I came from the only place on earth worth living.

The park also had a stage where people like the mayor made speeches on holidays and sometimes there were wrestling matches, which I thought would be more interesting than the speeches, but we never went to see the wrestling because Inger said it was vulgar, though when an orchestra played, we would take a blanket and sit on the grass, and that was okay. I wanted to visit the Cherry Hut that was just a little way up the highway because the face of Cherry Jerry was carved into the top of every pie, but Lene and Inger made their own pies and jams and saw no reason. The beach had swings and a slide near the edge of the water, but so did the big beach in Frankfort. One thing Beulah had that Frankfort didn't was the bathhouse, where you could change your clothes to go swimming, but I hated those little cubicles and the nasty public toilets with their wads of wet tissue on the floor. As far as I was concerned back then the only good thing that was ever in Beulah was the free show.

That was the big outdoor screen the town stretched between two poles right on the beach once a week all summer to show movies. There were speakers too, so even though we were outside we could hear the music and everything the actors said, along with the gunfire and galloping hooves, because most of the movies shown were westerns with stars like Slim Whitaker, Gabby Hayes, and Tex Allen. Everyone in town and for miles around would turn out with their blankets because the movies were free. The way the town paid for them was to let all the local businesses put ads up on the screen, which is how I knew about the jack-o'-lantern face of Cherry Jerry. First they would show a newsreel or a short and then the feature, and it was even better than the Garden Theater because out there in the fresh air you could almost feel the dust the big horses churned up from the mesas. Under all those stars and the indigo sky going black, you felt like you were right in the saddle with those cowboys out west, in the middle of all the galloping and shooting and zinging arrows, it all felt so real.

Years later, at a drive-in movie with my husband, our children asleep in their pajamas in the back seat, looking at the big screen through our windshield, I remembered the free show and was so aware that John Wayne's Wild West was just a Hollywood set that everything seemed tarnished. But that was my adult life. I lived it at half-mast.

Once we even saw the northern lights. You're not supposed to be able to see them in summer, but I swear we did. They were just like rainbow-colored curtains coming down, and after the movie was over we stayed to watch those big, iridescent swatches of light dance in the sky. It was something, better than any movie, even better than the Fourth of July.

Another time I remember they broadcast the fight between the American Joe Louis and the German Max Schmeling over the speakers before the show began, not the fight that Louis lost, but the one where he knocked Schmeling out in the first round and got to be heavyweight champion of the world, and even though we never went to the wrestling matches my stepmother and her sister were cheering along with everyone else because the American beat the German. The war hadn't started yet—it was 1938—but even the people of Beulah seemed to know one was coming, or maybe they were still mad at the Germans from World War I, I didn't know, I don't even know if everyone realized right away that Joe Louis was a black man—colored was what people said then, though it wasn't a term I'd much heard because there weren't any black people in Benzie County—but afterward people still seemed glad though not as glad as they would have been if the American was white, because the newscaster called it a brutal fight. He said that Joe Louis was straight out of the jungle, as primitive as any savage, and people didn't like that. They would rather he won just because he was American. But in those movies we watched out there at the free show the Indians were the savages, and they always lost. Because my father listened to the news whenever he was home I wondered what he would think, but he was on the lake, and to tell the truth I don't know that he ever went to a movie to see the cowboys beat the Indians. There are a lot of ordinary things I can't picture my father doing. But after the big fight whatever feature was playing that night came on—I think it was *Sagebrush Trail*—and I lay back on the blanket and looked up at a sky so full of stars it looked like they might spill over and fall to the ground while the music played and the credits rolled, and I thought about my father's ship, which wasn't the Bull of the Woods anymore because I had been on the *Manitou's* last journey. Now he was captain of the *Ashley*, out there somewhere on the lake beneath the same sky. He would be up in the pilothouse, and the watch would be on deck, and maybe some of the crew were out there smoking, and they would all be looking at the same stars while below, in the firehold and the engine room, the black gang would be feeding the big Scotch boilers and wiping down the crankshaft and hosing off the pipes or else the ones off duty would be playing cards with the deckhands around the long table in the flicker, because sooner or later everyone on the ship except the officers ended up playing cards or chewing the fat in the flicker, which was once just an empty hold sealed off behind a bulkhead that the black gang found and made into their own, jury-rigging a series of extension cords that swayed with the ship's movement and made the lights flicker on and off, which is how it came to be named. So I wondered if Amund and Nils and Malley and all the rest of the black gang wished they could be out there on the edge of Crystal Lake listening to the fight where the black man who was American knocked the German off his blocks, so hard he saw stars, or if they would care, and would they care that the cowboys whupped the Indians one more time, or would they just tip their heads back and drink in the unblinking stars of that vast ink-black sky?

28

The windrow where we had stuck went nearly to the bottom of the Passage. Earlier we had broken up the pack ice by backing, running one engine ahead and the other astern to create a circular current. That was what I had watched from the bridge when all the chunks began boiling up, but now we couldn't ram without peeling the hull, and we had ridden too far up on the ice to back off. So we waited, but after another day when nothing changed, the wind didn't shift, and we couldn't turn around to raise the aft and try crushing the ice with the propellers, my father ordered the crew to spud. I put on my scratchy wool leggings and my hat and coat, and Alv came back for a moment to help me with my boots. I wanted to go up to the boat deck to watch because the gunnel on the weather deck was too high for me to see what was happening just below. All the while Bosun kept yelling, "What's the matter with you whores? You never seen ice before?" So from the boat deck, where the lifeboats rested on their davits, I watched the men go over the side, down two long Jacob's ladders that were kept rolled up in the lifeboats, one by one, deckhands first, even the ones who weren't on duty, then some of the black gang too. They seemed almost merry as they descended with their ice saws and spud bars, long poles with a blade at the end. It was almost like watching a troop of soldiers preparing for battle, before they knew what a battle really entailed, because no one expected to die out there on the ice.

It was clear enough for me to see the little puffs of their breath as they called back and forth, even though I couldn't hear what they said. When I was smaller I sometimes tried to blow my breath out in different shapes like bubbles or smoke rings, but it always came out just the same, a formless little cloud, though if I wasn't wearing a scarf over my mouth sometimes the ice caught on my lips for a moment, and if I was fast enough I could lick up little prickles of my own breath before they melted, but sometimes it was so cold those little prickles stung my lips and made them bleed, not a lot, just specks like freckles on an overripe peach.

The men with the saws were cutting blocks out of the ice like the ice man did in our harbor, you could hear the rasping of the teeth, and the men with the spuds were hacking at the surface with their wide blades trying to create cracks. It looked like a regular party out there with so many men working, except the bosun, who stood at the rail yelling down, though I doubt they could hear him any better than I could hear them, and what I think is they enjoyed it, enjoyed the fact that they were doing something instead of just waiting, enjoyed being out there in the world instead of scrubbing and painting down below deck, enjoyed watching Bosun yell without having to hear him as much as they enjoyed ribbing each other while they worked—and they worked hard. You could see the slivers of ice flying into the air, and if it wasn't quite as exciting as watching the big chunks explode up out of the ice field when we backed, somehow the party spirit floated all the way up to the boat deck, and I laughed when I saw Walter join the bosun at the rail and heard him say, "This the big blow you were talking about?"

"It's coming," Bosun said. "Didn't say when."

"That's one way to cover a bet," Walter said. "Blow's always going to come sooner or later. Might even wait for spring."

"There'll be a blow all right."

I believed him because now I knew a ghost, even though I didn't know who it was or what it wanted, but it came every night, and so I knew it wanted something and that whatever it wanted it wanted from me.

I picked Alv out on the ice, because even from a distance and with all his heavy clothes you could see there was something still not quite formed about him. To my five, fourteen seemed old, but not on a ship full of men. He was slender, and even in his heavy clothes and despite his shadow of a limp, which was more apparent on the ice than on the ship, there was something fluid in the way the rest of his body moved, as if his bones had yet to fully settle. Some of the men were probably no more than twenty or so, but I could see what a difference there was between fourteen and twenty or twenty-five. Plus some of the men, like Bosun and Odd and the chief engineer, had to be forty or fifty or even nearing sixty like my father, but once a sailor hit thirty it was hard to tell because the lake weathered them so much. And that was the other thing. Alv hadn't weathered, his skin was as smooth as mine, which was one of the reasons the men teased him so much. So far he'd stepped into a bucket of paint and flung the contents of the pilothouse spittoon into the wind and come back to the bridge with his face dripping wet tobacco. Not to mention they thought he'd been seasick when what he had was cat scratch fever. He wouldn't have dared confess to them that what he really wanted was to play the piano.

It took a long time, but I could hear the ice cracking under the thud of the blades, and farther off I could see the men from the other boat down on the ice too, but finally the Bull of the Woods broke free, the men came back up the ladder and put their saws and spuds away, and then we ran alongside the other boat to make a pass, so close you could see the faces of the small crew on deck, and we waved back and forth like we were just passing by, but then we had to back again and try to make a channel for the other boat. It was a fishing tug named the *Lela*, but out there on the ice, no matter their size, the boats were all one fleet, like allies in a war. Sparks flew as the heavy tow cable spun out from the winch, and I stayed up on the boat deck to watch it all, how the tug was made fast once we'd broken up enough ice to pull it back off the windrow into the space we'd carved. Then my father found a small passage around, and it was like a procession, the two boats with our big ship in the lead, churning past the thick wall of ice, and it was a good thing that we were first because my father was such an experienced captain, and the Passage is so tricky, full of shoals and fickle currents, it wasn't enough just to slide by the windrow, because we could still run aground, and now that it was clear again I could make out a distant frill of green flecks in a white ridge that rode the edge of the frozen lake. That was South Manitou Island, someone said, so I listened as hard as I could but all I heard was the crunch and scrape of the ice and the ship bumping through the floes, I couldn't hear the cholera victims crying out for help, and I understood now why none of the passing ships came to their aid, because there was barely enough draft for ships as large as the *Manitou* even as far offshore as we were.

For a while we continued our procession, but then the *Lela* turned off to the west, and we continued north, because we would have to repeat the whole process to free the *Ashley*, and that's what we did, though that wouldn't happen till the next day, since it was going on dark. Alv's cheeks and nose were red with cold when he came to get me for supper, and he seemed to have forgotten all about the piano and his infected hand and how much he hated the ship and its crew because he said with pride, "Well, I guess I'm a *real* deckhand now."

29

$\mathcal{I}$t was my birthday. I wasn't five or six or even seven anymore, I was eight, which seemed a very grown-up number, and my stepmother gave me a party. There were always parties, those informal afternoon gatherings of women eating sweets, drinking coffee, and playing cards, but this was special, a birthday party with a cake and eight candles, and though my father was on the lake all the children in my grade came with their mothers because the women wanted to enjoy the party too, but the presents were for me, a whole pile of them wrapped in fancy paper tied up with bows. I was wearing a new green taffeta dress with black velvet stripes on the skirt and sleeves that matched the bow at the little turned-out white piqué collar, and I felt so pretty. I'd never had a party before, at least not one I remembered. My mother was in the hospital when I turned five, and then when I was six my father and Lene must have been busy getting married, maybe my birthday got lost in the shuffle. And for my seventh birthday I got whooping cough. These days you'd have to hire a whole circus to make up for it, but back then there wasn't nearly the fuss they make over children's birthdays now. It was a big deal just to have a frilly little paper cup full of candies for each of your guests and a game of pin the tail on the donkey, which was just an old sheet with a donkey drawn on it and tails cut out of black construction paper. By the time I was giving parties for my own children, the donkey game came in a kit, but at least you didn't have to rent a skating rink or bring in Barnum and Bailey. And circus or no, we had a good time. We played drop the clothespins in the bottle and blind man's bluff and stumbled all over both parlors. Billy fell against the piano stool and sent it scooting across the room, and all the grown-ups did was laugh. Then it was time for the birthday song and the candles on my cake.

"Make a wish," someone instructed, so I did and blew the candles out, all eight of them at once, which meant my wish would come true.

"What did you wish for?" one of the girls in my class wanted to know, and then they all tried to tease me into telling, but Lene said I shouldn't because if I told, my wish wouldn't come true. And anyway I couldn't tell my real everyday wish because that would hurt her feelings, after she went to so much trouble to give me such a nice party. Because one of my real everyday wishes was that my mother didn't die, but that wouldn't come true ever, no matter how many candles I blew out, and so on my birthday I wished for something that could happen, something that would.

So I thought it didn't really matter if I told, but I went along with it, and in my best birthday girl voice I said, "I won't tell you," but right then one of the mothers, whose name was Mrs. Lunde, said, "My goodness, Lene, she's getting to be such a big girl. Tell us, Fern, what do you want to be when you grow up?"

"She wants to get married, of course," another said, but still another, who wore too much scent and had the kind of marcelled hair that had gone out of fashion, said, "Maybe she wants to be a working girl. She could be a teacher or a nurse."

"A secretary," Mrs. Lunde suggested. "That's a nice job for a woman."

"Not for me," I said airily. "I'm going to be a wheelsman on a ferry."

That made them laugh, as if I'd said something cute. Then the third mother said, "No, seriously."

"I bet she wants to marry a captain," Mrs. Andersen guessed. "Just like Lene."

"No," I said. "I'm going to *be* a captain, but first I'll be a deckhand,

and then I'll be a wheelsman, and when I write for my captain's I'll change the rules and let the captain steer."

Again they tittered.

"The girl just idolizes her father," one of Lene's friends said.

The woman with the marcelled hair smoothed her skirt. "All little girls idolize their fathers."

It was true, I did idolize my father, but that wasn't what they meant and so I said, more forcefully, "No, I don't."

"I bet you get married." The first mother scanned the room, and her eyes fell on Billy Johnson. "I bet your future husband is here right now."

"Fern's got a crush," one of the girls in my class sang, and the others joined, singsonging "Fern li-ikes Billy."

My face flamed. "I do not!"

"Oh, look, she's blushing," one of the women said, and my classmates took up the chant again.

"I am not!" I stomped my foot. "I'm never going to get married, and I don't care what you say, I'm going to work on the ferries. I already know how." I looked around, at their mocking faces, and my voice began to rise. "I can tie a clove hitch and dog down a door, I know how to clear the scuppers and ring the engine room on the chadburn, I know how to spud and how to back, and I know everything, because I know way more than any of you!"

"Fern!" my stepmother admonished, because that was no way for a little girl, even a girl as big as eight, to talk to an adult. My cheeks stung, their faces blurred, and I shouted, "I am too! I'm going to be a captain! You just wait and see!"

Again they laughed, but an uneasiness splintered through the laughter, and when my stepmother spoke again, her voice was no longer chiding, its volume had dropped, and hidden inside its reasonableness there was an attempt to be kind that upset me more than any scolding could. "Don't you know that girls can't grow up to work on the ferries?"

The woman with the marcelled hair smoothed her skirt again. "The railroad has an office in Beulah. You could work as a secretary there."

"I hate Beulah." My lip quivered as if I had been slapped, and my voice fell to a whimper that was the worst betrayal of all. "Yes they can, I will too, and none of you can stop me." My eyes burned, I had begun to cry, because I knew then that what they said was true: I wouldn't grow up to be a sailor, I wouldn't be a wheelsman or a captain, because women weren't allowed. How many had I seen on the *Manitou*? How many worked on the *Ashley* or the *Beaver*?

"I will too!" I repeated, shouting now, and my stepmother's tone grew sharp. "That's enough, Fern," she said, but it wasn't, nothing was enough until I ran off to my room to cry and ruined my own party.

30

*E*ven though a lot of the men had eased up on him, it didn't matter that Alv had become a real deckhand because the bosun was as ugly as ever. And because I had promised never to let anything hurt him, the next day at noon dinner, when the bosun started in, I rose on my stool and snapped, "Stop it."

Alv tugged at my dress, trying to get me to sit down. The mess had gone completely silent. "He never did anything to you. So just stop."

"Well, I'll be darned," Walter said under his breath. Everyone had their eyes on the bosun, whose face was an angry purple, but instead of saying anything to me or to Walter or even to Alv, he turned to the other hands and growled, "What are you looking at?" By this time, Alv had gotten me to sit down, but he wouldn't raise his head. Everyone looked around like they didn't quite know where to fix their eyes or what to say or whether to say anything at all, and the whole while the bosun continued to glare at them without ever looking at me or at Alv or even at Walter, who whispered, "Good for you, sweetheart," but Alv didn't say a word, and we all finished our dinner as quickly as we could.

Except me. I'd lost my appetite because I knew right away that I hadn't made things better, I'd made them worse. I hadn't even been brave, because there was nothing the bosun could do to me. One by one the men left the table, until Walter was the only one still there.

"It's okay, honey." He patted me on my shoulder. "You didn't say anything everybody else hasn't wanted to say."

"I'm sorry," I whispered, my eyes full of tears. "Why is the bosun always so mean to him?"

"Oh, honey. Because he can be. Don't you know that's the way things work?" Walter gave me another pat, but there was no comfort in it, because Alv had left the mess without even glancing at me.

And I did make things worse, because the bosun was meaner than ever, often aiming a nasty smile in my direction as he started in on Alv. When he wasn't around some of the men who had begun to accept Alv, maybe even like him, began to tease him about hiding behind my skirts. And Alv still wouldn't look at me.

But I was wrong about not having anything to lose. Because I don't know who told, especially since my father was so opposed to hearing tales, but at suppertime he came to get me, and I had to eat in the officers' mess with him. Across the way I could hear the crew laughing and talking, and it was even worse than the night I'd spent in the closet at Billy Johnson's. I squirmed on my chair and pushed the food around on my plate.

"Are you sick, *lille*?" my father asked, but I only stared at my uneaten dinner.

"I want to eat with the crew," I said.

My father pushed his napkin aside. "The bosun is paid to do his job, Fern."

"He's a bully."

"A bosun doesn't keep his men in line by making nice."

"But he picks on Alv!"

My father sighed. "The boy is new. He has a lot to learn. You're a good girl to want to look out for your friends, but your friend will learn to look out for himself."

I returned my eyes to my plate as if the food I couldn't eat might disappear if I looked at it hard enough.

"Is it really so bad eating here in the officers' mess with me?"

I couldn't say yes—that would be impudent—but I refused to say no. "It's just so jolly in there. The men tell all these jokes and stories." I paused. "Do you know any jokes?"

My father's eyes crinkled as if he meant to smile, but instead he cleared his throat, his brow furrowed, and his voice grew stern. "I don't know what kind of jokes and stories they're telling, but not all sailors' jokes are meant for a lady's ears."

"But I don't want to be a lady. Please, Daddy. I won't say anything again. They're funny jokes. There's one about a pirate, and a whole bunch about these people named Lena, Ole, and Sven."

"Good Lord!" My father shook his head. "Those jokes are as old as the hills. I daresay they were telling them when my father was captain."

"Ole and Sven are at a funeral. But Ole can't remember the name of the deceased"—I stumbled on the unfamiliar world—"so he says, 'Sven, who died?' and Sven says, 'I don't know, but I tink it was da guy in da box.'" I waited for my father to laugh. Instead there was a sad, pained look in his eyes. "It's funny, Daddy!"

"You are not one of the crew, Fern." My father balled his napkin and laid it on the table. "The only reason you're aboard is that your mother is sick."

"Then I'm glad she's sick," I said.

His face turned so severe I thought he meant to spank me for saying such a terrible thing, but instead he said, "No, you aren't, and you mustn't say so. Your mother has had a very bad time."

"I know it," I said, though I didn't, not exactly, not then.

"And I can guarantee she would not want you sitting at a table with the crew listening to their jokes. It was my mistake ever to allow it in the first place."

"But I want to be a sailor when I grow up."

My father's shoulders sagged. "It's the Halvorsen blood, I'm afraid. Never could see another life for myself. But it's a curse for a man to pass down to a daughter."

"You told me to be nice to Alv. You said he could look out for me." I was wheedling now.

"So I did." He shook his head. "With all this ice you're in for a long trip, and I know there's not much to keep you entertained. It's all right to *pretend* you're a sailor. But when we get back and your mother is better, you'll have to do your pretending on land. Your mother can teach you"—he seemed at a loss for words—"something more appropriate for a girl. She can show you how to sew. You could make clothes for your dolls. You'd like that, wouldn't you?"

I was quite certain I wouldn't, but we still had to free the *Ashley*, and after that there would be the trip across the lake and back. So all that mattered to me was that day and the next and the miles and miles of lake that lay between me and having to become a lady landlubber stitching up clothes for stupid dolls. How could I bear to spend those precious days eating in the dreary silence of the officers' mess while the crew laughed it up and razzed one another in their own?

Later, after my father had gone back to the bridge, I heard Alv open the big refrigerator that was in the passageway between the galley and the passengers' quarters to get something for Whispers, and I followed him to the car deck.

"I'm sorry," I said.

"It's okay," he said as he crouched with the saucer.

"My father says I can't eat with the crew anymore."

"I'm sorry," he said again, but his voice was toneless.

"I just wanted the bosun to stop picking on you."

"I know it." At last he stood to face me. "I know you were trying to help. It's just that you can't, don't you see?"

"Are you mad at me?"

He tried to smile, but his mouth was sad around the edges. "No, I'm not mad."

I wanted to be relieved, but everything had changed, and there was no way to change it back. So we left it at that, but as I climbed the steps of the companionway, I wondered what would happen if I asked the ghost to make the bosun stop.

31

*B*ut I didn't do it right away because as soon as the ghost took hold of my toe that evening I lost my nerve, and the next morning I took breakfast with my father, all the time listening for the noise from the crews' mess, though breakfast was never as lively as dinner or supper because the men were always so sleepy, the ones who were tired because their shifts had just ended and the ones who'd just gotten up but weren't awake yet. And then, sometime between breakfast and dinner, we stuck in the ice again.

We still hadn't reached the *Ashley*, though we could see it in the distance, as if both ships had fetched up on a vast white desert. We were just off Pyramid Point, where the land turns east to skirt Good Harbor Bay, then points a gnarly finger north into the lake, crossing the forty-fifth parallel at the knuckle. The Point looked a lot like Sleeping Bear, streaked with sand and snow because most of the snow blows off those perched dunes, which are so majestic and stark alongside the snow-capped shadows of the woods that grow all the way down to the shore in the places where the dunes aren't quite so exposed or so steep.

I was in the observation room, playing with Manitou. We had scattered the pieces of the jigsaw puzzle across the floor and were pretending they were islands. I had drawn a face on a wooden clothespin Dick Butler gave me, which was just the right size to be a giant jumping from one island to the next. When I looked out the window one of the trees seemed to have separated itself from the woods and begun to walk out onto the ice, away from the Point, and even from such a distance I could see how deliberately it was moving, whatever it was, so I put on my coat and went up to the pilothouse, but my father wasn't there. The second mate, Otto Andersen, was in charge, and Odd was behind the wheel even though there was nothing for him to do while we were stuck.

"What is it?" I asked and pointed out the window, but the dark splotch was still too far away, and so the mate took a pair of field glasses from the chart desk drawer.

"Is it the snow wasset?" I wondered what a snow wasset would do to a ship that was stuck in the ice. We wouldn't sink, but we wouldn't be able to get away.

Odd snickered. He hadn't made the fuss over me that some of the crew had, but I liked him because he always seemed to be in a good mood. "Got a snow wasset fixing to eat us. Better fetch the bosun. Must mean we're getting ready for his blow."

The mate lowered the glasses from his face. "It's a moose." He didn't sound too sure.

Odd took the binoculars. "What the . . . ?"

They passed the glasses back and forth.

"It's a moose," Mr. Andersen repeated, and this time he was definite. "You ever seen a bull with a rack in February?"

"Devil's horns," Odd said, a little pocket of surprise inside his voice. "Heard of it but never seen it."

"Let me see," I begged, but when they handed the glasses down to me everything looked so blurry I gave them back and pressed my face to the window instead. It was still a ways off but close enough now that I could see it wasn't a tree, it wasn't tall enough, the body was too thick, and it had legs but was too big to be a deer. It was walking very slowly, but there was no mistaking that it was coming toward us.

"Is it the snow wasset?" I asked again, because in the wintertime when the lakes froze up Bosun said the snow wasset grew legs.

"It's the mark of Satan," Odd said.

"Mark of a bull been castrated," Mr. Andersen corrected. "See how the rack's misshapen? Bull gets castrated he grows a new rack, but it's deformed, and he doesn't ever shed it."

"Devil's horns," Odd insisted. "I guess you ain't heard the stories."

"Can't say I have." The mate's mouth twitched like he meant to smile. "I don't sit around drinking with the injuns like you do."

"Learn a thing or two if you did," Odd said. I was still watching the moose and wondering what it wanted, because nothing with devil's horns and the mark of Satan could be good. "Get an injun drunk he can tell a damn good story."

"Stories is right."

"Maybe."

Mr. Andersen took another look at the moose. "Look at the poor devil. Everything's froze up. Got no fat reserve left."

The moose was close enough now that I could see the crooked rack, the antlers that didn't match, and the clumsy face with its big donkey nose. There was a moose's head mounted on the wall in the log cabin restaurant that was on the way to Benzie State Park, and it had a proper rack, which looked like two tractor seats with big claws on the sides because even a moose that's made right looks stupid. I felt sorry for the one on the wall, there among the deer heads with eyes so dark and alert they seemed startled to be dead. The moose didn't look surprised as much as embarrassed.

"A moose wouldn't eat you, would it?" I asked.

"Moose with devil's horns?" Odd said. "No telling."

Mr. Andersen shot him a sharp look. "Moose don't eat meat," he said to me. "This time of year boats get stuck, sometimes a deer or a moose comes out looking for a crew to feed it."

"I seen a wolf once," Odd said. "Sailor shot it off the stern."

I felt my eyes grow big. "Was it hungry? Why didn't he feed it?"

"Cause it was a wolf," Odd said, and that made sense, because the wolf in "Little Red Riding Hood" ate the grandmother and the girl, and the only reason they didn't die was the woodsman who came along and cut open the wolf's belly. I wondered if there had been a pair of wolves on Noah's ark, because if there were, the wolves probably would have eaten all the other animals and Noah too, unless the lions ate the wolves first, and that was something I had never thought about, all those animals that wanted to eat each other cooped up together forty days and forty nights on an itty bitty ark. They didn't talk about that part in Sunday school.

Odd crouched down. He had a thin, oily smell like paint, but it wasn't paint, it was the firewater that gave him overfondness. "Don't you worry, because that is a very nice moose, and devil's horns to some is just a halo to others."

"Is that true?" I wasn't sure whether he was making fun or trying to be nice.

Odd straightened up. "What do you say, Matey? You think that's a nice moose?"

"I'll tell you what," Mr. Andersen said to me. "Why don't you run down to the galley and tell Sam we got a starving moose out there, see if he can't find a little something to spare for it?"

I ran so fast I didn't even close the door when I tore into the passenger lounge, yelling, "Sam, Sam!"

"What's this?" Sam turned from the stove. In the prep room Billy Cooke had left big lumps of dough to rise, and the yeasty smell along with whatever soup Sam had in the big pot made my mouth water, and all of a sudden I felt as hungry as the moose, even though I was almost too excited to notice.

"There's a moose, it's out on the ice and it's starving, and we have to find him something to eat!" I was hopping in place. "Oh, please, Sam. It's got devil's horns, but it's really a nice moose, and if we don't feed it it's going to die."

I wondered if we would take him aboard, but he was too big to climb a ladder and there wasn't enough room on the car deck, which was too bad, because I thought it would be fun to feed him out of my hand and have him nuzzle up against me and lick my face with his big moose tongue.

Sam's grin bared his big, square, yellow teeth. "Is that a fact now?"

"Mr. Andersen said to tell you. We saw it from the pilothouse, but I saw it first. I thought it might be the snow wasset, but the mate had binoculars, and it's a moose." I wondered if I'd made a mistake telling Sam that it had devil's horns. "What's castrated?"

Sam seemed taken aback because he didn't answer at first, and then he said, "Accident, most likely. That or a fight. Poor critter. Been a cold winter."

"Winter's always cold," I said.

"So it is. But some's colder than others."

And then, because I must have sensed some connection, I said, "What's a faggot?"

"Lordy, miss!" Sam's face turned bright red. "Nothing you need to concern yourself about."

"Because . . ."

"See here," he said quickly, "we got an emergency on our hands, moose starving out there on the ice, can't let that happen, now can we?"

I must have been satisfied or completely distracted by the situation because I said, "But what will we feed it? Mr. Andersen says mooses don't eat meat."

"And Mr. Andersen's exactly right. So we'll just get him some carrots."

"Can I help?" I began to hop up and down again. "Oh, I want to feed the moose." I remembered how the men had come up from spudding with their saws and poles, singing merrily, "We are climbing Jacob's ladder." Maybe Mister Andersen would let the crew get one of the ladders from the lifeboats, and Sam and I could go down on the ice to feed it out of our hands.

Sam winked. "Sure you don't want to take him a saucer of milk?"

I froze. I couldn't think of a single lie to tell, so I looked down.

"Got a little stowaway, do you?"

"Oh, Sam, you won't tell, will you? *Please*. Because the bosun . . ."

"Oh, I know about the bosun." Sam stooped to pat my shoulder. "It seems to me a growing girl needs a lot of milk. Don't you worry. Your secret's safe with me."

I was so relieved I almost cried. "Oh, thank you, Sam!"

"So how about we find a meal fit for a moose." He opened the walk-in refrigerator and came out with a couple heads of cabbage and some carrots that he put in a mesh bag that he handed to me, then ducked inside his cabin to get his heavy jacket, and we went down the passageway through the crew's quarters to the afterdeck. The moose had come much closer while I'd been inside the galley, so close I could see his patchy coat.

"Holy cow!" Sam said.

"It's the devil's horns," I said.

"Poor critter." Sam reached into the bag for a cabbage, but I tugged on his sleeve.

"Let's get one of the ladders from the lifeboats. I want to pet him. *Please*."

"Sorry, kiddo. You need to keep your distance from a moose. Otherwise he might charge." Sam hurled the first cabbage. When the moose reached it, his nose set to twitching as he chewed, and up this close he looked so massive it was hard to figure how anything could get so big just eating vegetables. Sam handed me another and boosted me to the rail. I threw as hard as I could, but the tightly bunched head wobbled to a stop just beside the hull. "That's okay." Sam set me down. "He'll get it."

By now the crew must have heard, because Roald and Axel were on deck, and when the moose finished Sam's cabbage and came up close for mine, Sam boosted me again so I could see and let me throw a turnip that rolled across the ice.

"Good thing Captain's daughter's not pitching for the Tigers," Roald said.

Sam set me down again. "Moose got legs. Far as he's concerned that was right over the plate."

"Got devil's horns too. What are the chances?" Axel picked up a carrot, and then Roald did too, and it seemed like everyone wanted to get in on feeding the moose, but then there was a shadow to the side and a sharp crack that hurt my ears. The moose seemed to stumble, it was so fast you couldn't tell what happened, but I swear he looked right at me before he fell. And this moose didn't look like the one in the restaurant at all, not embarrassed or stupid, either one. Just sad.

Dick Butler was standing on the deck with a pistol in his hand and a big grin on his face. Bosun and Loke were there too, though I hadn't seen or heard them come out.

"Now what did you want to do that for?" Loke said, and when I looked back there was blood starting to run out onto the ice.

"Don't know about you, but I'm hungry enough to eat a moose," Dick said, and I felt terrible because it was almost the same thing I'd thought back in the galley smelling Billy's bread and Sam's soup.

"Aw, can it, you just had breakfast," Loke said.

Sam's voice sharpened. "What's the matter with you? Poor beast was starving, and the girl was feeding it."

"It's a freak," Dick said. "Thing had devil's horns."

"Wasn't hurting you."

"It was too close to suit me. What if it charged?"

"Wouldn't stand much chance against a 360-foot steel hull, now would it?"

"Says who? The hull is leaking, we're stuck again, not even under-way. Food's likely to run out before we ever make port."

"I never let you men go hungry yet." Sam turned away.

By now my father had come down from the wing and around the deckhouse. He looked out at the moose and back, then at Dick. "You," he said and held out his hand for the gun. The moose was trying to struggle to his feet, and I imagined a rank musk of game in the air along with the thick smell of blood, though there was an offshore wind, we were so high up, and it was so cold it's likely the only thing I smelled was the brittle air. My father fired. The moose fell back, and this time didn't move. "Next time you take it in your fool head to kill something, you kill it clean, you hear?" My father's blue eyes turned to flint. "And you don't go killing anything off my deck unless I say so, sailor, is that understood?"

"Yes, sir." Dick's voice was sullen.

Neither the bosun nor any of the men had said a word since my father appeared.

"Moose is the best game meat there is." Dick's voice rose to a whine.

"This isn't a hunting party," my father said.

"Yes, sir." Dick looked around at the men as if to find support, but still no one spoke, and finally he walked to the hatch and went below. My father was still holding the gun.

"No sense letting the meat go to waste," he said to the bosun. "Send a couple of the men down to dress it. We'll wait to start the engines until they've got it up here." Without looking at me, he strode back to the wing.

"Don't know if I want to eat a moose with devil's horns," Axel said.

"You ain't eating the horns," Bosun answered, which surprised me, given how superstitious he was. "You and Roald, go fetch the Sami boy. You'll need two sharp knives, two axes, and a saw. You can tell the little pussy what to do if he don't know, but make sure he dresses it himself. Boy needs to grow a little fur on his balls."

"It's cold. Why don't you come back inside?" Sam said to me as Roald went up to the boat deck for one of the Jacob's ladders, but I didn't move. I wanted to go down the ladder with the men, but I knew Sam wouldn't let me, so I figured to go up to the boat deck and watch, the way I had when the men were spudding.

Axel laughed when he saw what I intended. "Bloodthirsty little thing, aren't you? Better hope your friend doesn't slip with the knife. He could be sprouting devil's horns himself."

"I wish Dick didn't shoot it," I said. "But now it's dead, I want to see." I wondered if we would keep the head with its misshapen rack. We could hang it on the wall of the passenger lounge. And maybe deer would come out too, and pretty soon the lounge would look just like the log cabin restaurant. And if there *was* a storm that would be something, all those heads tumbling down off the wall, eyes staring every which way, antlers tangled up like a fight. I was so excited by the moose that for a moment I forgot about the wet coal and not eating with the crew.

Roald pitched the rope ladder over the side, and the wooden rungs clattered against the hull. Then he, Alv, and Axel mounted the gunnel and went down. I watched as they tied the legs and turned the moose over on his back. Then Alv peeled the pelt from the jaw to the tail. I was surprised how white it was inside, not bloody at all. And when he cut out the windpipe that was white too, white on white, striped with bright rings. Years later, the first time I found a whelk egg case at the ocean, I remembered the windpipe inside the dead moose and couldn't explain to anyone why the lump in my throat turned my voice to gravel. That was when the moose began to visit me in dreams. I stayed up on the boat deck to watch the whole thing, the dark gush when they bled it and emptied out the entrails. Alv used a hatchet and a saw to cut the animal into quarters, but it wasn't nearly as gory as I expected, except for the blood that ran out on the ice, turning pink and watery at the edges, and the steaming purple mess of guts. I wondered if it smelled bad up close. I sniffed the crisp air for a hint and believed I could at least smell the hide. Axel and Roald stood aside. Their mouths were moving, they would be giving Alv a hard time, though I couldn't hear what they were saying, but he did the whole job himself until it was quartered, and then they helped him cut it into parts like the round and the loin, because even a quartered moose is too big for a man to bring up on a ladder. It took a long time, but I watched the whole thing, and when they were done they left the head with its devil's horns and the gut pile and the feet and the fur and brought all the rest of it up, and Bosun made sure they kept the breakfast loins opposite the backstrap intact, because that was the best meat, and the best meat always went to the captain. And after they were done my father had the engineer start the engines and the wheelsman turn us around so that we could empty the aft ballast tanks and raise the stern to break up the ice with the propellers, and we got unstuck, and then pulled up close to the *Ashley* and broke her out, all the while Sam was fixing up our supper of roast moose with potatoes and carrots and onions, and I don't know how the breakfast loins tasted, because in the commotion over the moose my father seemed to have forgotten I was supposed to eat with him, but the roast, even the roast off a starving moose, was better than any meat I've ever eaten, better than Sunday's *svinestek*, and at the first bite I stopped thinking about the poor moose with his sad eyes and clunky nose, forgot all about the way he looked at me before he fell, like maybe he thought it was my fault. I didn't think about any of that as soon as I tasted that first bite because back in the crews' mess I guess I really was hungry enough to eat a moose.

32

*A*lv's swollen hand might have made him a little slow to learn his knots, but one thing he knew was how to dress game. He'd grown up hunting with his father, though his father always yelled and told him he couldn't do anything right. "But I guess I did," he said to me. "I guess I did all right this time, and a moose is a whole lot bigger than a deer."

I wished his father could have seen, though it wouldn't have mattered because Alv couldn't do anything to suit him, just like he couldn't do anything to suit the bosun. But Axel had never been hunting and Roald said the biggest thing he'd ever dressed was a squirrel, and neither of them had any idea how to dress something as big as a moose. So the whole while we were eating and exclaiming, Alv's face glimmered with pride. And when the men called him "Moose Boy" and laughed it was a different kind of laughter. Except the bosun, who didn't laugh, didn't even smile, didn't say a word, though he ate just as much as everybody else. Even Dick Butler glanced up from his plate and said, "I'll give the little fairy this much, he knows how to dress game."

It was the oddest thing. Because Dick Butler shot the moose I got to eat with the crew again and things beween Alv and me went back to the way they had been. It was one of those bad things that make everything good.

And maybe because of that, maybe because everything seemed right again, that night I got my courage up while I lay waiting like I always did for the ship to stop its shrieking and moaning and go quiet, for the air to change, and the ghost to steal into my compartment. This time I sat up, though I was careful not to disturb my foot, but even so I felt the ghost's hand slide from my toe to the arch. "Please?" I said. "I need your help. I need you to make the bosun stop being so mean to Alv." Soft as it was, my voice seemed to empty out the air, but then it closed in, so dense I could scarcely breathe, and my voice dropped to a whisper. "I know you want something, if you could just tell me what, but you're the only one I know to ask." I was so terrified my whole body trembled. "Just this once? Please?" The hand tightened around my instep, inching past my heel until it gripped my ankle. And then it was morning, I woke to the smell of eggs and bacon, and Manitou was beside me on my pillow just like always, it was like nothing had happened, except my head ached, my ankle hurt, and when I got up to get dressed and put on my socks, there it was, all black and purple and blue.

33

*T*he blow came after we had freed the *Ashley* and turned west, after we passed between North Manitou and South Fox islands and found open water. The sun had come out, and it was so clear that from the pilothouse you could see for miles, but there was no land in sight, only ice and the inky-blue water spilling little whitecaps between the floes, because out there the ice had a lot more cracks, it wasn't quite so solid, and the day promised to be the fairest one yet until the barometer began to drop. We were at breakfast in the mess when I felt the change of pressure in my ears and the crew's voices began to sound funny, and I realized it was because my own voice was ringing, like an echo in a phone with a party line, which is the only kind of line people had in those days.

"Told you there'd be a blow," Bosun said, and his voice seemed to echo even more than theirs because the room had suddenly gone quiet as all the men felt it. They knew what was coming even if I didn't, not yet.

"Oh, why don't you go to hell with your omens and ghosts," Dick Butler said. It was something none of the deck crew would dare say. Dick Butler only thought he could because he didn't work for the bosun, he worked for John Larsen, and the chief engineer wasn't there. But all of them worked for my father, and there was only one thing you were allowed to say to the captain, and that was "Yes, sir." So I guessed that Dick knew Bosun wouldn't go whining to my father that someone from the black gang talked back to him because another rule was no fighting. A ship is close quarters, even a ship as big as the *Manitou*, and I had learned that not all the men felt the bond of being on it together, they got on each other's nerves but had to find a way to get along. Oddly, I don't think anyone disliked Twitches, who was at the end of the table muttering to himself as usual, because he did his job and didn't bother anyone once you got used to the constant buzz of his voice, he was like a bee in the background, and when I asked Alv what it was like to bunk with him, Alv only shrugged and said, "Well, he talks to himself, but he doesn't expect anyone to answer, he's not so bad, he minds his own business and doesn't snore, but if he did I'd just put my pillow over my head."

Even before he killed the moose Dick Butler had a nasty streak anyone could see, because the men were always pranking each other, short-sheeting their racks, putting salt in the sugar box, that sort of thing, but what Dick passed off as pranks, like tripping Alv and making him put his foot in a bucket of paint the first day to keep balance, wasn't meant in fun, though the black gang stuck together, so none of his own ever called him out. And now that the men had enjoyed their fine moose dinner with more to come, they seemed to have forgotten how ornery he was to kill it, and my father wasn't there, so he was back to his cocky self.

Except when I looked at him again I realized he wasn't feeling cocky at all. There was a seam of worry behind his eyes, and I knew he was thinking about the leak and what would happen in the storm. He might like to be right, but he'd rather be wrong than go down in a storm.

Because I had free roam of the ship I had seen him pinching out his butts on the car deck more than once. Of course, I didn't really have free roam, I just took it, and as long as I stayed out of Bosun's way no one ratted me out, that was what they called it when they told on one another, which they never did, because if you ratted someone out it made you a rat, and the officers had no more use for rats than they did for the men that got ratted on. I still didn't know who had ratted me out to my father because most of the crew had got to be fond of me. I don't think Twitches noticed I was there, and maybe the bosun didn't like me and neither he nor Dick had much use for Alv, but the rest of the black gang took to me like I was their special pet. Except for the bosun, men on a ship kind of like having a woman around even if she's a little girl. So Dick Butler never practiced his mean streak on me, even though he had to know I'd seen him smoking on the car deck. Instead he went back and forth, because sometimes he was nice, like when he told me little secrets about playing poker or gave me the clothespin. And there was another thing, something I never told Alv—once when I went down to the car deck, I saw Dick put out his cigarette and drop it in his pocket, and then he pulled a little ball made out of crumpled paper out of another pocket. The ball was attached to a length of string, and he crouched down and bounced that paper ball around until Whispers came out to bat at it, and every time he did, Dick jerked the string, and this went on long enough that I realized he must have played with Whispers before, and I thought about what he'd said about cat scratch fever. He must have discovered the kitten on one of his smoking trips, maybe even before we did. For all I knew, he could be feeding Whispers too. And maybe he knew that I knew and that was why he was so nice to me sometimes.

Axel had been in the middle of another Ole and Lena joke, but when he felt the pressure drop and the bosun said, "Told you," he just stopped. His harelip tensed, and then he said to Dick, "Why don't you go to hell yourself," and the bosun didn't say a word. I supposed he felt it served Dick Butler right. But Axel wasn't mad. He was scared. Everyone was.

My father appeared in the doorway, on his way from the officers' mess. "Well, boys," he said, "I believe we may have to tolerate a bit of weather."

"Storm's coming, all right," Holgar said as soon as my father left, and then for a minute all the men were talking, how long it would take and how hard it would hit, and who would be the first to know, was it the captain up in the pilothouse, who didn't bother to share the weather information he got with the crew, though in those days before radar that information was scanty at best, the deck watch, or who? My father's brief announcement was all the crew could expect. They would be left to read the signs for themselves, though I wondered if they felt the signs the same way in the engine room and the firehold.

"They'll know soon enough if a bulkhead goes and the water starts rising," Roald said.

"Going to need every bit of that coal." Holgar glanced at Dick, his face clouded with worry.

But mostly the men broke off talking. Other times they told stories about storms they'd been in, like the one where a wave pitched all the way up over the pilothouse, pulled the deckhouse loose, and left it floating around like Noah's ark, or the time the carload of Buicks rolled off the stern of the *Ann Arbor 4*, taking the wooden seagate with it, the waves tore all the stanchions loose, and the upper deck dropped so low the steam pipe to the big whistle broke and if the chief engineer hadn't crawled on top of the boilers and shut off the valve, the ship would have sunk right there in the lake instead of later at the dock, where the whole crew was saved. That was before their time, at least most of them, though they all talked about it as if they'd been there. But no one seemed inclined to recall past mishaps now as we lingered in the mess because there was nothing to do but wait to see how bad it would be. The watches would double-check everything, the steward's crew would see that all the dishes were stowed away, and each of us would make sure we'd secured our cabins and anything else we were responsible for, but for the moment the crew seemed caught by a spell of paralysis so deep they didn't even feel like talking. I might have piped up, because for all their stories and despite the leak, the idea of a storm still excited me, I might have asked if they thought the deckhouse would come loose or the cars bust off their jacks, if the engine room would flood and the engines fail, but I didn't. I would like to say that I had enough sense not to, enough sense to know that every man was wondering if this would be the big one, if he'd ever see land and the people he'd left behind again, but I think I was just afraid that the bosun would yell at me. Especially after I'd asked the ghost to make him stop treating Alv so ugly. He wouldn't like knowing I'd sicced a ghost on him. Even the thought of it made my ankle throb.

Once Holgar told a story about a ship he'd been on where a new deckhand was so afraid of drowning he'd worn a life jacket to bed and when he was off duty he just sat in the mess with that same life jacket on and wouldn't speak to anyone, it was like he was already communicating with the dead, and when some of the men began to rib him, asking what he'd signed onto a ship for then, he couldn't answer and turned so white he looked like he was already his own ghost, and the first port they reached he went up the street and was never seen again. So I wondered if all the men who seemed suddenly too lead-limbed to move were thinking about drowning and began to wonder what it would feel like, was it just like when you got a mouthful of Lake Michigan while you were swimming and started sputtering and choking? But that was summer. In winter the water was so cold you would freeze to death before you had time to drown. And that part didn't sound nearly as enthralling as floating around in a deckhouse or watching the railcars bust loose.

Bosun cracked the silence. "You ladies going to sit here waiting for doomsday or do your jobs?" He glared at Alv. "There's a bucket of soogee with your name on it, boy. You want to leave a clean house you get swept overboard." Which was silly, since a bad storm would turn everything topsy turvy, and who cared whether the wreckage was clean or not.

I wanted someone to open the purser's office so I could fetch the little brass message tubes in case anyone wanted to write a letter, but I could tell it wouldn't be a good thing to ask.

So one by one the men rose and went off to their posts, the watches to make sure nothing was open and nothing was loose, the deckhands to their cleaning, the black gang back to stoking and wiping. They had to try to dry out the coal and make sure there was plenty at the ready, because a blow always put a strain on the boilers as the captain tried to keep the ship from falling into the trough of the waves, but even the black gang moved as if in slow motion, as if the dropping pressure made the air so thick it weighed them down, and I learned the first thing about the kind of storm that gives warning: that the worst thing of all seems to be the waiting, though when the storm hit I would learn the second thing, and that is that the first thing isn't true.

34

$\mathcal{W}$e were rocking almost gently among the floes when the wind suddenly shifted to the southwest and began to pick up. "Here she comes," Odd said, and though a tingle seemed to pass through the room, for a moment the men actually relaxed on their stools. Odd was in the mess playing poker at one end of the table with Axel, Holgar, and Roald, which is where the deck crew sometimes gathered between meals when they were off duty, though more often they went down to see what was happening in the flicker. I was at the other end playing a card game we'd made up all by ourselves with Alv. It had been hours since we felt the barometer begin to drop. All morning we had waited, then eaten a noon dinner of moose hash, though the long morning sapped the men's appetite in spite of the apple pie still warm from the oven. But I ate it all, every crumb. "What's the difference? Going to puke it all up anyway when she blows," Holgar said, watching me, then reaching for his pie.

"*You* are," Odd said, because he almost never ate dessert. He preferred a nip to a sweet, that's what the other men said. What Odd said was, "Liquid sugar goes down easy. Don't even have to chew." Other times he bragged, "A little whiskey's what keeps a man sober. Get behind that wheel, close one eye, and you ain't never going to see more than one horizon."

"Go ahead, eat your pie," they said to Alv now. "You're the one going to puke for sure." They were joking, but the morning had worn

173

lines into the fine muscles on their faces as their fingers tensed on the cards and the barbs they hurled at one another grew sharper until the air itself seemed to bite at the same time there was a slackness to it, a flabby indecision the ship's sudden yaw seemed to give shape, but then she straightened and the air slackened again.

"You know to tie yourself down if Captain has to turn?" Holgar asked Alv and me.

"What to?" I asked.

"Whatever you got. He'll give a signal, and you find something, because she's going to tilt so far you'll think upside is down, when that prop comes out of the water this ship's going shake so hard you'll feel like you've been knocked to kingdom come, and sweetheart an earthquake's got nothing on that."

I swallowed as I pictured Alv and me lashed together to a chair like prisoners. My father hadn't said anything about that when he stopped by the mess to say that we would have to tolerate some weather. Later he had called down to suggest that I ride it out in my cabin, but the storm was taking its time, and I didn't want to miss it all by myself in the passenger quarters.

"You ever been in an earthquake?" Roald asked Holgar.

"No, but I been on a ship went broadside. Rolled so far over her spars went under. Swept the watch right off the deck."

"Quit your yap," Axel said. "You're gettin' on my nerves."

"Just trying to impart some useful information to the rookies."

"*Impart?* You been reading a dictionary instead of that raggedy Sears catalog?" Roald asked. The catalog belonged to Dick, but all the men passed it around for something to do. I liked to look at the pictures of the toys.

"Yeah, well shut it," Axel said, and this time Holgar didn't say anything back.

I don't know where the bosun was, below deck maybe, checking for the third or fourth time that his crew had secured every mop, brush, and bucket once he called a halt to the soogeeing and painting he'd ordered right after breakfast.

Some of the hands at the table were on duty, but they hadn't cleaned or painted very long. "Painting with a gale coming on," Slim had snorted as he passed through on his watch. "That's a good way to take a bucket in the face." But all Bosun said was, "You don't say when she hits, I do, and she's going to take her time, just long enough to make all you ladies wet your pants." Alv told me about it when he came up, because almost as soon as Slim had passed through the engine room, Bosun had put them to work stowing away all the supplies they'd just gotten out. So we went to join the other men in the mess and play cards.

Before that, when Alv was still below, I had gone into the observation room with Manitou to watch for the storm, but when nothing happened except the popping in my ears, when the sky stayed so stubbornly blue, the whitecaps no bigger than ruffles, I got bored and went back through the passenger lounge to make extra sure nothing was loose in my cabin. That's when I noticed that no one had secured the brass eyes on the back of the leather chairs. I set Manitou in one and pulled it to the wall so the hook could reach, and then the bosun came in.

"What do you think you're doing, girlie?" It was the first time he'd spoken to me since I'd called him out.

I straightened and tried to sound like one of the men. "I'm dogging down the ship, sir."

He looked at the hook reaching up to the chair, and to my astonishment he laughed. "Well, I'll be," he said, then seemed to catch himself. His eyes moved to Manitou, sitting in the chair, and the grump came back to his face. "Better get a move on then. Storm don't wait for no teddy bears lounging around."

"Yes, sir." I moved to the next chair, then crossed in front of him to fasten the ones on the other side. I'd never been alone with the bosun before. Sometimes when he was around I tried to make myself invisible, but now there was no crew to blend into, and all of a sudden I didn't want him to ignore me. So I said, "Sir. Do you think the storm is my fault?"

"Storm's a storm," he said.

"But you said women are bad luck."

"Storm's bad luck, but it's the kind of luck you can count on, just like death and taxes."

I didn't like that he said death. "There's a ghost in the managers' cabinet," I said. "It comes out at night. Do you know who it is? It won't tell me what it wants."

His eyes squinched, and the lines between the little rolls of fat on his forehead deepened, though the dome of his head stayed smooth as ever. "You seen the ghost?"

"No. I just feel it."

"I heard of it," he said slowly, "but don't anyone on the ship know who it is."

"You like ghosts," I said.

"I know some. Ain't the same thing as liking."

"What about the ghost on St. Martin Island who wants to find his children? Do you know him?"

"Well, see, miss," he said, "a ghost don't ever get what it wants."

I liked that he called me *miss*. But I wanted to be sure that he knew the storm wasn't my doing, not mine and not Whispers's, whom he didn't even know about, because Dick Butler had kept the secret too, and there weren't any preachers aboard unless the ghost was a preacher, but if the ghost was a preacher it ought to be able to pray for what it wanted.

"Well, sir, I believe it was the *Chicora*," I said.

His gold tooth winked. "That's right. But ghost ship don't bring the storm, just warns you it's coming."

I thought for a minute. "Do you think this ghost is trying to warn me?"

"Can't say," he said just as I spotted Alv in the passageway from the mess, and Bosun spun around like he felt who it was even before he saw him. "What are you gawking at, boy?"

Which seemed an unfair question since Alv hadn't even entered the lounge yet. He wasn't looking at anything.

"Captain sent me to check on Fern. He says for her stay in her cabin."

"Might check the chairs while you're at it, you little pussy." Bosun gestured toward the wall. "Girl already done all your work for you." He moved toward the wood-paneled wall next to the purser's office, which was rounded at the end so there wouldn't be any sharp corners if a storm flung someone down the passageway. I supposed that was why there was no knob on the narrow door I'd noticed just inside the passenger quarters when Alv first brought me in to choose my cabin. The bosun crouched in front of it to reach through the hole, but his hand was too big, and after a minute he stood and turned around. "Girl. Come over here. See if you can fit your hand through."

I reached in.

"Now twist it up and feel against the wall to the left. There's some keys. I want the one in the middle."

"Yes, sir," I said, feeling along the grain of the wood and nap of folded towels until I touched metal.

Bosun said nothing as he took it, just unlocked the door to the purser's office without looking at either of us, and neither of us told that my father had let Alv have a key, though I guessed he gave it back, because he only needed it to let me into my cabin that first time. And what the bosun did before he came out, I saw it even though he did it like he didn't want anyone to know, was pocket one of the little brass message tubes sealed with cork. He handed me the key. "Put it back." Then he looked at Alv and said again, "What are you gawking at?"

"Nothing."

"Ain't nothing to see," Bosun said. "So you just go on and tell the captain his little girl is just fine."

"Yes, sir."

"Me and the captain's daughter here just been having us a conversation," Bosun said, and I thought that meant we weren't done yet, but then he started down the passageway behind Alv, so I called after him, "Sir!"

He turned. "What?" There was a snarl on his face now.

"I don't believe the ship will go down." I'm not sure whether I meant to reassure a superstitious old man or convince myself. I liked the idea of a storm, but the tension that strained the men's faces and hands all morning had begun to frighten me, and I was glad to know where the key was so that I could take one of the tubes for myself, and if I had to I would get Alv to help me write my last will and testament—those were words the men sometimes bandied about. But the idea didn't seem so appealing anymore.

"No," he said. "She'll take a beating, but she won't sink."

Do you promise? I wanted to ask. But this was the bosun, and I was going to be a sailor, so what I said was, "No, sir."

35

The lull lasted a minute or two. Then the mess went dark, the sky outside turned black, and even before the ship rolled, the wind shook the deckhouse so hard the plates in the galley rattled behind their cages. Waves were slamming the ship, and when I tried to look out the window I fell. A couple of the men staggered, and the others clutched the table. You couldn't stay on your stool without hanging on to the table, and we could hear the chairs in the passenger dining room that weren't bolted to the floor hurtling against the walls. I wanted to go up to the pilothouse, but my father would be busy, and I was supposed to be in my cabin, so I decided to go back to the observation room to get a better view. The alarm bleated as the men fought their way to whatever stations they were supposed to take in a storm, most of them below in case the ship took on water or the railcars came loose. My sea legs wouldn't balance, so I crawled through the passageway. Manitou slid across the floor of the lounge, and I tried to grab him, but he slipped out of reach. That scared me worse than anything the men had said, and I started yelling, "Manitou! Manitou!" but he couldn't hear me, I couldn't hear myself over the lashing waves and all the things flying loose. The ship was yawing, my father and whatever wheelsman was on duty would be fighting to keep us from going broadside, and the lights overhead were flickering, the floor was skidding around, it was like the earthquake Holgar talked about, but I couldn't find anything to tie myself with, everything was moving so fast. Back then, before radar, lake captains often preferred to beat into the wind for fear of running out of lake, going aground and breaking up in the surf, but the wind had shifted so quickly waves were coming up beneath the stern, lifting us so high it was like the bottom of the earth falling out when we dropped, but the wind was still rising, and then we weren't plunging so much as pitching. The chairs in the lounge were sliding back and forth on their hooks, but the hemp chairs in the observation room didn't have hooks, and by the time I reached it one of them had already been thrown into the lounge, just missing me as it crashed into the wooden column that enclosed the spar, the others were upside down and sideways, scooting around, there were checkers and puzzle pieces everywhere, and the sky had been blocked out by snow, I couldn't see the lake, even though I could hear big cakes of ice being hurled against the hull. I didn't want to be alone, so I crawled back into the lounge, where Manitou skidded just beyond my reach again, but then we collided, and I grabbed him up by the ear and tried to hold him against me with one hand and keep crawling, but the stern rose so high I was thrown all the way back to the observation room when the wave crested, and then nearly to the galley as we rose again. I was still clutching my bear, but there was no one in the galley or the messes, everyone was on the bridge or below, working to keep the ship out of the trough or the fires stoked and the cars from coming loose, or else they were in their cabins, hunkered in their bunks, holding on. I didn't know where Alv was. Ahead of me Axel staggered and fell, then crawled along the crew's passageway, he was trying to get to the head, and it was Hail Mary even though most of the men were Lutherans, he was yelling and puking both, and I was at the door that opened to the weather deck and the hatch to the car deck, I was yelling too, and even though we couldn't hear each other I knew he was telling me not to open it, and I was asking him to help me get it open, and then somehow it flew open, and both of us pitched through, onto the icy deck, where I was hit with a spray of sleet in the second before I struck the back of the doghouse and fell all the way down the companionway to the car deck, where some of the cars had come loose from their jacks and were rolling back and forth on the tracks, and there wasn't enough room, the cars that broke loose were threatening to knock the others off their jacks too. Holgar was moaning, and there were some other men sick, but they were trying to get the cars secured before they derailed, and then above the screeching wind and roar of the lake we heard something blow. It was the bulkhead between the engine room and the flicker. My body ached so much I couldn't even tell which part was hurt, I'd lost Manitou again, but I kept crawling along the icy car deck to the engine room hatch, which came open like something sucked it right off its hinge, I heard it hit one of stanchions, or maybe it was one of the cars. I didn't think about Whispers because you couldn't think, but I hung on to the companionway rail and half slid down the stairs. There was water on the floor of the flicker, but it hadn't come up over the lips of the cabin doorways, though the row of sinks against the wall was pulling loose and in the engine room the water was rising. The black gang was fetching dry coal by hand off the top of the pile in the hold, and the pumps and fans were running, but they were ankle-deep in the frigid water. Down here you couldn't hear the wind as much, only the noise of the engines and hiss of the pipes, but each time the ship lurched, it seemed as if the firemen would be flung into the furnaces, though somehow the other men held on to them, and they kept slinging coal into the fires. Dick Butler grabbed me and pulled me back to the companionway. "Up," he ordered, "up," and I crawled up the steps to the car deck, where some of the stanchions were starting to buckle, but still I couldn't find Alv. It was so cold the spray turned to ice, the scuppers had clogged, and water was sloshing over the rails and between the cars. "Up," Dick kept saying, he was still behind, pushing me, because with the cars busting loose the car deck was dangerous, and waves were exploding over the seagate, making the job of trying to anchor them even harder. I wondered if the men would try to raise the gate and push some of the cars off, like they did on the *Milwaukee*, but Dick kept prodding me from behind even though I knew he was needed below, and the deckhouse would be dangerous too, the deck would be riding up and down now that the stanchions were giving. The companionway was cockeyed, but I managed to climb it and pull myself back through the hatch to the deck, where the freezing waves were breaking over the aft pilothouse, and the wagon they used to load groceries had come loose and went skidding past, but Dick got me into the deckhouse and we staggered and crawled through the aft passageway back through the galley, where the rack that held cups had come loose from the wall, and broken dishes littered the floor, and when we got to the lounge and my cabin somehow he found a life jacket that would fit a child and buckled it on me, even though he had to know that anyone who went into the water would lose consciousness within seconds, or maybe he thought I would somehow climb onto a floe and hang on even though the floes were all being smashed into one another and flung against the steel hull.

"You stay here and keep safe," he said.

"But the coal is wet. What if the furnaces go out?"

"We don't want that to happen. So right now your job is to stay up here and pray for us."

"All of us?"

"All of us," he confirmed.

"Alv too?" I couldn't help asking.

"Yes," he said. "Alv too."

Then he zigzagged and gripped his way down the passageway, back to where he was needed to stoke the fires along with the firemen so we would have enough power to ride the storm out.

I crawled back to the observation room, but there was no horizon, no lake or sky, and I couldn't see the snow, because we were all turned around, we were in the trough and rolling over, and I slid down the floor to the wall, and what I was looking at, I realized, *was* the lake, it was above us, but finally we righted. I wanted Alv. I wanted my mother and my father, and I worked to get the door cracked and slipped through to the deck and up the icy ladder to the officers' quarters, where I crept up the inner staircase to the pilothouse. We were out of the trough and pitching again, and when I peered in, the helmsman, Pete this time, was clutching the wheel to keep balance, and my father was hanging onto a chadburn, I could see galoshes and the navy wool of his trousers ballooning above them. A watch was beside him, one of his galoshes was flapping, and Loke was saying, "Pumps can't keep up. We're taking too much water over the stern, hull's leaking, engine room's flooding, bulkhead's gone."

My father shouted. "Goddamn wind rattailed. We'll have to turn."

My father called down to the car deck to warn the men and ask someone to go above to the crew's quarters and let the rest know, took a second to swear, then rang for the engines and seemed to count the waves to make sure we didn't go broadside on the seventh, and when he was ready he yelled at Pete, "Hard left and pray she makes it."

The ship went over to starboard and shook so hard I fell down the stairs. We were broadside then, so far over, the wall was underneath me and the waves were breaking overhead, then slowly we righted again and began to beat into the wind. Waves were slamming over the bow, pounding the deckhouse, and over the ripping of the storm I heard a shatter of glass. The whistle cord had broken off, and each time it swung the whistle wailed.

When I got to the crew's mess Odd and Holgar were clinging to stools. "We're all in," Odd said, but it was hard to hear over the bellowing wind. Holgar's wrist was broken, you could see, the way his hand was splayed out on the billowing oilcloth. Everything else in the mess had fallen in spite of the wet dishtowels Sam had put out to try to hold things down, but then Mr. Andersen, the mate, staggered in and said, "Boys, we've always brought you home before, and we need you now if we're to bring you home again." So they both got up, Holgar with his broken wrist and Odd, and followed Mr. Andersen down the aft passageway to give it their last.

No one slept. No one ate. The coffee urn had toppled. For as long as I could, I kept crawling around the ship, but it didn't stop, and finally I did what my father said and got into my bunk and pulled my blanket up and held on to the side, but it wasn't possible to sleep, and time didn't pass, there is no such thing as time in a storm, there is only the next wave. I can't say how long it went on, only that when the wind began to subside, though the ship was still tossing, just not quite as violently, I went to sleep at last. When I woke it was daylight, and the storm was over, the ship damaged but aright. There was a strange silence, as if everyone on the ship was dead or else holding his breath to see if it was just a pause or really done. When it was clear that it was through I stepped out into the passenger lounge, but there was no one there, just the chairs and puzzle pieces from the observation room flung all around. Alv came to find me. He had been on the car deck, working to keep the rest of the cars from breaking loose. His face was streaked with black, the sleeve of his Carhartt jacket torn off—which was something because those jackets are strong—his gloves lost, his hand swollen up again. He began to right the observation room chairs and put things in order.

"I can't find Manitou," I said.

"We'll find him."

"I *can't* find him."

He turned from the chairs. "Oh, Fern."

"What if he washed overboard?"

"Come here," he said and pulled me into a hug, then sat in a chair he'd righted.

"I want my bear."

"We'll find him," he promised again.

"How do you know?"

"Because he would have had to go aft or on the bridge to wash overboard. Can he climb stairs?"

"Not by himself."

"Well, then."

"But what if he slid aft? I told him to stay with me. He didn't listen. He was a very bad bear." I sniffled. "Do you think I'm a bad girl?"

"I think you're a very big girl to be so little." He patted his lap and pulled me up. "It's over. You're safe."

184

My whole body ached, but now I knew it was my arm. "You hurt your bad hand."

"Banged it up is all. Piston in the starboard engine jammed when we came out of the turn. We have to put into port."

I twisted on his lap. "Are we there?" I meant Menominee. Because if we were docking in Menominee we must have gotten through Death's Door in the storm. We'd missed the man with the green light, and it was so rough if he'd come out to look for his children he might have been swept away.

He laughed. "Nowhere near. Captain had to change course to keep her afloat."

"But we burned up all the dry coal."

"We'll take on more when we get to Manistique."

"The cups in the galley broke. Everyone's going to need coffee, and now there's no way to drink it." I began to cry. "I was *looking* for you."

He stroked my back.

I dried my face against his good sleeve. "It was Dick Butler brought me up from the engine room. Even though he was needed below." I couldn't get over it.

"He's got a good side, I guess," Alv said. "Not that I ever see it."

"He told me to pray for you."

"I bet."

"He did. He told me to pray for everyone, and I asked if that meant you too."

"So did you?"

I nodded. "I prayed to Jesus. Do you think he listened? Because I never pray when they tell us to in Sunday school, and he might know."

"I guess he must have. We're alive."

"Were you scared?"

He seemed to think about it. "No." I could hear the smile that lit his face, this time for real. "No, no, I wasn't. I was too busy."

"I might have been a little bit scared," I admitted.

"Of course you were. You were by yourself."

"Do you think Whispers is okay?" It was the first I'd thought about our kitten since the storm began.

"Cats have nine lives."

"But what if this was his ninth?"

"Well," Alv said with deliberation. "If I was a cat and I had learned anything from my other lives, I don't think I'd stow away on a boat with a bosun who hated cats. Especially if I was black cat."

Slowly I nodded. "I think you're right. He didn't know any better, so this must be his first." We were both of us wet and cold, but I took comfort in the rough canvas of his jacket. "What if your hand is hurt so bad you can't play the piano?"

His breath stirred my hair. "Ah, Fern, I guess that wasn't really going to happen. I'll be a sailor."

"Me too," I said, just as my father opened the door to the lounge and scooped me up.

"She's okay, sir," Alv said. "A little hungry maybe, but Sam will fix us up."

My father kissed the top of my head. "We've had a bit of weather, *lille*, but it's okay now. You've been brave *liten jente*."

I buried my head in the wool of his uniform, which was all wet because a wave had shattered the pilothouse windows, and with a muffled voice I promised, "Daddy, I did what you said. I never left my cabinet."

36

*W*hat a liar I was.

37

When you own property on an Atlantic beach, you remember the names of the storms, not just the ones that struck, sending the ocean washing down the streets along with mattresses, appliances, and roofs, but the ones that threatened before they turned course or petered out, though not until you'd spent hours in front of the nightly news, tracking the radar images of the hurricane's advance. Ed, my husband, and I hadn't yet bought the cottage at Wrightsville Beach when Hazel hit in 1954. The first storm we sweated was Donna, watching TV back in Raleigh. I recall Bonnie because that year we had a bad nor'easter too and the north end of the island lost several feet of beach. And everyone in North Carolina remembers Floyd because it caused such terrible flooding down east. Oddly, the worst property damage Ed and I suffered was not at the coast but in Raleigh, when Fran came inland to knock the power out and topple the big willow oak in our front yard, sending it through the roof into a second-floor bedroom and totaling both of our cars. Bob was a Gulf storm, no risk to us, but we tracked it anyway because it seemed such a novelty to be following the first storm named for a man.

Then there are the catastrophic storms no one can forget: Andrew, Hugo, Katrina.

But on the Great Lakes even the worst storms come and go unchristened.

188

38

*B*ut I see I've failed to say much about my husband. I met Ed shortly after I finished college, where I learned to be a teacher instead of a sailor, and for a few years I taught first graders how to read out of the successors to my Elson-Gray primer, those Dick and Jane readers with their insipid family, Mother, Father, and little sister Sally, along with their pets, Puff the cat and Spot, who was, yes, now a dog. How privileged and oh-so-very-white they were, a bit of mischief the worst that ever befell their small, perfect world, though on the surface of it most of my students seemed to come from families just like them, and later you might have mistaken ours for one too. Those were more innocent times, people like to say, and I suppose they were if you consider that innocence is just ignorance dressed up in nice clothes. What harm, I have often wondered, did the lie those books told do to the children whose secret guilts, fears, or longings went unrecognized? This would have been the midfifties, an era that painted itself in the same bland colors as those books despite the dark tones beneath the surface. Did I err, I wonder now, in never telling my children about my childhood? And though you might think that over the years they would have asked, the truth is children have very little curiosity about their parents' lives—they're much too absorbed in their own. I know almost nothing about my own mother, but I have to wonder how much more I'd know if she had lived. And what was it about my own children that I failed to see as I went about the business of being a good wife and mother? I left teaching while I was pregnant with Ellen—in those days you weren't allowed to teach once you began to show. Ed was an electrical engineer who got in on the ground floor of electronics, he made a good living, I didn't have to work. Later I volunteered for the hospital, but I was home to sign the permission slips, bake the cupcakes, and chaperone the field trips as my children ascended through school. I didn't return to teaching when they grew up because I felt I'd been away too long or maybe because I felt it had never been my true calling, though I suppose when I chose to teach first grade it would have been out of some desire to reclaim my own ignorance, to recreate that illusion of innocence by observing it in my students.

What can you say to probe deeper in a world so full of surface?

What are you afraid of? What do you want that you know you'll never have? *What have you done that you can never tell?*

And what do you say to your own children when they come home each night, for in a way they are lost to you their first day of school, when they enter a world that excludes you and begin to accumulate secrets you don't know enough to ask and if you did, would they answer? Instead you greet them with those lame standard questions: *How was your day? What did you do in school?* and they respond with stunted words that say nothing. What feelings did they hide, those two children I loved as unconditionally as I had loved Alv, even though they grew up to become strangers, the way children often do.

I moved east, first for boarding school, then on to Wheaton College, where I was finished, certified, and stamped with approval. On graduation the president presented each of us young women with a favorite recipe written out in calligraphy on parchment that was rolled just like a diploma. Mine was for hamburger pie, and to tell the truth my family loved it, though by the time Ellen graduated from college she would have hit the roof if the chancellor dared to gift his female grads with recipes. There is a sea change between us that I can't overcome as much as I would like. If I told her that I once longed to become a sailor, she would wonder rather impatiently why I didn't, would insist I just didn't want it enough, didn't try. But for all the liberation she claims, the truth about Ellen is that she is domestic by nature and was from the start. Oh, she can criticize the toy kitchens, the Tiny Tears and Betsy Wetsies Santa brought because she doesn't remember they were what she wanted. She was nothing like me, a girly girl, all baby dolls and frills, who at the age of three was already mothering her little brother. But these are things she would not like me to remember, even if she hasn't really changed and now wants to mother me, much as she resents it.

Ed grew up in Plymouth and went to MIT. He too was an only child, and my children cannot know how deeply I regret that we could not provide them with cousins. Having had none myself I know what a wonderful gift that would have been. Ed's parents were still alive when we married, and they lived on until their early seventies, when they died in quick succession, heart attacks for both, sparing us the need to care for them in their old age, the way Ellen thinks she needs to look out for me, though boss me around is more like it. I don't mean to sound flippant. Small as Ed's family was, I welcomed it and was welcomed into it. And then we created our own.

We met at a party in Cambridge. I had gone on from Wheaton to teach in Boston, where I enjoyed the old graveyards, the narrow streets of the North End, the riverfront, and easy distance to the Cape, though for me the ocean never quite equaled the lake, not at the north shore, not off Cape Cod, and not later in North Carolina, but that is hardly the fault of the ocean. That first year out of school I shared a two-bedroom apartment on Charles Street with three other women, all teachers like me. We had fun, but you wouldn't exactly call it wild times, nothing like the extended youth my grandchildren are enjoying. There were parties on the weekends, and at one of them Ed and I struck up a conversation about a particular kind of tree that grows in the park between Storrow Drive and the river, though what tree—what its name is—I can't remember. We talked about the trees, about the river and the Harvard boys who were endlessly out rowing for crew, we fell in love and got married, and then when we had children we talked about them. I have said that Ed was a kind man, and he was. I have no regrets about our marriage, though through those years of raising children and even after, the children seemed to be the middlemen around whom the marriage was conducted. But that is not so unusual, I think.

We had a good life, an ordinary life, and I guess that is what surprised me. Ed took a job, and we moved to North Carolina. We had two children, and there was to be a third, but I miscarried in my fourth month, and after that we were through. I loved Ed, I loved my children, bossy little Ellen and that quiet, scientific boy, Paul, who seemed to have been engendered by that first conversation Ed and I had at the party, for he was endlessly fascinated by nature, the plants and the bugs, and we were surprised that he didn't major in biology; instead he took premed, met a Frenchwoman, and became a doctor in Nîmes. But I grieved for them too, for even in that more innocent time in a city such as Raleigh they lacked the freedom I had known, that easy access to the woods, to the lake, and to the river. Raleigh was too far inland, there was no river, no lake, no endless horizon. But then, as I say, who knows what secret lives my children lived? We took them to the state parks, to the Blue Ridge Parkway and the Smokies, we hiked, in the summer we went to the beach, Ed and I bought the cottage at Wrightsville, and later, when they were older, we traveled out west so they could see for themselves the grandeur of our country, the Black Hills, the Grand Canyon, Painted Desert, Bryce, the Arches, the Tetons, Yellowstone, Glacier, Yosemite, the Olympics, Mount Rainier, the Columbia River Gorge, Big Bend, Joshua Tree, King's Canyon. It was my first time to see those wonders too, but we saw all that majesty as tourists, they didn't grow up with it in their hearts and in their blood. It was their country, but it didn't belong to them the way this little corner of Michigan once belonged to me. Perhaps Raleigh did, though they left it soon enough of their own volition. There was the beach, of course, three hours away back before the interstate, but there wasn't much wildness to Wrightsville even then, and we didn't live there, we owned a cottage that we rented out and used ourselves only a few weeks each year.

And then one day they were grown up and gone, and I mourned the way all mothers do. Ed retired, and we traveled. We toured Europe, even went to Norway, to the northern coast, where some of the Sami still practice their traditional way of life, though by now the greatest number of Sami live in Oslo, so assimilated most Norwegians bear some Sami blood. Ed enjoyed Karasjok, but I felt dispirited, sampling authentic Sami cuisine, hearing traditional songs, then buying souvenirs at the Sápmi cultural park. Somehow I had imagined discovering Sami herding reindeer and living their lives instead of demonstrating them for tourists, though I didn't let on. Never in the fifty-nine years of our marriage did I let the past gurgle up in my throat, because I had swallowed it whole, just like the snow wasset once swallowed ships and their crews. My husband was a man who allowed me to live at the surface, and I was grateful to him because the surface was the only place I felt I could survive.

Of course, there was a war to worry about when our son was a teen, but it ended before he had to register. And though Ed suffered at the last—he had cancer—his suffering was mercifully short. I miss him, though I missed him more when I still lived in the house we'd shared in Raleigh, when I would turn around to tell him something only to remember that he wasn't there, though what I meant to tell him, I can't say. Little things. They're what a life is made of, that quotidian of grocery lists and holidays, the bird feeder outside the window, the dogwoods in spring and tomatoes from the garden in summer, the succession of dogs and cats, the TV shows we followed, and news of the day, and then, before you know it, it is gone, all of it, even when you live a life as long as mine.

When Ellen was born, the wife of one of Ed's colleagues warned me that a mother's life is made up of long days and short years, but that is true for everyone, not just mothers. One moment you are a girl standing on the shore of a great lake and the next you are an old woman.

39

My father went down in the Armistice Day storm of
1940, which began late in the morning of the eleventh with southeast
winds and rain that quickly changed to hurricane-force winds from the
southwest and driving snow. At least that is how it began for him. In
fact the storm had begun four days earlier, when a low pressure center
off the island of Vancouver moved inland, destroying the new Tacoma
Narrows Bridge. A secondary storm developed in the southern Rockies,
and on the Texas panhandle winds reached 66 miles an hour. Today's
meteorologists describe such a storm as a Texas hooker, a low pressure
system that moves east, then hooks around to the Upper Midwest. But
in those presatellite days, without television or internet, we didn't track
storms the way we do now, and by the time word reached the Chicago
weather office on the tenth, it had closed for the night. In Minnesota
the holiday began with such mild weather duck hunters celebrated by
turning out in shirtsleeves and light jackets. Before the storm was over
more than fifty of them would freeze to death. That same morning in
Chicago the temperature fell from 63 degrees to 20 in an hour. But at
8 a.m., when my father left Menominee for Frankfort, he must have
anticipated blue skies and a pleasant journey.

It seems unimaginable now that no word came over the radio.
Surely the destruction of the Tacoma Bridge would have been reported,
though perhaps it was not considered national news or if it was I don't

194

suppose anyone in the Midwest thought it of concern to them. At any rate my stepmother paid little attention to the news. She listened to her music shows and took things as they came. And if my father had any premonition at all, the most he would have said to his crew was, "Well, boys, it looks like we may have to tolerate a bit of weather." To us, my stepmother and me, he would have said nothing; he wouldn't have wanted us to worry. He knew how sudden and fierce November gales can be, when cold air sweeps down from Canada, bumping against warmer air from the plains. Sailors call the resulting storms the Furies. But my father was a prudent captain, despite the railroad's pressure. He would never knowingly risk the lives of his crew. Even when the *Manitou* had a leak the engineer failed to report, he brought us through the storm.

I was at school when the temperature in Frankfort began dropping and the wind began to howl around the building. At noon we walked home with the wind whipping at our backs, unaware that at the north end of the lake, at the Lansing Shoals light, winds would soon reach 126 miles per hour. Farther south, off Pentwater, the *William B. Davock* and *Anna C. Minch* went to the bottom. Another vessel in the same vicinity, the Canadian *Novadoc*, ran aground and broke in two in waves so tremendous the coast guard refused to go out to rescue her crew. At Ludington the Pere Marquette ferry *City of Flint* was unable to make the harbor entrance and had to be scuttled on the beach. Two other fishing tugs and a motor cruiser sank at the far southern end of the lake. My father's ship was caught in open water on its return from Menominee. She went down with all twenty-eight of her crew somewhere between St. Martin and the Manitou Islands.

When the officials from the railroad office in Beulah came to call on the evening of the thirteenth, the news came as a confirmation of what we already knew but would not say. To do so would have seemed like a jinx, because as long as it was not official we could hope that we were wrong, that communications had simply been severed and tomorrow my father's ship would come home, perhaps with an engine gone and a broken spar, everyone on board somewhat shaken but all accounted for, all alive. The power had gone out in Frankfort, and there was no school on the twelfth as we began to dig out from the blizzard. Throughout the day of the twelfth my stepmother was unusually quiet, though she went about her daily business as best she could. Without lights, without her radio programs, we went to bed early. Sometime Wednesday afternoon the power was restored. By then I was back at school. Even without electricity our classrooms got plenty of light through the windows and the building was heated by a coal-fired boiler. The bathrooms in the basement were always dark and creepy, but that day if you had to go a teacher took you down with a flashlight. Yet even when the electricity came back on the sounds in the halls seemed muted, the teachers' voices subdued. It wasn't possible to live in Frankfort without knowing someone on the ferries. Neither the coast guard nor the railroad had heard from the *Ashley*, which had been assigned to my father after the *Manitou* was lost. Many of the crew from the *Manitou* still sailed with my father. Morten Johannessen had been given his own ship at last, but the other mates and the wheelsmen had gone over to the *Ashley* with my father. Axel was a watch now, and Nils a water tender. Amund had moved up from water tender to third engineer. Even the bosun, Rudy, had gone with my father.

But the storm was over, the winds had calmed, and we went about our lessons as if nothing could be wrong. At the same time everything felt off, and as we recited, our voices seemed to take on a strange echo, as if the barometer were dropping and we were waiting on a storm instead of watching through the window as the janitor picked up debris from a storm that was done. But perhaps I was the only one staring out and listening to strange echoes, perhaps my classmates were simply thinking about what they would do in the free hours before supper after school let out. They had never been through a storm out on the lake. And yet I thought less about the way the *Manitou* had pitched and yawed and nearly sunk than I did about my father standing in his cabin and telling me the *Ashley* was unlucky. Boats talk, he'd said; a captain always knew. Even so he had taken command without complaint—I think he was thankful that the railroad didn't hold him responsible for the loss of the *Manitou*—and when I asked what the *Ashley* had said to him after his first voyage—this was in the year after my mother died and before he married Lene—he had patted my head and said, "Now, *lille*, don't believe every silly superstition you hear."

"But you said," I protested. "The railroad shouldn't have changed her name. You said it was bad luck."

"Aye," he said, "but I'll tell you a secret. I still call her by her right name, and she likes that, so she behaves herself for me."

For the life of me, I cannot remember what that real name was, though perhaps he never told me, perhaps I never knew. My head tipped warily to one side. "So she's not unlucky anymore?"

"Not a bit of it. After all, I'm her captain, she listens to me."

Because I was young enough to want to believe him I accepted what my father said and didn't think of it again until those long days of the twelfth and then the thirteenth, when I sat at my desk unable to focus on my arithmetic, hoping that my father had already docked in Elberta, only no one thought to send word because I was at school and it was important that I learn long division. But then it was lunchtime, and I walked the three blocks home, where Lene served me a cold roast beef sandwich with an apple, and because she said nothing I knew it wasn't so, knew she'd heard nothing, and didn't dare ask if there was news.

That night the railroad men came from Beulah in their gray fedoras and heavy topcoats, climbing the four sets of steps to the front porch and knocking politely on the front door.

Lene rose from the loveseat in the front parlor. "I believe you have homework," she said to me.

"No, I don't," I said, but she repeated, "You have homework," which meant I was to go to my room, and she waited while I climbed the stairs before she opened the door. I tried to listen from the upstairs hall, but she ushered them into the back parlor, where they would have sat on the uncomfortable maroon sofa to deliver those details that they knew. The *Ashley* had left Menominee bound for Frankfort Monday morning. She had passed St. Martin Island and was in open water a bit southwest of where we had fought the blizzard and storm not four years before when she sent a distress signal, then disappeared. The bodies of Billy Cooke and Holgar had washed up a few miles apart west of Seul Choix Point, and a life preserver stenciled with the name of the *Ashley* had been found floating in the bay. The ship was presumed to have sunk with all hands.

I had crept back downstairs, standing behind the half-closed pocket doors between the front and back parlors, and I heard nearly every word. There was nothing about the message tubes, and I wondered if the bosun had gone to the purser's office to pocket one before the storm hit, if a message might still wash up to tell us what went wrong besides the weather. Billy Cooke, whose name had been such a source of merriment among my father's crew, had baked the apple pie I had gobbled in the mess, where many of the men who'd now gone down had sat waiting along with me for the storm that nearly sank the *Manitou*. My father's actions, his and the crew's, had saved us, and I wondered why they hadn't saved him now. Did they have to turn? Did the engine seize? Did the coal get so wet the firemen were unable to maintain pressure?

My stepmother simply nodded, though when she rose, gravity seemed to push her back down, as if her legs had turned to cement. I slipped into a corner, and I don't know whether she was aware of me or not before she closed the front door and turned around, whether she knew that I had heard it all and seen her nod when the railroad men told her they were sorry. We hadn't spoken of the storm since I had come home from school in that screaming wind two days before, and she had gone about her business, cooking supper and cleaning up with her usual vigor, though except for the sound of her scrubbing and wiping, the house was silent. In the corner of the front parlor the piano had stood untouched, the lid lowered over the keys, and the stool seemed so strangely still, as if we were accustomed to it spinning of its own accord. And in the back parlor even after the power came on when it was time for her shows the radio sat mute. I was acutely aware of every sound I made, my breath shooshing in and out, my footsteps on the stairs, even though I tiptoed.

She didn't speak at first after showing the railroad men out, making sure the porch light was on and watching as they descended the porch steps and then those four more flights to the street, their hats bobbing in the golden hoop the streetlight cast onto the snow, the beams of their own flashlights dancing on the scraped white bits from the shovel. Only after they'd reached the sidewalk at the bottom without either of them slipping or falling did she turn around.

"Well, Fern," she said, "we shall have to make the best of it."

40

Just as the men had predicted, Bosun picked Alv to go first when it was time to jump the clump at Manistique. My father went into the aft pilothouse and used the chadburn to instruct Odd as we backed up to the slip just inside the river while the deckhands strung a cable outside the stanchions on the weather deck and attached a manila line that ran down to the car deck at the stern. Already the seagate had been raised, and as the stern swung in alongside the pilings, Alv's face went pale, though I didn't know if he worried that his bad leg might give way when he landed or that the line would snap. Even though the Annies didn't use bosun's chairs when they tied up to unload, the crew had told him again and again that the new boy always went first on the chair because that was how the bosun found out whether the rope was rotten. Freighters carried safety blocks, but not the ferries. "Come through the worst storm ever been only to die at the dock 'cause the railroad's too cheap to buy a goddamn block of wood," they warned Alv, like it was a fate meant just for him, but you could see that Axel was nervous too, the lines in his face drawn tight, even though the men all agreed it was actually lucky the ship had taken on so much water because if a ship rode too high she would catch the wind like a sail, and then the crew would have all it could do to get her tied up. "Open your eyes, you stupid jackass," Bosun yelled as Alv grabbed the line, took a deep breath, and jumped, Axel and Holgar right behind him. Then the three of them were teetering on top of the pilings, pulling the line and then the cable while Twitches took up the slack with the winch because he was the strongest hand, and if the cable sank it would be too heavy for the men to haul. As soon as they had secured it to a bollard, their shoulders dropped with relief, but the bosun kept yelling, "Faster! Get the lead out. What are you waiting for?"

Then they had to unfasten all the chains and turnbuckles and jacks to unload the railcars that clanked and rumbled across the metal apron. After that the deckhands had to untie the ship so we could tie up alongside the other dock where the ship would be repaired. This time they used the chair, and once again Alv had to go first, but the rope held, and he dropped to the dock, and after we made fast, a square I hadn't noticed in the hull opened like a secret door, and the rest of us walked through it down a gangway from the car deck to the dock. It was the first time I'd set foot on land in over eight days, and I looked around for caribou—somehow I had imagined them lining up to meet us—but all I could see was the river and the railyard and the squatty red lighthouse at the end of the east pier. It didn't look all that different from the Lower Peninsula.

Now that the cars were in the yard the stanchions could be straightened. The starboard engine had to be repaired, the bulkhead between the flicker and the engine room replaced, and the sinks that had pulled loose fastened back to the wall. The hull would be patched until the *Manitou* got back to Elberta, because a proper job of hull work required a ship to go to dry dock, and there was no time for that now. But before they could do any of it the stern had to be raised and a cofferdam built around it so the crew at the shipyard could pump the water out. A normal round trip was supposed to take fourteen hours, but we were already more than a week out and now we would have to spend more time in Manistique. So during the day we had time to go up the street, but at night we came back to the ship because the railroad didn't want to pay for a hotel, even though the repair work went round the clock with so much clanging and banging we all had to sleep with our pillows over our heads.

But the first thing we did was go to the doctor so the injured crew members could be treated. He put a splint on Holgar's wrist and a cast on Malley's broken leg and with a nod toward a door that must have opened to the surgery, said we were lucky no one got frostbite. The best part was I got to wear a sling because my humerous was fractured. That was my armbone. I had broken my other arm when I fell on the ice the year before, so now I guessed they matched, but the doctor said that children's bones knit so fast I'd be healed before I could say Jack Robinson. So I said, "Jack Robinson" before I thought, because I didn't want my arm to heal, I wanted to wear my sling forever. I was impressed to have broken something with such a big name, which I repeated for everyone in case they hadn't heard, but then Axel said it was just my funny bone, because it was my "humorous, get it?" and Holgar suggested in that case Axel might as well stop telling me jokes and everyone else too since he'd told them all six times already. Alv had found Manitou like he promised, and when I told the doctor my bear was hurt, the doctor wrapped a big white bandage around Manitou's arm, which he liked so much we had to show it off to everyone on the crew plus all the people we met on the street.

Afterward we went to a bar that wasn't far from the railyard, even my father, who drank a beer with his men and thanked them for the courage they had shown in keeping the *Manitou* afloat through what he still called a bit of weather, and everyone was in a jolly mood because we'd come through the storm and now we had some days off and the boat would be fixed even if the railroad wasn't happy about the expense or lost time, but "what do they expect?" Pete said. "Act like God, but if they got that kind of power, how come they didn't hold back the storm?" The men hoisted a glass to my father for his steadiness under fire, and John Larsen said we owed our lives to him because he'd ordered the engines twisted for the turn, had rung for full speed ahead on the starboard engine and full speed astern on the port, and if he hadn't we probably wouldn't have come about, so I was proud of my father and lifted my glass too because the bartender had brought me a fizzy new drink called a Shirley Temple for the little girl who sang and danced in the movies, so I sat on my stool and sang along with the men even though I didn't know the words, but when they came to the chorus I belted out, "Way hey up she rises, way hey up she rises, earl-lie in the morning!" But then my father took me back to the boat, "before things get rowdy," he said, and Alv came along with us while the bosun stayed at the bar with the men, all drinking together like they'd always been the best of friends. My father told me again what a brave little girl I had been, and then he went to his cabin to write a report for the railroad, and Alv and I snuck back down the gangway to explore the railyard, hunting for Whispers's car. I had worried what would happen to him after the storm, but Alv trapped him in a box before we unloaded and put him inside one of the cars that had lost its seal, then closed the door tight so that he couldn't get away. The cars looked so much alike I was afraid we wouldn't find it, but a few still had unbroken seals, and my kitten was meowing so loud we could hear him several cars away, though he quieted right down when Alv slipped him some food. But Alv wouldn't let me take him out because if he got away in the yard we'd never find him. I stood outside the car and explained about the storm so he would understand why Alv had to put him in a box and why he had to wait a little longer, because once the stanchions were braced with steel rods the deck crew would have to paint them to keep them from rusting, there would be all kinds of things for the deckhands to do to get the ship ready.

Alv kept busy doing laundry and putting things back in place, though not so busy some of the crew didn't haul him up the street to get a tattoo. Later he rolled up his sleeve and showed it to me. It was a blue anchor, like nearly all the sailors had, but he said not to touch it because it was sore and the skin around it was red, though I could tell by the way he kept looking at it over his shoulder that he thought the pain was worth it even if it hadn't been his idea.

"I want one," I said, but he shook his head.

"I don't care if it hurts. I wouldn't cry. And you know where to go. You could take me."

"Captain would skin me alive. Girls don't get tattoos."

Even though I knew it was true, my father wouldn't like it, and I didn't want to think what my mother would say, I blew a big disappointed breath out through my lips and vowed, "Well, next time I'm going with you, and then we'll see."

Mr. Strom, the mate who was filling in for the sick purser because he was good with numbers, ordered new supplies, so I got to watch the steward's crew, the cooks and the porter, haul all the new groceries across the deck in the wagon that had broken loose in the storm, we got new mugs to replace the ones that broke, and then, when everything was fixed, the leak patched as best it could be from inside, the deck crew got busy painting, and after the coal we had left was dried out with fans, we had to take on more because we'd burned up so much fighting the ice and then the storm, so we had to back up to the apron again, and before the railcars were loaded, several coal cars came on to dump their loads with a roar of choking black dust. Then the railcars were loaded, the boilers began to thump, the seagate came down, and this time there was nothing between us and Menominee except Death's Door, and after all we'd been through, Death's Door would be nothing, Axel said, which wasn't what he'd said before, but after the storm everything changed, we were all just so glad to be alive and on our way it was like we were already there, and everyone, even the bosun, seemed to be humming a happy tune inside, a whole chorus that everyone could feel even if it made no sound.

41

So we made the best of it, Lene and I, or so I thought, though things were not the same without my father. He'd been away so much, you wouldn't think his absence could make such a difference, but it did. It wasn't as if we'd spent our hours in anticipation of his arrival, because it was nothing we could count on, a certain time, a certain day. And yet there was something so draining in knowing that he would never come home.

I had never gotten used to thinking of him on the *Ashley*, not even when Lene and I were taking picnics up to the Elberta bluff to watch it depart. I'd loved the *Manitou* so much, whenever I pictured my father on the lake, it was always on the Bull of the Woods. I would close my eyes and see the Annies' trademark cutaway prow, see all the brightly polished brass in the pilothouse and the cords for the whistles and the sign for left and right that once made me wonder about getting turned all around, and Odd or Pete on the thick mat of latticed wood behind the wheel, my father in his uniform, bending over the chart desk or sitting on the chair with his newspaper. But the *Ashley* had been built for the Grand Trunk, it didn't have the cutaway prow, and I didn't know what its pilothouse looked like inside. What I pictured was Alv, face turning pale as he clutched the manila line to jump the clump in Manistique. I saw the men I knew, the men I'd played cards and once gone to a bar with, gathered at the long red table in the flicker, where I could trace in my mind every nick in the paint, every groove and fingernail-sized dip in the wood, the same way I knew the red-checked oilcloth in the crew's mess and the scratchy feel of my wool blanket, and the way the cables smoked and sparked on their winches when they were let out, knew the smells, bread baking in the galley, Sam's soup on the stove, the oil in the engine room, wax on the wood paneling in the deckhouse, and the acrid sting of the soogee. I wondered if the *Ashley* had a linen closet with a hole where the knob should be and if the blankets in the passenger cabins were green, was there a special compartment for the managers, did it have a ghost, and if I was aboard and closed my eyes would everything be in the same place? I didn't know, because my father had no call to take me across the lake again, and so I never went aboard the *Ashley*, which made it hard to imagine at the bottom of the lake, to walk its passageways and skim down the steps of its companionways in my mind, to read the brass plates above the cabin doors and know who they belonged to, though no one knew where each man was on the ship when he drowned, or maybe they didn't drown, because when icy water hit the boilers they would explode, though no one knew for sure whether the boilers on the *Ashley* exploded or not and I didn't want to think about that. I preferred to think that the ship was intact on the lake's deep floor.

That's what I did at night those first weeks, tried to walk myself through the watery passageways and along the car deck and the weather deck and on up to the boat deck, where I pictured the lifeboats still on their davits. I would imagine it all, just as if the ship were on the surface, but then the chair in the pilothouse would begin to float around, the cup rack in the galley would fall, the sinks would pull away from the bulwark between the flicker and the hold, and I wouldn't be able to go to sleep, or else I would fall asleep and another image would appear in a dream and wake me up. It was almost like the first time the ghost came to me on the *Manitou*, because in the morning my pillowcase and Manitou's fur would be damp and that's how I knew that I'd cried. I was too old to be sleeping with a teddy bear, but after my father went down I rescued him from the top of my chest of drawers and brought him to bed, because he had been aboard the Bull of the Woods, he had crossed the lake, gotten stuck in the ice and lost in the storm, he'd escaped the fire, and if I no longer pretended that he could talk, I could still talk to him. One of his eyes had come off, but each night I whispered into the ear that no longer had any silk plush on its edge at all, though I can't remember what I said. It was a hard time.

It was an equally hard time for Lene. She too had trouble sleeping or else fell asleep and woke up with a bad dream. Sometimes at night I could hear her moving around the house stealthily—perhaps she was afraid to wake me—with none of her daytime vigor, though that too seemed to wane. She cooked our meals and kept the house clean, though somehow there seemed little point to either. She still visited with her friends, but their conversations lacked the old lilt, there wasn't nearly as much laughter, and she never ever sat down to the piano. She listened to her radio shows but without the visible pleasure they had given her before, and I couldn't stand to listen to the radio at all, because I would strain to hear the sound of my father rustling his newspaper or tamping his pipe through the drone of the newscasters, though probably I was luckier than Lene, for I was a girl still, I had school and homework and a few classmates I could call friends. We had our sports, after school we went sledding and skating, at birthday parties I dropped clothespins in the bottle and pinned the tail on the donkey, just as I must have when I came back from the other side of the lake, so numb with guilt and grief and no mother, I barely remember that first year back. I was nine and then ten, Lene made an effort and gave me a party even though my birthday was little more than two months after my father was lost and we never spoke of the one I had ruined two years before. Still there was something missing. I don't mean my father, not exactly, for he had rarely been available for parties. Rather, his absence left something missing in us.

The third mate from the *Manitou*, who had become my father's second mate on the *Ashley*, had a daughter two years ahead of me in school. Her name was Doris Strom, and though we hadn't been friends before that winter, two years being a great gap in age when children are so young, after our fathers were lost she sought me out. She lived on Forest Avenue, and together we often walked the two blocks down Leelanau to Fifth Street, where she turned off to go home. It was an odd friendship, because we almost never mentioned our fathers even though it was our fathers who brought us together—rather we chattered about school, and because she was older she would tell me who the cute boys in her grade were, and sometimes she would ask about the cute boys in mine, which was something I hadn't paid much attention to. "Oh, you will," she would say airily, and we would go on to talk about the teachers, which ones were mean and which were nice. And sometimes when the weather turned warm that spring she would coax me into going to Collins Drugstore for a soda. There was a war on in Europe now, but America was not yet involved, and we paid little attention to the world beyond the fourth and sixth grades and the pursuits of our leisure.

Yet every now and then she would say, out of the blue, "Do you think our fathers went to heaven?" And I would be startled by the question because even though Lene and I still attended the Scandinavian Lutheran Church, even though I stared at those stained-glass windows behind the altar every Sunday, sat through the sermon, and went to Sunday school, I never thought about my father in heaven, I only thought of him at the bottom of the lake with all the fishes I once imagined I would see if I could look through a glass window on the ship's floor. I couldn't picture him in the clouds among a bunch of angels playing harps. Instead I wondered where he had been when the *Ashley* sank—down with his men, trying to lighten the ship by pushing the cars off their rails into the lake, or up on the bridge like Peter Kilty, knee-deep in water, waving good-bye. What happened after you sank I didn't know, and yes I wondered, did you stay where you were, or did you bob around the ship, because if you were in your cabin or in the mess, you would probably still be on the ship, though if you were outside on the bridge or on deck the current would surely pull you off.

After they found the first two bodies, Billy Cooke and Holgar, they only ever found one more, Axel, along with just enough wreckage to be sure the ship had gone down. It was months before I stopped hoping that someone, maybe the bosun, had written a message and sent one of the brass tubes overboard. I wanted those few last words—*We're all in, good-bye*—no matter who wrote them.

Another time Doris said, "My mother cries all the time."

Lene did not cry, not in front of me, though she may have cried in the privacy of their room with its big old-fashioned wooden sleigh bed where only she slept now, still on her same side. What she did with my father's things, I don't know. She left his tower office intact, but one day his extra uniform and other clothes were no longer in their closet, and I grieved over their loss as if they were my father. The only criticism I'd ever heard the crew voice about him was that he wore his uniform too often, but they didn't understand how much a part of him it was.

Nor did Lene try to comfort me, though to her credit I may not have appeared to need comfort, any more than she did. We went about our business, just somehow a little more mechanically, and that was how we mourned. We went to the Garden Theater, though more often I went with friends now. We went to visit her sister in Beulah, though I was old enough to stay by myself and usually chose to remain home. Billy Johnson asked me to be his girlfriend, and I said no because I didn't want a boyfriend, I wasn't interested in boys, but then I wondered why he asked, was it because he felt sorry for me? His father was a banker who went to work every morning and came home every night, his mother cooked their dinner and sometimes sent pastries or other little treats over for Lene and me, so he hadn't been the death of her after all, and whether he would be when he got a little older, when the mischief of boys grew more serious than throwing a cat in the bathtub or digging up a flowerbed for worms, when they did more than dare one another to cannonball off the diving board or climb to the iron railing in front of the lighthouse's second-story door, I was not to find out.

Because near the end of the school year, before it was warm enough for the free show or swimming in the lake, I came home one afternoon to find Lene waiting for me in the front parlor, where the lid over the keys of the August Förster piano remained down, the sheet music on its rack untouched.

"This house is too big," she said.

But it wasn't, oh it wasn't! Not for me.

"It's too much to keep up. There's other families would enjoy it." She was seated on the loveseat, and her back was very straight, her hands folded in her lap. I was still holding my schoolbooks, for I'd meant to head upstairs, but now I put them on the newel post and sat on a straight-backed chair next to the piano. The pleats between her brows had deepened since my father died, and little pouches of weariness sagged beneath her eyes.

"I've decided to sell it and move back in with Inger," she said.

A chill ran down my arms, and I hugged them closer to me. The house in Beulah was too small, it was so dark, Lene and I would have to share a room, and there was hardly any yard, just the buggy field across the street with its drainage ditch and the highway overpass that cut us off from the woods.

"I hate Beulah."

"Now, Fern."

"I don't want to move," I said.

"But Fern . . ."

"How can you make me move away from the lake?" My voice began to swell. "That's where my father is! I want to watch the ferries, I want to walk on our beach and canoe down through the marsh to the river, I want . . ."

She cut me off. "I wasn't thinking that you would move with me."

I stared at her. There were strands of gray in the dark-blonde hair that waved along her broad face, and her gray-blue eyes were set at the same time they were expressionless. She had a habit of penciling her brows, and they made her face look hard.

"Inger's house is too small, and she's not used to children."

You're not telling me anything I don't know, I sniffed to myself, so distressed I didn't even think what that could mean—did she intend to have me move in with the Johnsons or with Doris Strom?

"And you're getting to be such a grown-up girl, I thought maybe we should send you to school."

"I go to school," I said.

"I mean to a school for girls where they live, a boarding school." She leaned forward. "You wouldn't get an education here like you will there. It's an opportunity not many girls get. You should be grateful."

"Where is it?" I asked suspiciously.

"Pennsylvania. A town called Lititz."

"What a stupid name." My hands clenched in my lap. "I don't want to live in Pennsylvania." I'd learned the states in school, their capitals and major products. Pennsylvania's was Harrisburg, and its product was coal. I imagined living in a dark hole beneath the earth, my face blackened with dust and streaked with sweat, just like I was one of the black gang, but without a ship, without a lake. Pennsylvania was a desert full of black holes.

"Linden Hall is one of the oldest and best schools in the country."

It didn't occur to me to ask how she knew about it or to realize that she must have been planning her move for some time, sending off for brochures and information. No doubt she wanted to move because of the memories the house held, but she didn't say so, and I gave her no credit for her grief.

"No!" My stomach burned, and acid churned inside my throat. "I can't leave Frankfort. I love it."

"But you see you can't stay." She sat back and crossed her legs. "When I sell the house . . ."

"You *can't* sell it. It's not yours."

"But it is," she said.

"This is my father's house, it's *my* house. This is my HOME!" I was shouting now. "I was here first."

211

"Your father is dead, Fern. And I miss him as much as you do. Maybe more. When you're older you'll understand what there is between a man and a woman."

"My mother is here!" I cried, though the truth is I didn't know where my mother was. No one had ever taken me to see her grave.

She uncrossed her legs. "Well, I've made up my mind." Her voice was even. Mine was the one that that quickened and rose.

I did cry then, but it did no good, nothing moved her because she had decided, decided what was best, I just hadn't understood that, lame as it was, the best of it wasn't what we were already making.

"We can write letters," she offered. "I *will* miss you, Fern."

But I was too angry to pretend that I would miss her. Because I was an orphan, never mind she was my stepmother—"your mother now," my father had said, but neither of us had ever been fooled by that, no matter how polite we were—and there was nothing left to miss except the biggest loss of all, and that was the lake.

42

*T*he buoyant mood with which we left Manistique didn't last because there was still so much ice clotting the way, and as the day crept along and the men began talking about Death's Door again, their voices lost animation and grew thin. Much as they joked, they hated going through Porte des Morts, which was much narrower and rockier than the Manitou Passage, even though both were feared as graveyards for ships.

"Two months and we could take the canal," Axel complained in the mess.

"Ice can't be any worse in the canal," Holgar added. This was the Sturgeon Bay Canal, which had been built in 1890 because so many ships had been lost to Death's Door, but Holgar was wrong—the ferries never used the canal before late April because the ice was impassable, and in winter captains nearly always chose Death's Door, the passage between Gills Rock and Plum Island. The only other possibility was to go around Washington Island to the north, passing between it and Rock Island, which, according to Odd, "ain't the end of the earth, but you sure as hell can see it from there," or between Rock and St. Martin Island, and that was the problem, too many islands, too many shoals, not enough draft, not to mention the ice, which thickened as we neared Pilot Island and the Door County peninsula.

"Gives me da willies every time." Hans, who was normally not so superstitious as some of the others, and no one was as superstititious as the bosun, pronounced the word *villies*, and I practiced it that way myself. "Gives me da villies," I would say to Manitou or when I was talking to the boxcar where Alv had kept Whispers hidden, though I would always add, "You vill be fine, you vill see, ve vill come tru it because our captain is da best. He brought you tru da storm, remember?"

"Who are you talking to?" Dick Butler asked once, coming from behind a railcar to startle me when I thought I had the car deck to myself. His clothes gave off a stale stench of smoke. Everyone on the boat had his own special odor, from Odd's whiskey to the bosun's sour breath, Alv's sweet boy smell, and my father's aroma of authority.

"Nobody."

"Talk to yourself, do you?" he asked, but it was just swagger, because he'd seen me take note of the butt he dropped into his pocket.

"Don't you?" I responded, because I did talk to myself, not just to Whispers and Manitou.

"Can't say I do," he said and went back down to the flicker, where I knew the men would be grumbling about Death's Door just like they had been doing up in the mess. I wondered if Dick knew that Alv had hidden Whispers, or if his mood had soured because he assumed the cat had been lost when we got to Manistique.

That night at supper Bosun said, "There's ghosts from lost ships call you by name," and then he told us how he'd once worked on a ship out of Alpena that had gone through a terrible storm on Huron that had washed the purser, first cook, and watch overboard. It had taken out the port engine and snapped the forward spar, but the ship had been repaired and put back into service, and on moonless nights he claimed the missing crew members came back aboard, reported to their stations, and slowly went about their duties, the watch prowling the decks, the cook sifting flour in the galley, the purser counting money in his office, and then they would simply vanish or sometimes you could even see them climbing noiselessly over the side to return to their watery graves. "But it warn't no apparitions," he insisted, and I believed him because I knew how quiet my ghost could be. "That dead cook, he'd come aboard, and in the morning the new cook would go into the galley and find the dough already mixed and risen."

Loke hooted. "What I say is come back as a ghost might as well make yourself useful."

Bosun also claimed to have seen one of the Flying Dutchmen, those old sailing ships that wrecked in Death's Door. "Come up on the crest of the wave and there it was, three masts and sails set, moon so full you couldn't mistake it, just east of Gills Rock this was, but we lost sight when the wave topped, and at the crest of the next it was gone."

Loke might have argued and some of the other men too, but not after we'd all seen the *Chicora* and then, just like Bosun said, there was a blow, and even if it took a few days every man aboard agreed it was the worst February storm anyone had seen.

I thought about my ghost, who hadn't come the whole time we were docked in Manistique, maybe because the repairs went on all night with so much racket and all that coming and going. So much time had passed the bruise on my ankle had faded to a sickly yellow, but I hoped the ghost would return tonight. An uneasy metallic taste seeped from the slippery flesh inside my cheeks because the ghost had gotten angry when I asked it to make the bosun stop picking on Alv, and what if that was why it disappeared? I dreaded it, but even so I wanted it back. I had to know what it meant to warn me about.

"Blow was going to happen no matter what," Walter insisted, but there wasn't a man on the ship who believed him now, except possibly my father, but my father always ate in the officers' mess with the mates, and he was not one to court superstition, though he'd told me himself that ships speak. Most of the time you couldn't tell what he thought, unless he'd heard something he didn't like, talk about going down or about the crew and their various resentments, and then he would say, "There'll be no more of that, boys." And I was always astonished how a quiet word from him stuck, because they never ever talked back, not even the bosun, though I never really saw my father and the bosun together until we were on the ice in Green Bay. What it was, I thought, was that captains never liked their bosuns, and probably the bosuns never liked their captains either, but they each had their jobs to do, and the captain was happy to let the bosun boss his deck crew around because the deck crews and nearly everyone else hated the bosun, but he got the job done, and the men spent their anger on him, keeping a kind of awed and distant respect for the captain.

So long before we got to Death's Door the men joshed and told stories, but underneath their banter, just like underneath the ice, which looked solid but was always moving with the currents, there was a narrow ribbon of fear. Still we made our slow way through the ice without getting stuck, even though we had to back now and then and once, as we got closer to land, raise the aft to use the propellers to churn up the ice, and no one even speculated on what would happen if we caught another storm or a gale or if one happened inside Death's Door, where the ship would surely be smashed against the rocks, though when the conversation fell off and the mess or flicker grew quiet, I could feel the men thinking, because fear gives a quality to the air, a faint electrical prickle. So maybe that was it, maybe that was what the ghost had to tell me. Another storm was on the way.

But then the men began to say they thought Manitou was good luck—not the bosun of course—but the rest of them joked about it, saying, "Wasn't the captain, was the captain's daughter's little bear brought us through the storm."

"Let me hold him a minute," Nils said to me, and then they all wanted to take turns, and it was a sight, these weathered sailors sitting at the long, red table in the flicker holding a teddy bear with a big, white bandage on its arm in their laps. "You been hoggin' him. Give him over," Axel said, because he was down to his last pennies. "I need some *cards*, damn it." And the men seemed to think it was the funniest thing ever when he took the next hand with a full house, aces over eights, and after that whoever was holding Manitou took to bluffing—maybe, because mostly the others would fold and we never got to see the winning hand. Once Dick even staked me and let me tuck Manitou behind my sling to play my own hand, and I didn't have anything—by then they had taught me to read the cards—but one by one they all folded, and then I had ten whole cents to myself, and even though I knew they had just let me win, I whooped and hollered and did a little victory dance, but when it was time for bed I made them give my bear back, because even though I hoped the ghost would return now that all the racket was over, I didn't want to face it alone.

"You're awfully popular," I told him as I took a cookie from the galley and drank a glass of milk for my bedtime snack. "Just don't let it give you a swelled head. Because it wasn't you that brought us through the storm. It was my father twisting the engines, and don't you forget it. All you did was get lost."

That night we saw the beacon that marked Plum Island, but as we worked our way toward Cedar River there was more resistance from the ice. It didn't move so much with the currents now, it went deeper, and my father gave the order to sit out the night because a smear of clouds had closed around the moon, and visibility was so poor he wanted to wait until morning to tackle the big job ahead.

We were in Wisconsin now, because we had to sail through Wisconsin to get back to Michigan and Menominee, on the far side of Green Bay. It was even a different time here, someone had said, Central, a whole hour earlier, which meant we had sailed forward in space only to slip backward in time, and I couldn't stop remarking about it because the idea seemed impossible, the world so much bigger than I'd known, so big there would be places where yesterday was today and today was tomorrow. I had never been farther than Traverse City and Glen Haven, but here I was in a whole new state on the other side of the lake, where a forest fire had sent the mother bear and her two cubs over to us, and what if that had never happened? There would be no Sleeping Bear, no

Dunesmobiles, no Manitou Islands, no Manitou Passage, and even though I still didn't understand why the mother bear wouldn't have turned around to save her two cubs, it seemed to me that the world I knew, the world I loved so much, hadn't come out of Adam and Eve the way the Sunday school teacher said, but out of that fire, and though I didn't know the story about the phoenix, it seemed that was the way it should be, it seemed right.

43

I found my grandparents' graves in the Norwegian Cemetery out on M-115, across from the township hall and turnoff to the airport. Now it is called Crystal Lake Township East, but back when my father's parents were interred it was still the Norwegian Cemetery, then, when they began to let Swedes and Finns in, it became the Scandinavian Cemetery, then the Lutheran Cemetery, and finally the township took it over, though they might as well have kept the original name since Norwegians bought up nearly all the plots first thing. My grandparents are buried side by side near the back. *Henrik Halvorsen, born in Norway, died November 17, 1913.* I hadn't known my father was named after his, and for the first time I wondered what my father's boyhood been like. Had he loved Frankfort the way I did, or did he just love the lake? *Katrin Halvorsen, wife of Henrik Halvorsen, born in Norway, died April 8, 1918.* So my grandmother had outlived her husband by four and a half years. Seeing that, I wondered where they'd lived, if they had passed the tower house on Leelanau Avenue down to my father, or had he bought it himself, and if so which house had been theirs, another of the grand homes on Leelanau, one on Forest or even Michigan Avenue, where there would be a view of the beach? I knew all the old houses, I would recognize it. And wouldn't that be strange, to stand outside of one of those dwellings I'd passed every day as a girl and realize that my father had grown up there?

Of course I could find out. The Benzie Shores Library would have histories of Frankfort. There would be a record of deeds at the county courthouse in Beulah, and I made a mental note to check them, but I wasn't looking for my ancestors. I had stumbled across my grandparents only because I was searching for my mother.

I found her in Crystal Lake Township North, not far from where Michigan Avenue intersects with M-22, the road that takes you north, past the western end of Crystal Lake, to the turnoff for Point Betsie, and beyond, through the national park, which wasn't a national park when I lived there as a child. If you keep going on M-22 you will reach Leland, where in-season excursion boats run to the North and South Manitou Islands. In fact M-22 will take you all the way around the Leelanau Peninsula, to the very tip and back down to Traverse City, where people once claimed to have seen a sea monster in Grand Traverse Bay. But that is the long way around.

When I didn't find her stone in Crystal Lake East I thought she might not have one, might simply have vanished, her existence unmarked, but afterward I was glad, because the Norwegian Cemetery is so flat and barren. Why my mother was buried in North I don't know. I never visited her grave as a child, if there was a funeral I must have been thought too young, and in September of 1941, when I was ten years old and my stepmother sold the house on Leelanau Avenue to move back to Beulah, I boarded an Ann Arbor train for Toledo with a suitcase full of clothes and in Toledo I changed trains to travel on to Lititz. I graduated from Linden Hall and went on to Wheaton, then to Boston and Raleigh. That first year in Pennsylvania I missed the lake so much I hated the state, the school, and especially my schoolmates. The girls made fun of my midwestern accent, though why that should be so—after all, they came from all over, though most hailed from the East—I don't know. Probably my accent was just an excuse. I didn't fit in. I didn't try. I was too much inside myself. Still as the years went on, because I had been an only child and had no family left, I came to enjoy living in a dormitory with a roommate and so many other girls, not all of whom I liked, of course, but then not all of them liked me. Lene and I exchanged occasional letters, but I did not travel back to Michigan when she died, which was shortly after I graduated college, while I was living in Boston. I have no idea where she and her sister, Inger, are buried.

Crystal Lake North is what you want the cemetery where your mother is interred to look like. It has hills and tall trees and big family plots marked off by borders of stone or crumbling cement terraced into the slopes. Though it is scarcely older than Crystal Lake East, it looks much older, and you don't want a cemetery to look new. My mother lies somewhat off to herself at the top of a hill, at the edge of the woods at the north end, and I can't think how her stone got there if my father didn't pay for it, though whether he visited it I cannot say, any more than I can say whether he imagined that he would someday lie next to her at the edge of those woods so like the woods behind our house where I played as a girl and that's why he chose that plot instead of one near his parents in Crystal Lake East or even another one in North, on the side of the same hill or at the foot, where the Civil War veterans sleep with their wives. Or perhaps even as she was laid to rest he thought the only proper way to be buried was at sea. Or after he and Lene married maybe he imagined that he would be buried beside my stepmother instead. I have said before that Lene was not an unkind woman, and in that summer before I left Frankfort and my childhood behind, I'm sure she would have taken me to see my mother if I'd asked. Why didn't I? I wonder. I suppose I was too angry to ask anything of her at all.

And I am glad that my father lies at the bottom of the lake, for I wouldn't want to think of my mother here alone with my father next to Lene. When Ed died he was cremated, and per his wish I scattered his ashes along the beach at Wrightsville, where we owned a cottage for so many years, though Wrightsville was always far too built-up to suit me. I believe it was illegal—that's one of my complaints about Wrightsville with all its rules and regulations about no dogs on the beach come summer and when and where you can walk them in winter—but when the sand starts to blow around who's to mind a few ashes in the mix? We had sold the cottage several years before—too much upkeep, and after Ed retired he wanted to travel—so I had to drive to the southern end of the island and feed a parking meter, to time his dispersal before the meter ran out, and what kind of place is that? Better to go down with your ship at sea.

I know that my mother chose to die. Once, when we were children, Billy Johnson told me she killed herself, though if that was true surely I would have heard more about it, bits and pieces of rumor, whispered fragments following me down the school halls or the street. It is kinder to think she had a postpartum infection, what they used to call puerperal fever, though I suspect her depression was so deep she simply chose not to live, that she just lay in the sleigh bed in my parents' room with her face to the wall until she expired. We were gone so long even if she meant to see me again she would have lost the strength to wait. I can't imagine that neighbors wouldn't have checked on her, but perhaps she sent them away. And perhaps no one knew how seriously ill she was. My father told me himself that she'd perk up, and he must have believed it. He had to. It would change everything if he didn't.

At any rate, there's no one left to ask, if anyone ever knew. Even Billy Johnson is dead, along with his parents, buried in another part of Crystal Lake North, and now his son is our mayor.

Her stone is simple, no mottoes, no hearts, no flowers, thank heaven none of those skulls you see on the stones in Boston's old graveyards. It's enough to be dead, you don't need the sour face of your bare bones etched above you. Just her name, Silje Halvorsen, and the years that she lived, 1911–1936, no months or days because she was an orphan and perhaps the exact date of her birth was unknown. She died while we were at sea, and I don't know who found her or when. I'm not even sure how long my father knew before he told me. Communications between land and ship were so unreliable back then. We had a ship-to-shore, but it was so full of static it was almost of no use.

But there it was, is, the grave I traveled over a thousand miles and more than seventy years to find. I crouched to brush a few leaves off the stone, which felt cool to my hand, a little mossy, a bit porous, with a faint moldering scent of earth and last year's leaves, the smell of deep shade, but there wasn't much tidying to do. And nothing to say except, "Mother, I've come home."

I wanted to say *mama*, but the word wouldn't come. I don't remember her, and she remembers nothing. Because when my father offered me as a reason for her to get back up, I was not enough to keep her alive.

*I*f the ghosts from the hundreds of ships lost to Death's Door called anyone's name that night, I didn't hear. Even the ghost from the manager's compartment failed to visit, though I had been so sure it would come back at least one last time, and I wondered what happened. Was it so frightened by the storm that it stole down the gangway and went up the street like the sailor who'd been so terrified of drowning? Maybe it was slipping through the woods with the caribou I never got to see. But what if it was lost? And what if it was still angry? It would never tell me what I was now certain I needed to know.

When the sky began to pale, the engines pounded into action. The wind had picked up, out of the west, and though the ice was denser you could feel movement beneath, and up ahead the current had forced a geyser of spray through a hole in the surface. It was my first ice devil, and I ran up to the bridge to get a better look. Below, in front of the ship, the prow made a spiderweb of cracks, and as we thrust forward the ice in the passage began to buckle and roar, we were able to force our way through by backing, there was land close all around us, then finally we were through Death's Door, past Washington Island, inside Green Bay, making the turn toward Chambers Island and Menominee. My father called the engine room so the firemen could get up full steam, and then just before the turn he rang the chadburn for full power, because it's nearly as hard to turn a ship in the ice as it is in high seas, though we didn't have to come about like we had in the storm. Pete spun the wheel several spokes to the left, we swung to the southwest, and then we were back to fighting the ice, backing off and ramming, running up on it and backing off again, slowly breaking our way through Green Bay. It was overcast, but visibility was fair, and I could see the ice-covered escarpment that was Wisconsin off to port, those unforgiving rock cliffs where the Winnebago had ambushed the Potawatomi or maybe it was the other way around, because it was so long ago no one seemed to know, though that didn't keep Red and Roald from arguing about it. By then we were coming up on supper. I was still fascinated by the time difference, and it delighted me to think that it could be five o'clock and four o'clock at the same time because if the line ran right down the middle of the ship, it would be suppertime only on one side of the table. So I took a portside stool and exclaimed to the crew across the table, "I'm eating before you are," but then Roald spoiled it and said that Menominee was on Central Time, just like Wisconsin. "Time don't change on a ship," Bosun added, which made sense because my father would wear his pocket watch out if he had to reset it every time the *Manitou* crossed the lake. But it was like the bosun to want to spoil things even more.

"Just don't get ahead of yourself," was what Holgar said to me.

After supper there was another windrow and another ship stuck up ahead. By then we were nearing Chambers Island and the Strawberry Passage, though we would turn before we reached the Strawberry Islands and skirt Chambers Island to the west because only a small boat could navigate the shoals to the east. There was no moon and a fog had set in, we could no longer see the Door Peninsula, and though Axel claimed that on a clear day you could see Wisconsin and Michigan both, neither could have been much more than a line along the horizon with the water tower at Menominee sticking up, until Wisconsin receded as the water tower grew and you got closer to the river and the Menominee lighthouse appeared. My father called for rest again, so that we would be fresh and have enough light to free the other ship before making the last sixteen miles to Menominee.

"We're almost there," I whispered to Manitou as we settled down for the night. I was sleepy. I'd been up early, in the pilothouse when my father made the turn into the bay, in the mess, on the car deck talking to Whispers, and down in the flicker, where the men were dealing yet another hand and Malley was still playing a sad song on his harmonica at the end of the table when I went up to bed.

"Tell your nursemaid he gets to jump the clump first again," Dick Butler called after me.

He was still sore about Alv being above deck, and even when the others brushed him off he wouldn't let it go. "You tell the little faggot this time when we take him up the street we're going to see he gets turned into a man. Takes a man to do a man's job, don't he know?"

"Ah, can it, would you," Amund said and drew three cards. "You want to be on deck so bad, go sign on some other ship and just don't tell 'em you know your way around the engine room and a firehold."

"Sweet dreams," Dick called after me as I climbed the companion-way back to the spar deck and my cabin. He was in one of his nasty moods again, and Nils replied, "Might be you don't come back with us from Menominee. Be a whole lot more peaceful."

And the funny thing is I did have sweet dreams, which is to say I slept soundly and didn't have any dreams at all. I'd cheered up considerably through the light of day. "Ghost ship don't bring the storm, just warns you it's coming," Bosun had said, but he was just a superstitious old man, because we'd come through Death's Door just fine and were practically to port, and who cared what a ghost that was such a scaredy-cat it ran up the street because of a bit of weather had to say?

It was not yet light when I woke. I had left the little stool by the sink folded down in case the ghost came back, all tired out and wanting to sit, but I knew it hadn't. I would have felt it if it had. I was kneeling on the stool to brush my teeth when I realized I smelled smoke, but it wasn't the kind of smoke like Sam cooking bacon or the stale stink from Dick Butler's clothes. It was a thick, smudgy smell that seemed to hold something sharp inside, and I was trying to pin it down when the general alarm began to ring, and I rushed outside still in my nightgown, where the men were gathering on the weather deck.

"Fire on the car deck," someone yelled, and just then flames splashed a bright reflection into the doghouse over the hatch, which was open because men were scurrying up the companionway from the flicker and the engine room, the golden light from the heat fluttering across their faces. The distress horn was blowing along with the general alarm. Below the fire was cracking and popping, and the deck seared my bare feet, but there was no pulse from the engines because my father had already signaled for them to be turned off and the ship to be evacuated. Despite the pumps the fire had leapt out of control so quickly the last of the black gang had to come up through the escape hatch. The air was damp and cold, but you couldn't feel the damp or the cold because the deck was so hot it warped the air, sending wavy shimmers up through the chill. Smoke smeared the sky, and even though we were in sight of land we were much too far from shore for a breeches buoy even if we'd been close enough to a station for the Coasties to get the cart with the Lyle gun down to the beach. Instead some of the deck crew were hooking the rope ladders, the Jacob's ladders from the lifeboats, over the gunnels, and the mates were on deck, lining us up. "Quick," Casper Strom, the third mate, said to me, "Get your coat and boots. We're going to the ice." By now smoke was tumbling out the ports below and from the funnels up above the boat deck, squeezing through the scuppers, choking the air in thick, oily black clouds, and below the flames weren't popping and cracking so much as they were licking and roaring. My eyes burned, I had begun to cough, and as I rushed to my cabin my soles felt as if they were melting off my feet. By the time I was back, struggling into the sleeves of my coat, my galoshes unzipped, my father was on deck. He took my hand and snatched Alv from the line for one of the ladders. Manitou was tucked safe inside my good arm, still wearing his bandage, because he didn't take it off at night like I did my sling, and in my haste I had left my sling and my shoes behind. "Take her off first," my father said. "You go ahead so you can catch her if she slips. Do you understand? That's an order. My daughter gets off the ship first." He bent to kiss me and zipped my boots. "Don't be afraid, *lille*," he whispered. "Alv will see that you're safe." Then he was gone, and I cried, "Daddy!" When I turned around Alv had already hoisted himself to the rail and was motioning Holgar to boost me.

"Whispers!" I screamed. "Alv, what about Whispers?"

He dropped back to the deck. "I'll get him," he promised. "Holgar, take her off like the captain said. I'll be right back." Alv ran toward the doghouse on the afterdeck, so Holgar went down first, and it was Bosun himself who lifted me to the rail to follow Holgar down the ladder that swung against the ship with our weight. Men were scrambling down the other ladder, and when I looked up I saw the soles of a heavy pair of boots a rung above. Then we were on the ice, which was so cold through my rubber boots without my shoes my feet forgot all about the sizzling deck. Flames billowed up through the hatch toward the deckhouse, and the sound was like a thousand trains rocketing through a crossing all at once. It was all the paint and whatever was inside the rail cars, the tons of coal and coal dust, the ship went up so fast they couldn't even man the pumps. My father must have signaled the ship ahead to port because it was already putting down its Jacob's ladders for us. On the ice the men were running, slipping, trying to get away in case the *Manitou* exploded. Bosun picked me up, running with me pressed against his barrel chest, my legs bouncing against his thighs, and over his shoulder I watched the flames writhing through the ports. They were shooting from the deckhouse now, and even on the ice my face flushed with the heat. When the bosun must have felt we were a safe distance, he stopped and turned around to see. "It warn't your fault, none of it, just remember that, miss," he said, and I don't know why unless it was because he had said women were bad luck on a ship or he thought my father wouldn't make it off, but then my father was there, the bosun was handing me over, I was in my father's arms, still clutching Manitou. My father's jacket smelled like fire, there was soot in his eyebrows and streaked along one cheek, his whiskers smelled singed.

"Fern," he said. "About your mother . . ."

But I wasn't listening. The ladders had burned through and were puddled on the ice beneath the hull midships, and we were all there, watching the fire consume the Bull of the Woods. Holgar took a picture, you could hear the popping of the paint cans through the roar, and we were walking now, the long, slow walk to the other ship that was stuck off Chambers Island, where we would wait for the *Beaver* to come free us and take us home. "Your mother . . ." my father said again, but I didn't hear him, I was screaming, a jagged shriek ripping up from my lungs through my throat. Because Alv wasn't on the ice, he wasn't walking to the other ship or running, either one. The deckhouse had collapsed, the ladders burned through and fallen, there was nothing left to be saved, and Alv wasn't there.

45

I never told. Not about Alv. Not about Dick Butler, who survived along with the rest of the crew. He even survived the Armistice Day storm because he left the boats after we got back to Frankfort. Or else he did what Amund said and signed on some other ship for some other line and never mentioned that he knew his way around an engine room and a firehold.

My father never forgave himself, of course. He'd been so certain that Alv got off first. And even so I never told.

46

I never told on Dick Butler because that was the code. And how could I tell on him after, when I hadn't told before? Because if I'd told before maybe none of it would have happened.

But if I had told on myself? It wouldn't have made any difference for my father. He was a captain, last man off the ship, no matter what. He blamed himself. And I know what he, you, or anyone would have said: "But you were only five years old."

And it is true. I was only five years old. But there can be no forgiveness without blame. *Someone* has to acknowledge the harm that you have done. Because guilt casts a long shadow, it does not accept excuses, and guilt that goes unspoken is a wound that needs air. So I have to wonder—if I had told would it have made a difference for me? Did I choose not to tell because I was afraid or because I was afraid to be let off the hook? *I* sent Alv back. It was the last secret we shared. Maybe I wanted to hoard it.

I don't know, I can't say, because the ghosts I want, the ghosts that I have waited for, waited and waited, will not come. They will not tell me what they want. They will not tell me what I needed.

But lately I have had this dream. We are crossing the lake on a great ship, Alv and I. Both of us are grown. Sometimes I am the captain, and he is my crew; other times he is the captain, and I am his crew. Together we stand in the pilothouse, looking out the windows high above the deep blue of the lake, which rocks the ship like a cradle in its delicate white lace of waves, just the two of us, gazing out at the vast, unbroken world of water. It is a perfect summer day, sky the color of cornflowers, a bright band of clouds laid just above the horizon. Below, in the passenger lounge, there is a piano, an August Förster upright with candle sconces and insets of burled wood, on its legs shiny brass eyes so that it can be dogged down if the ship begins to roll. But of course it never does, and when the sky grows dark, it is only evening shadowing in. Because on this ship there are no storms, no fires, no stowaway cats, no spoiled and willful little girls. And so together we stand to watch the sun slide beneath the waves as the low scud of clouds turns lavender and pink and gold, lingering until the last ember of daylight turns to ash. *Then* we go below. He seats himself at the keyboard, and I choose a leather chair, propping my elbow on its arm, cheek resting against my palm as I cock my head to listen. And in the chords he plays I hear the thrum of the engines and kiss of waves against the hull, the cries of the gulls circling overhead and trill of a redwing blackbird in the marsh, there is a soft clatter of reeds as I dip my paddle into the river, wind ruffles through the woods, stirring the feathers of the grosbeaks and cardinals and greening new leaves. Across the harbor the foghorn sounds its deep call, and through it I hear a bright splash of waves against the base of the lighthouse, the patter of raindrops on the sand, and the wet, heavy silence of falling snow. What he plays is the song of my childhood, but then, as he lifts his hands from the keys and looks up, there is one last echoing note. It is the sound of those two cubs, the North and South Manitou Islands, waking from their long winter's sleep with a yawn as they stretch themselves and make ready to climb the steep dune to their mother.

But of course it's not a dream at all, only a notion I took that year so long ago when we went to the ice. Before I knew that I was the ghost, come to warn myself, and the ice tore a hole through the hull of my heart.

Acknowledgments

An earlier version of chapter 1 was published under the title "When I Was Five" in *The Best of the Fuquay-Varina Reading Series 2014*, and an adapted version of chapter 13 appeared under the title "HOMES" in *storySouth* 38. My thanks to the editors.

Across the Great Lake is a work of fiction, and throughout the research and the writing my goal remained plausibility rather than historical accuracy. There was an Ann Arbor ferry, the *Ann Arbor 5*, that was nicknamed the Bull of the Woods for its superior ice-breaking ability, but the ship I have given that nickname is fictional, and everyone aboard is a product of my imagination. The *Ann Arbor 4* did sink beside Frankfort's south pier in 1923, and its chief engineer's watch survived the winter frozen on the bulwark, but whether he put it up to the ears of the children of Frankfort I can't say. Although I have read an account of the old Frankfort water tower's bursting and flooding the town, official records suggest that it merely sprang a leak. There are reports of a mate firing a wheelsman who went home, got drunk, came back, and refused to leave, just as Don Barnard recalls an uncle with a big nose who insisted that keeping it out of other people's business gave it a chance to grow. I am indebted to the several writers who shared memories and information that I transformed into fiction.

The following books were extremely helpful to my knowledge of Frankfort, the ferries, Lake Michigan, the Armistice Day storm of 1940, and Great Lakes lore: Dennis A. Albert, *Borne of the Wind: Michigan*

Sand Dunes; Charles M. Anderson, *Memo's of Betsie Bay: A History of Frankfort*; Don Barnard, *Growing Up Stories: Growing Up in Benzie and Manistee Counties, Mich. in the 1930's*; Florence Bixby and Pete Sandman, *Port City Perspectives: Frankfort, Michigan at 150 (1850–2000)*; Victoria Brehm, *Sweetwater, Storms, and Spirits: Stories of the Great Lakes*; Grant Brown Jr., *Ninety Years Crossing Lake Michigan: The History of the Ann Arbor Car Ferries*; M. Christine Byron and Thomas R. Wilson, *Vintage Views along the West Michigan Pike: From Sand Trails to US-31*; Charles F. Chapman, *Seamanship*; Art Chavez and Bob Strauss, *SS City of Milwaukee*; Jerry Dennis, *The Living Great Lakes: Searching for the Heart of the Inland Seas*; Fred W. Dutton, *Life on the Great Lakes: A Wheelsman's Story*; Arthur C. Frederickson and Lucy F. Frederickson, *Early History of the Ann Arbor Carferries, Frederickson's History of the Ann Arbor Auto and Train Ferries*, and *Pictorial History of the C & O Train and Auto Ferries and Pere Marquette Line Steamers*; Skip Gillham, *Ships in Trouble: The Great Lakes, 1880–1950*; Bernie Griner, *My 90 Years in the Northwoods: From Pomona to the Betsie River*; Jonathan P. Hawley, *From Artisans to Artists: Betsie Bay's Historic "Island" Story* and *Point Betsie: Lightkeeping and Lifesaving on Northeastern Lake Michigan*; Nelson Haydamacker with Alan D. Millar, *Deckhand: Life on Freighters of the Great Lakes*; Richard N. Hill, *Lake Effect: A Deckhand's Journey on the Great Lakes Freighters*; George W. Hilton, *The Great Lakes Car Ferries*; Lords Commissioners of the Admiralty, *Manual of Seamanship: 1932*, vol. 2; Jim McGavran, *In the Shadow of the Bear: A Michigan Memoir*; Loreen Niewenhuis, *A 1000-Mile Walk on the Beach: One Woman's Trek of the Perimeter of Lake Michigan*; Eugene Edward O'Donnell, *The Merchant Marine Manual*; N. A. Parker, *History of Crystal Lake Township*; Tom Powers, *In the Grip of the Whirlwind: The Armistice Day Storm of 1940*; William Ratigan, *Great Lakes Shipwrecks and Survivals*; Benjamin J. Shelak, *Shipwrecks of Lake Michigan*; Kathleen Stocking, *Letters from the Leelanau: Essays of People and Place*; Frederick Stonehouse, *Haunted Lake Michigan* and *Haunted Lakes: Great Lakes Ghost Stories, Superstitions, and Sea Serpents*; Louis Yock, *Lost Benzie*

234

County; and Karl Zimmermann, *Lake Michigan's Railroad Car Ferries.* Websites too numerous to mention provided much additional information about ships, the Great Lakes, and local history.

For their assistance with my research, I am grateful to Linda Spencer, executive director of the S.S. City of Milwaukee National Historic Landmark and Museum, and to Bob Newcomb, who led me through the ship more times than I can count; to the Frankfort Chamber of Commerce; to Amy Ferris of Crystal Lake Township; to the staff of the Benzie Area Historical Museum; to the principal of the Frankfort Elementary School; to the pastor and secretary of Frankfort's Trinity Lutheran Church; to Tom Mendenhall of the Manitou Island Transit Company; and to Henrik Bjarheim, David Betts, Stephen White, Phil Richardson, and Gary Greer for their input on the Norwegian and the nautical. Many thanks to Janice Fuller for reading the last chapters and offering suggestions.

I owe a great debt to Grant Brown Jr., whose history of the Ann Arbor railroad car ferries, *Ninety Years Crossing Lake Michigan*, which I read while researching an essay about Frankfort, so fascinated me I couldn't let the material go, and who answered many questions from a stranger, often taking time to research the answers and interview old-timers who had worked on the ferries. I wouldn't have written this book without having read his, and I couldn't have written it as plausibly without the generosity of his input, though any mistakes are mine.

Always I offer thanks to I. D. Blumenthal, the Blumenthal Foundation, and Wildacres Retreat, where this novel was begun and a first draft completed, and to my many friends there, who were its first audience. I am grateful to the North Carolina Arts Council for a writer's fellowship grant that funded an invaluable last fact-checking trip to Michigan and Wisconsin. Many thanks to Amber Rose, Sheila Leary, Adam Mehring, Michelle Wing, Ann Weinstock, and especially Raphael Kadushin of the University of Wisconsin Press. I can't imagine a better experience in publishing. Thanks also to Caitlin Hamilton Summie for assistance with publicity.

To my family: my husband, Michael Gaspeny, and our sons, Al and Max, I want to say how fortunate I feel to have your love and support. And to my husband, who has cheered for the Tigers all his life, special thanks for the information about Father Coughlin and Hank Greenberg, for your suggestion that a cat or a dog might stow away on the ship, and for the enormous care you put into reading and offering suggestions on how to improve the manuscript. You are all over this book. *You.*

Lee Zacharias is the author of four previous books, including *The Only Sounds We Make* and *Lessons*, a Book of the Month Club selection. Her work has appeared in the Best American Essays series. Born in Chicago and raised in Hammond, Indiana, she is professor emerita of English at the University of North Carolina Greensboro.